"THE author of the justly famous Travis McGee series . . . knows everything dangerous that there is to know about people. . . . He scares the hell out of me. . . . In a John D. MacDonald novel, you learn how a lot of things work. . . . Some of the lessons are not at all good for you, but they are as fascinating as staring at a cobra."

Gerald Walker,
The New York Times

Finished
1 Mar 76

"TO diggers a thousand years from now . . . the works of John D. MacDonald would be a treasure on the order of the tomb of Tutankhamen."

—Kurt Vonnegut, Jr.

"WITH his exceptional talents as a storyteller, there's no problem he can't handle and handle well."

—Rex Stout

"A CRIME writer who never lets the customer down."

—*Saturday Review Syndicate*

"HIS books are narcotic and, once hooked, a reader can't kick the habit until the supply runs out."

—Clarence Petersen,
Chicago Tribune Book World

THE DREADFUL LEMON SKY

John D. MacDonald

A FAWCETT GOLD MEDAL BOOK

Fawcett Publications, Inc., Greenwich, Connecticut

THE DREADFUL LEMON SKY

THIS BOOK CONTAINS THE COMPLETE TEXT OF THE ORIGINAL HARDCOVER EDITION PUBLISHED BY J. B. LIPPINCOTT COMPANY.

U.S. Library of Congress Catalog Card Number 74-23085

Printed in the United States of America

First printing: September 1975

1 2 3 4 5 6 7 8 9 10

For each true friend of Travis McGee

Life is not a spectacle or a feast:
it is a predicament.

—SANTAYANA

1

I WAS in deep sleep, alone aboard my houseboat, alone in the half acre of bed, alone in a sweaty dream of chase, fear, and monstrous predators. A shot rang off steel bars. Another. I came bursting up out of sleep to hear the secretive sound of the little bell which rings at my bedside when anyone steps aboard *The Busted Flush*. It was almost four in the morning.

It could be some kid prowling the decks for a forgotten camera, portable radio, or bottle of Scotch. Or a friendly drunk. Or a drunken friend. Or trouble. I could not know how long I had slept past the first ting of the bell. I pulled on a pair of shorts and went padding through the blackness, past the head and the galley, through into the lounge to the locked doorway that opens onto the sheltered deck aft. The handgun which I had slipped from its handy recess before I was totally awake felt cold in my grasp.

I heard a small knocking sound, secret and tentative. "Trav?" A husky, half-whispering girl voice. "Trav McGee? Trav, honey?"

I moved over to where I could see through glass at

an angle, just enough to make out the girl shape of the
small figure huddled close to the door, out of the
brightness of the dock lights. She seemed to be quite
alone.

I called through the closed door, "Who are you?"

"Trav? Don't turn on any lights, huh? Please!"

"Who is it?"

"It's me! It's Carrie. Carrie Milligan."

I hesitated, then sheathed the revolver under the
waistband of the shorts, cold against belly flesh. I unlocked and let her in and locked the door again.

She hooked one arm around me and hugged her
small self tightly against me and let out a long breath.
"Hey, hello," she said. "No lights. Okay? I don't want
to get you involved."

"Lights will get me involved?"

"You know what I mean. If somebody was close, if
they knew I came over toward this way and they
watched and saw lights go on here, then they'd want to
find out."

"So I can black out the captain's quarters."

"Sure. It'll be easier to talk."

I took her by the hand and led her back through the
darkness. Just enough light came in so that the lounge
furniture made bulky shapes to left and right. When we
reached my stateroom I released her and pulled both
thicknesses of draperies across the ports. Then I turned
on a light, the reading lamp over the bed which makes
a bright round pattern on a book and leaves the rest of
the room in darkness. It shone on the wrinkled sheets
of recent dreams and bounced off, illuminating her in
soft light.

She had hugged me with one arm because she held a

package and her purse in the other. The package was the shape of a shoe box, wrapped in brown paper, tied with cord.

"I know, I know," she said, backing away from the light. "I'm not wearing very damn well. I'm not lasting so good. What's it been? Six years. So I was twenty-four, right? And now I look forty."

"How's Ben?"

"I wouldn't have the faintest idea."

"Oh."

"Yes, it's like that. I haven't lived with him in . . . over three years. I threw him the hell out."

"Oh."

"Stop saying 'Oh.' You know, I felt a little pinch when I saw this great old boat. I really did. I didn't know I could feel anything like that, related to Ben. I thought it was all gone. But we were happy aboard this crock. It was the only really happy time, I think. Shiny new marriage, and not a dime in the world, but a great boat to have a honeymoon aboard." She sat in the chair in the corner by the locker, out of the light. In a different voice she said, "I should have settled for you."

"You figured I wouldn't marry anybody," I said. I sat on the bed, facing her.

"I know, I know. What I don't know is why I was so red hot to get married. So I married Ben Milligan. Jesus! Know what he was, really? He was a child bride. His mother spent twenty-five years picking up after him, waiting on him, telling him how great he was, and then she turned him over to me. Whine, whine, whine. He couldn't hold a job. Nobody appreciated him. Bitch, bitch, bitch. He had like fourteen jobs in two years, and the last part of that two years, he didn't even *look*. He stayed home and watched the soaps on TV. He did all that body-building stuff all the time. Muscles on muscles. When I came home from work, I was supposed to cook, or at least stop on the way home and buy pizza or hamburgers. Trav, couldn't you tell what he was like?"

"Sure."

"Couldn't you have said something?"

"And lose an eye?"

"Okay, so I was in love. Thank God for no kids. I think it was him, not me. But he wouldn't go see a doctor about it. He got very grumpy that I could say anything might be wrong with the perfect body. Look, McGee, it was all a long time ago. All forgotten. I didn't come here to talk about my great married life. I was thinking on the way here, I don't *really* know Travis McGee. But you made me feel close to you, way back. I had to find somebody I could trust. I went through an awful lot of names. I came up with you. Then I started thinking, Maybe he's got somebody aboard with him, or somebody lives aboard, or he's away, or he's married. My God, it's six *years*. You know? I stepped aboard and six years were gone. You look great. You know it? Absolutely great. You haven't changed at all. It isn't fair. Look at me!"

It happens to people. They get up to the point of explaining the mission and can't make it, so they go into a talking jag. She needed help. There was a thin edge of anxiety in her tone, and the words came too fast.

So I gave her some help. "What have you got in the box?" I asked.

She exhaled harshly. Almost a gasp. "You get right to it, don't you? What have I got in the box? In this here box, you mean? Once you said you had a safe place for things. Do you still?"

"Yes."

She came over and put the package on the bed beside where I was sitting. She grasped the cord and popped it with a swift sure motion. She stripped the brown paper off. Meyer says whole tracts could be written about character revealed in opening a package.

"What I've got in this box," she said, "is money."

She lifted the lid. It was money. It was packed in tightly. Used bills, some loose, most tied into tidy bricks with string, with adding-machine tape tucked under the string. "I've got here ninety-four thousand two hundred dollars. Plus ten thousand for you, for keeping it until I want it."

"No need for that."

"It's worth that to me. And I'd feel better."

"Can I ask any questions?"

"Hardly any. That's part of the fee."

"Stolen?"

"Like from a bank or payroll or something? No."

"And if you don't come back?"

"I'll be back to get it before . . . what's today?"

"Early early in the morning of May the sixteenth, a Thursday."

"Okay, if I don't come get it before the fifteenth of June, or get some kind of word to you before the fifteenth of June, then I'm not coming at all. So it should go to my sister, Susie. Do you remember my maiden name?"

"Dee. Carrie Dee."

"That was short for Dobrovsky. She uses the whole name. Susie . . . Susan Dobrovsky. You get it to her.

That's part of the fee. And not telling anybody at all about me being here. That's the rest of the way you earn ten."

"Where is your sister?"

"Oh. Sorry. She's in Nutley, New Jersey. She's younger. She teaches nursery school. She's now like about the age I was when I knew you before. Twenty-three? Yes. Two months ago. She's nice, but . . . dumb about things. She doesn't know how things are yet. Wouldn't it be nice if she didn't have to find out? Look, will you put this in a safe place and keep it for me?"

"Yes, of course."

She swayed, took one dizzy step, and turned around abruptly and sat down on my bed beside the box, bouncing it, spilling the bricks of money. She shook her head. "I'm dead for sleep. And I'm dirty, Trav. I've been in these same clothes too long. I can smell myself. These clothes, they ought to be buried. For the ten thousand, dear, could I ask for three more things?"

"Like a bath, a place to sleep, and a change of clothes?"

"I'm a size ten."

After she was throat deep in the big tub, sploshing and sudsing, scrubbing her cropped pale hair along with the rest of her, I located an old surplus ammo box, the kind with the rubber gasket and the flat metal lever that fastens it safely tight. I moved the money, all except the ten thousand, into the ammo box and put that forward in the flooded area between the double hull. I added the ten to my own cache, mentally adding another four or five months to my retirement. I retire whenever I can afford it. When the money is gone, I go back to work. Salvage work. Retirement comes when you are too old to enjoy it completely, so I take some of mine whenever I can. What good are beaches without beach bums? What would the little vacationing lady urchins do for their holiday pleasures were not some of us out there wastreling away? After the large money was all stowed and quite safe, I went digging into the big locker drawer under the bed in the guest stateroom. It is always packed with girl clothes. They get left aboard. They are purchased in the ports I can reach with my old houseboat, and they are left aboard for another time. No trouble to have them cleaned and put them away. And having the supply facilitates spur-of-the-moment decisions.

I found her some navy flairs and a pink sleeveless turtleneck shirt. And I found the kind of terry robe which fits anyone. It fit her and dragged on the floor behind her. She helped me make up the guest bed. She was yawning with every second breath. Her eyes were glazed with fatigue. When I went in not more than three minutes later to ask her if she'd like some hot chocolate or a drink, she interrupted the question with a long, gentle, purring snore.

I stood for a few minutes leaning against the doorframe, looking at her in the semidarkness, remembering her. I remembered the pre-Ben Carrie Dee, a pretty girl who worked at Peerless Marine and was seen now and again at some of the parties in and around Bahia Mar. We are never the best judges of what is meaningful and what is trivial in our lives, I guess. The accidents of time and place change the script, and later we say it happened on purpose.

Carrie didn't happen to me on purpose. Or I to her. There was a TV crew at Bahia Mar making a commer-

cial. The Alabama Tiger had them at his permanent
floating house party every night of the week they were
there. The boss fellow was squat and hairy and very
loud. Mod clothes and a glossy wig and a conviction
that his profession and personality made him irresist-
ible. I went topside at midnight on the *'Bama Gal* to
get some air and see if there were any stars to look at.
Boss Fellow had a girl down on the deck by the overturned dinghy and was mauling her around, riding her
clothes up over her hips as she kicked and bleated and
yelped, her protests lost in the Tiger's two hundred
amps of speakers.

I plucked him off her and, while he flailed and
cursed, I carried him to a place along the rail where I
could get a clear drop into the boat basin. He made a
mighty splash after the twelve-foot drop. When I was
sure he could swim, I let him fend for himself. It was
Carrie, and she was not in great shape. She was ripped
and scuffed and close to hysterics. She was certainly in
no shape to rejoin the party, so I walked her back to
The Busted Flush and found some clothes that would
fit her. She spent a half hour alone in the head, getting
herself back together.

It had shaken her badly. He had come all too close
to taking her. She looked spooked and sallow. By all
the accepted rules of human behavior, she should have
been so turned off by the near rape she would have felt
neuter for quite a while. And I should have been reluc-
tant to give her any new reason for alarm. But in some
strange way the episode became a stimulant. We sat
and talked, moved closer and talked, moved closer yet
and kissed, and I took her to bed. It was a very gentle
time, and very sweet in a strange way. In body lan-

guage she was saying, *This* is the way it should be. And I was saying, Replace that memory with *this* one.

It was an isolated episode. Except perhaps by glance or by fleeting expression, we did not mention it again. Knowing her in that biblical sense changed my status with her to that of benign uncle. She sought me out to ask my advice about how she should live her life. She was so determined, months later, that I should approve of Ben Milligan, I think she convinced herself that I had approved. She wanted a good life. It is not an unusual hope, but a very unusual attainment.

I pulled the door shut. I made myself the drink and dressed while I worked at it. After the drink it was time for juice and coffee. After coffee, it was time to go find her purse. False dawn let a little light into the stateroom. I moved silently on bare feet and found the purse at the pillow end, shoved between mattress and box springs. I eased it out and took it to the galley and opened it at the table in the breakfast booth, under the light.

And hello to you, Carolyn Milligan. Florida registration receipt on a two-year-old Datsun, tag number 24D-1313. I found the car keys and put them in my shirt pocket. The occupation, which used to be given on the driving license, no longer appears there. Assume she is still a secretarial type. I copied down the tag number of the car and the address as given: 1500 Seaway Boulevard, Apt. 38B, Bayside, Florida. Comb, lipstick, dental floss, matchbooks, payroll stub, airplane tickets, used. Misc. intimacies. So Mrs. Milligan worked for Superior Building Supplies in Junction Park in Bayside, Florida, and she made $171.54 per week

after deducts. She had been in Jamaica, at a Montego
Bay hotel, in April. She had six hundred and some dollars in the purse. And a Master Charge card. And three
kinds of pills. Everybody has three kinds as a minimum
allowance. It is the creature adjustment to a rapidly
changing world.

By then real dawn had arrived, and I locked up the
Flush and walked through the deceptive coolness and
the varying shades of gray, looking in the lots for her
car. I found it. Bright orange. Imitation leather.
Thirty-one thousand miles on it. Nothing significant in
the glove compartment. A case of twelve bottles of an
industrial abrasive in the trunk. Tru-Kut, it was called.
I opened one, wet my fingers, rubbed and snuffed. Industrial abrasive. A milky white solution that smelled
like men's rooms, overly sanitized, and contained a
gritty cutting agent. So secretary makes deliveries for
the boss fellow of Superior Building Supplies.

Nothing else of any moment. The tires were new,
doubtless recently replaced. Windshield starred by a
kicked-up pebble. Half a tank of gas. I relocked the
car. Nobody seemed to be paying any attention to me.
Over on charter-boat row they were getting ready to go
rumbling out of the basin and roar out to the edge of
the Stream. Early birds were beginning to arrive to get
the shops ready to open. The early maid shift was re-
porting to the motel housekeeper. The early bird who
gets the worm works for somebody who comes in late
and owns the worm farm.

I sauntered back to the *Flush* by a different route. I
unlocked it, slipped keys in purse, slipped purse under
mattress while she still snored on and on into this new
day. By morning light she did indeed look as if she had

not weathered the years too well. New deep lines bracketed her mouth. Her eyes were pouched, her chin slightly doubled, her skin grainy. She frowned in her sleep. By my count, she was thirty. The body was younger, the face older than thirty. Some great-looking couple, those two. Ben and Carrie. Travel-poster people. Photograph them on red bikes in Bermuda, and you would sell tickets on the airplanes. Too much boyish petulance in Ben's face. Too much pseudo-masculine heartiness in his manner. His momma had loved him, all too well.

2

CARRIE slept through the morning and into the afternoon. At three I went in and put my hand on her shoulder and shook her gently. She made a blurred noise of complaint and then gave a great start and snapped her eyes open. She looked terrified. Then she knew me and the lids got heavy again and she put a fist in front of a creaking yawn.

"Whassamarra?" she said. "Whatimezit?"

"Three P.M. on Thursday, love. Keep sleeping. You seem to need it. I'm going to lock you in and go over to the beach for a while."

"Look. When you come back. Wake me up again? Okay?"

"Sure."

It had taken such a great effort of will and so much pain to get back in good shape, I had vowed never to let myself get sloppy again. And that meant hot sun and sweat and exercise every day, no tobacco ever again, and easy on the booze, heavy on the protein. Meyer was involved in writing a long and complicated dissertation on the lasting effect on international currencies of

18

the Arab oil production disputes, and he quit each day at three and joined me on the beach to get in his daily stint. Meyer never looks fat and he never never looks slender. He is merely broad and durable in a rubbery way, and hairy as an Adirondack black bear.

He believes in exercise in moderation. He says that he is not interested in celebrations of masochism, and so, aside from a part of the swimming, we do not see much of each other until the exercise hour is over.

He was already sitting on his towel at the hightide line when I finished sprinting the last hundred yards of my one-mile run. When I stopped puffing and panting and groaning, I took a final dip and then stretched out close by.

"You ought to run a little," I told him.

"Would that I could. When the beach people see you running, they know at a glance that it is exercise. There you are, all sinew and brown hide, and you wear that earnest, dumb, strained expression of the old jock keeping in shape. You have the style. Knees high, arms swinging just right, head up. But suppose I came running down this beach? They would look at me, and then look again. I look so little like a runner or a jock that the only possible guess as to what would make me run is terror. So they look way down the beach to see what is chasing me. They can't see anything, but to be on the safe side, they start walking swiftly in the same direction I'm running. First just a few, then a dozen, then a score. All going faster and faster. Looking back. Breaking into a run. And soon you would have two or three thousand people thundering along the beach, eyes popping out of the sockets, cords in their necks standing out. A huge stampede, stomping everything and everybody in their path into the sand. You wouldn't want me to cause a catastrophe like that, would you?"

"Oh, boy."

"It might not happen, but I can't take the chance."

"Meyer."

"Once it started, I could drop out and they would keep on going. The contagion of panic. Once you see it, you never forget it."

"Meyer, do you remember Carrie Milligan?"

"A thundering herd of . . . what? Who?"

"About six years ago. I loaned Carrie and Ben *The Busted Flush*. Not to take on a cruise. Just to live aboard, during a honeymoon."

"And told me to keep an eye on them. Very funny. I think I saw them come out into the daylight once. Let me see. She worked in the office over at Peerless Marine. Pretty little thing. I forget why you loaned them the *Flush*."

"I owed Dake Heath a favor and that's what he asked for. He was her half brother and he wanted things nice for her. Carrie and Ben were broke and so was Dake. So I broke a rule and said okay."

"To answer your question, yes. I remember her. Why?"

So I told all. I had promised Carrie not to tell anyone. But all rules are off when it comes to Meyer. Also, it was a form of protection. When somebody comes up and gives you that much money to tuck away for safekeeping, special precautions are in order. Checking the purse and the car, for example. And telling Meyer everything, including my checking the purse and the car. If the law moved in, I wanted to be able to give some plausible answers, with somebody to verify them if need be. Also, if somebody grabbed Carrie and bent her until she told them where to look for money, it would be nice to have Meyer know exactly why my luck had, at last, run out. And it will run out. Maybe not this time, or the next time. Sometime, though. And like everybody else, I will go down with that universal plea blazing in the back of my mind. "Not me! Not yet! Wait!"

Meyer was curious about the money, so I described the stacks to him, each neatly tied with white cotton string, each of mixed denominations, each totaling ten thousand. And, of course there were the loose bills, probably from a broken stack, which could mean that she had spent fifty-eight hundred. Each stack had an adding-machine tape stuffed under the string. Yes, all apparently from the same machine, but I hadn't examined them closely. It was used money, but reasonably clean and tidy. Under black light, it might fluoresce. Or somebody might have a list of serial numbers. Or it could all be funny, printed in a small room by night.

"You know her better than I do," Meyer said.

"I don't know her well."

"Have you formed any opinions about her and about the money?"

"Like what? Like did she steal it? I don't know. She's not a bum. She's a worker. Something happened that makes her feel she's got some sort of a right to the money. She arrived physically and emotionally exhausted. She didn't know if she was being followed. She thought she might be. Anyway, I'll hold it for her. If she comes and gets it, no fuss, it's a very easy ten, so easy I'll have an uneasy conscience."

A late-afternoon breeze riffled the water out beyond

the lazy breakers and hustled some candy wrappers down the wet brown beach. Two tall young ladies came sauntering by, brown, brawny, and bikinied, as confident and at home in their bodies as a pair of young lionesses, their hair sun-streaked and salt-tangled, their hips rolling and canting to the slow cadence of their long walk in the sunshine.

Meyer smiled his smile and sighed his audible sigh. It is both a pleasure and a sadness to watch the very young ones walk by. They know so very little, and so frighteningly much. They are on the edge of life, thinking they are in the midst of it. Pretty soon we got up and snapped the sand off the towels and went trudging back across the pedestrain bridge. We parted, and as I stepped aboard the *Flush* I had the sudden strong feeling that harm had come to Carrie, that harm had come aboard, a feral, crouching, bone-gnawing creature.

But all was well. Such hunches happen all the time, for every one of us. We forget them all—except when one turns out to be right. Then we say, I knew! I knew!

She waited to be awakened, waited there with brushed hair, touch of lipstick, new smudge of eye shadow. She faked a sweet awakening from her drowse to pull me down into the mint taste of my own toothpaste, murmuring, "Hello, hello."

It was supposed to be very easy. No need for talk, for claiming and disclaiming. All inevitable because she had made it so through contrivance and through the directness of invitation. Worm my way out of the swim pants and glide sweetly into the lady. Thank you, ma'am. The good-boatkeeping seal of approval. Only a total fink person would decline an offer so frankly made. But the problem of her motive got in my way.

Was this supposed to be in addition to the ten? Was it supposed to cloud my mind and make me less curious? Was she setting up some justification or rationalization of her own? The problem of playing somebody else's game is the problem of finding yourself stuck in a role you can't play. You can't say your lines.

So I disentangled her and sat up from the steamy kiss and smiled down at her and thumbed a strand of hair back from her round forehead. "You certainly needed a lot of sleep."

"I guess I did," she said, looking sullen.

"While you were sleeping, I was thinking."

"Goody!"

"Let's say it gets to be June fifteenth and Carrie doesn't come for her money. Don't you want me to try to find out why you couldn't make it? Or who kept you from making it?"

"It wouldn't matter a damn to me by then, would it?"

"That's what I'm asking."

"The answer is no. Just get the money to my sister. That's all."

"And she'll want to know where it came from."

"Tell her it's from me."

"Maybe she's so straight she might not take it. Then what?"

She bit her lip and looked thoughtful. "I could write her, I guess. Phone her. Something to clue her a little."

"Want to clue me too?"

"No. I don't want to talk about it and I don't want to think about it, okay? It's my personal problem."

"You're paying me enough so you can ask for help."

"I better not try asking for anything else, huh? A girl

shouldn't make it too obvious. Not and get turned down."

"I just get suspicious of free gifts."

"Some gift. From a fire sale. We had us one night, a long time ago. Remember? I was okay for you then, but not now. Not the way I am now. It was a dumb idea. Sorry, fellow."

I took her hand and then despised myself for checking to find those little fingertip calluses acquired from operating office equipment. McGee checks everything, as do all paranoids.

I kissed her slack, cool, unresponsive mouth, and as I straightened up she said, "No charity, thanks. The impulse has come and gone."

"Suit yourself."

"Am I doing something to spoil your day?"

"You don't leave me any options. Any move I make is wrong."

"That's the way it goes. Check with an expert."

"At least I can tell you that you are still very attractive to me, Carrie."

"Sure, sure, sure."

"I mean it."

"Six years ago you meant it, but that was a different girl, six years ago."

"You confuse two things. Okay, I didn't react the way I was supposed to. My guard is up. What do you expect? After six years you show up with a bundle of money and want me to keep it for you. You claim you've shed Ben. I stay alive by keeping my inputs open. Is it gambling money? Is it street money? Is it ransom money? I know some people who are hungry enough to nail me, they'd unearth a girl from six years ago and use her to get to me, to set me up. Marked money. Counterfeit money. Nearly everybody can be manipulated. McGee is alive and well because he is very very careful about a lot of things. Carrie, if you had been Miss Universe stretched out here waving your eyelashes at me, the word would have been the same word. Whoa! Look out for free gifts. I check everything I can check. What I found in your purse about working in an office matches the fingertip calluses on your hands. The industrial goop in the trunk of your car tastes and smells like legitimate industrial abrasive solution."

She spun quickly and stuffed her hand under the mattress, looking for the purse.

"It's there," I said. "I put it back."

She sat up, hauling the sheet up under her chin. She stared at me. "Jesus! You *are* jumpy."

"And alive. Be glad you are leaving your money at the right place, if you still want to leave it here."

"I still want to leave it. It could have been more."

"It's a tidy sum. You are overpaying me."

"I'll decide that. Look, don't worry about the money. Okay? It isn't marked or anything. It's sort of . . . my share of some action. But somebody might grab it." Suddenly she grinned. "Hey! Thanks for giving me back my pride."

"Any time. Want some steak and eggs?"

She looked wistful but refused. She wanted to be on her way. She wore the borrowed clothes and carried her soiled ones in a brown paper bag. She waited for full dark before she left. She marched away under the dock lights, taking a roundabout route to her car. I expected her to look back, but she didn't.

There was a residual affection for her. The six years had aged her more than she could reasonably expect and had tested and toughened her. Her eyes were watchful, her merriment sardonic. There are too many of them in the world lately, the hopeful ladies who married grown-up boy children and soon lost all hope. They are the secretaries and nurses and switchboard people, the store clerks, schoolteachers, cab drivers, and Avon ladies. They lead the singles life. Lots of laughs and lots of barren mornings. Skilled sex, mod conversation, and all heartaches carefully concealed. They are not ardent libbers, yet at the same time they are not looking for some man to "take care." God knows they are expert in taking care of themselves. They just want a grown-up man to share their life with, each of them taking care. But there are one hell of a lot more grown-up ladies than grown-up men.

I wished her well. Lonely ladies can get into damned fool capers. I wished her very well indeed.

3

So two weeks went by. A pair of lovely weeks in May. A steady breeze off the Atlantic kept the bright tacky strip of Florida seacoast reasonably free of smodge, fugg, and schlutch. Old parties tottered out of their condominiums and baked themselves black in the white high glare of the beaches, pleased that their eyes didn't water and they could breathe without coughing.

On the tube the local advertising for condominiums always shows the nifty communal features, such as swimming pool, putting green, sandy beach, being enjoyed by jolly hearty folk in their very early thirties. These are the same folk you see dancing in the moonlight aboard ship in the tour ads. These are the people who keep saying that if you've got your health, you don't need anything else. But when the condominiums are finished and peopled, and the speculator has taken his maximum slice of the tax-related profits and moved on to crud up somebody else's skyline, the inhabitants all seem to be on the frangible side of seventy, sitting in the sunlight, blinking like lizards, and wondering if these are indeed the golden years or if it is all a big sell,

an inflation game that you have to play, wondering
which you are going to run out of first, your money or
your life. The developers leave enough to go wrong in
each condominium apartment that it becomes an odds-
on bet the money runs out first. Nursing homes are a
big industry in sunny Florida.

Anyway, it was Meyer who picked it up, a minor
item on a back page, and brought it over to the *Flush*
on the thirtieth day of May. It was early afternoon and
I was topside, wrestling with too many yards of white
nylon canvas, and with a borrowed gadget which, when
properly operated, puts brass grommets into the fabric.
I was irritated at how slowly my self-imposed chore
was going. I was dripping sweat onto the grommet machine and the clean white nylon and the vinyl imita-
tion-teak decking.

"Now what?" I asked sourly.

"This is what," said Meyer, and handed me the clip
he had torn out of the paper.

PEDESTRIAN FATALITY

The City of Bayside registered its fourth
traffic fatality of the year when Mrs. Carolyn Milligan was struck and killed at 10:30 Wednesday
night while walking on County Road 858 just
inside the city limits. Roderick Webbel, driver
of the farm truck which struck and killed the
Milligan woman, claimed that he did not see her
until the moment of impact when she apparently
stepped from the shoulder of the road into the
path of the vehicle. Mrs. Milligan, who lived
alone at 1500 Seaway Boulevard, was employed
by Superior Building Supplies, Junction Park,
Bayside. Police are investigating the accident and
no charges have been filed as yet.

A fat drop of sweat fell from the tip of my nose and made a dark pattern of a sloppy star on the newsprint, the same color as the sweat smudge from my fingers. Meyer followed me into the shade of the canopy over the topside controls.

I leaned my rear against the instrument panel and propped one bare foot on the pilot's chair. The breeze began to cool me off.

"Accident?" Meyer asked. When I stared at him he said hastily, "Rhetorical question, of course."

"Of course. And who the hell knows? Damn it, anyway!"

I am cursed by an imagination which turns vivid when I wish it would turn itself off. She had been sturdy bone and sinew, sweet flesh and quick blood. She had been scents and secrets. Then a great bewildering bash, a tiny light in the back of the brain flickering out, as spoiled flesh, crushed bone, ripped connective tissue went slamming off into the roadside brush, spraying blood as it spun.

"Meyer, she gave me the orders. Just get the money to my sister, she said. That's all, she said. She said that if she couldn't come back and get the money, she wouldn't give much of a damn who kept her from it."

"And," Meyer said, "she paid you to do just what she said."

"I know."

"But?"

"I look at it this way. Two thousand would have been more than fair. It would have paid my way to Nutley and back, with a nice hunk left over. So she's got eight thousand worth of service coming."

"Posthumous service?"

"Which she didn't want." I doubled my right fist and gave myself a heavy thump on the top of the thigh. Painful. "It is the merry month of May, Meyer, and the lady is going to be dead for a very long time. I would be doing what she wanted. Giving the money to the sister. And making certain there are no strings attached, nobody following the scent, nobody mashing the sister too."

"I admire your talent for instant rationalization."

"This is not romanticism, dammit."

"Did I say it was?"

"By the expression on your face. Patronizing, amused, superior."

"You are reading it wrong. The face is just some skin and fat and muscle stretched over bone. I was actually looking apprehensive."

"About what?"

"About what you might be getting me into."

"You can stay right here and work on your treatise."

"I'm at a stopping point, waiting for translations of some Swedish journals to arrive. I could struggle through them myself, but . . ." He shrugged and went over and picked up some of the canvas, inspected a grommet. "Is this crooked?"

"Very."

"Then it won't look very good, will it?"

"No. It won't."

"Travis, do we know anybody at all in Bayside?"

"I keep thinking there was somebody."

So we went below, and while I checked out the book in the desk, Meyer opened a pair of cold Tuborgs. No friends in Bayside. None. Meyer blew across the top of the Tuborg bottle, a foghorn note far away. "So why are we up there fussing around?" he asked.

"A question which will be asked."

"Insurance?"

"Possibly, but it doesn't feel right."

"Good old united Beneficent Casualty and Life. Those are such beautiful blank policies. I can type in all the——"

"I know. I know. But it could be a dead end. Accidental death, fellows. And these days you get checked out too often. It just doesn't feel right. I think that when she was here two weeks ago I borrowed some money from her. Maybe I gave her a promissory note. I'm in shape to pay it back, but I'd just as soon not pay it back to her heirs and assigns, not if I can get my hands on the note I signed."

"And you take some cash along. For credibility."

"Right! Maybe we both borrowed it and both signed. We're a pair of real-estate gunslingers trying to cheat the little dead lady's estate. We'll pay up if we have to. But we'd rather not."

Meyer closed his eyes and thought long and hard, taking a deep draft on the Tuborg as he did so. He nodded. "I like it."

"We'll take all the cash along," I said.

He looked startled. "All?"

"We'll operate from this gallant watercraft. In comfort. Even in certain vulgar luxury. Go pack your toothbrush, my friend."

After he left I checked my Waterway Guide and picked out what looked like the best of Bayside's several marinas. It was called Westway Harbor, operated by Cal and Cindy Birdsong. I phoned and got a young

man in the office named Oliver. Yes, he had a nice slot
for *The Busted Flush,* one that would take up to a
sixty-footer, one with water, electric, and phone hook-
up and about a hundred feet from the facilities. I said
we'd check in on Friday, probably around noon. The
fee sounded a little bit on the high side. Oliver wanted
to know how long we would be with them, and I said it
was hard to say, very hard to say. He told me to look
for a high round water tower north of the center of
town, and when I was opposite it, I was to look for
their private channel markers and they would lead me
right in, and he would be there to direct me to the slip.
"You can't miss it," he said.

By the time I'd notified the office we were taking off,
exchanged a few lies with Irv Diebert, picked up the
laundry, arranged with Johnny Dow to take the mail
out of the box and hold it, unplugged the shoreside
connections, topped the tanks, and tied the *Muñequita*
well off in the slip, tarped and snug, it was after four
o'clock. We chugged out to the channel and turned
north.

At drinking time I left Meyer at the wheel and went
below and broke out the very last bottle of the Plymouth gin which had been bottled in the United King-
dom. All the others were bottled in the U.S. Gin People, it isn't the same. It's still a pretty good gin but it is
not a superb, stingingly dry, and lovely gin. The sailor
on the label no longer looks staunch and forthright, but
merely hokey. There is something self-destructive
about Western technology and distribution. Whenever
any consumer object is so excellent that it attracts a
devoted following, some of the slide rule and computer
types come in on their twinkle toes and take over the

store, and in a trice they figure out just how far they can cut quality and still increase the market penetration. Their reasoning is that it is idiotic to make and sell a hundred thousand units of something and make a profit of thirty cents a unit, when you can increase the advertising, sell five million units, and make a nickel profit a unit. Thus the very good things of the world go down the drain, from honest turkey to honest eggs to honest tomatoes. And gin.

I put cracked ice in two sturdy glass mugs, dumped in some sherry and dumped it out again, filled with Plymouth gin, rubbed peel around the rims of mugs, squeezed oil onto surface of gin, threw peel away, and carried mugs up to the topside controls, where Meyer was using his best twelve-syllable words on a yuk who had pounded by us, lifting a nine-foot wash behind him. I saw it coming and had time to prepare. I did some twinkle toes myself: three to port, three to starboard, never spilling a drop.

We clinked glasses, took the testing sip, then the deep single swallow. Delicious. The birds were circling, the sun needles were dancing off the water, and the *Flush* was lumbering along, slowed imperceptibly by a fouled bottom. It is unseemly to feel festive about checking out the death of a dead friend. But there is something heartening about having a sense of mission. A clean purpose. A noble intent, no matter how foolish. Behind us, a couple of slow hours back of us, the 17,000 resident boats and the thirteen big marinas of Lauderdale, where 150,000 people grow ever more furious in the traffic tangles. Ahead, some murky mystery locked in the broken skull of a dead lady. The knight errant, earning his own self-esteem, holding the palms cupped to make a dragon trap. Peer inside. S'right, by God, a dragon! But what color, fella?

Before nightfall I found the anchorage I had used before, a sheltered slot between two small mangrove islands. Fortunately nobody had yet built a causeway to either island, or erected thereon one of those glassy monuments to the herd instinct. I nestled the houseboat into the slot and went over the side and made four lines fast to the tough twisted trunks of mangroves, at ten, two, four, and eight o'clock. The night air was full of bugs homing on my earlobes, screaming their hunger, so we buttoned the *Flush* up, testing night breezes and screens until it was comfortable in the lounge.

While Meyer was broiling a very large number of very small lamb chops, a skiff went churning across the flats, heading out toward the channel. The people aboard were yelping like maniacs, making wolf yelps, panther screams, rebel yells. I heard the crazed laughter of a woman. And then there was a sharp authoritative barking. Thrice. *Bam, bam, bam.* Tinkle of glass inside the lounge. Sharp knock against paneling. The skiff picked up speed. The woman laughed in that same crazy way. I stopped rolling and got up onto one knee, then raced topside and yanked the shark rifle out of its greasy nest. No point in firing at one small light far away, the sound fading.

"Why?" Meyer said, beside me.

I didn't answer until we were below again, out of the bugs' hungry clasp. "For kicks. For nothing. For self-expression. Good ol' Charlie shows those rich bastards they don't own the whole goddamn world. It was a handgun and it was a long way off, and having one hit us was pure luck."

"It could have been between the eyes. Pure luck."

"Stoned and smashed. Beer and booze and too much sun. Uppers and downers, hash and smack, all spaced out. Take any guess."

Meyer went quietly back to his broiling. He seemed moody during the meal, working things out his own way inside that gentle, thoughtful skull. The misshapen slug had dented the paneling but had penetrated so shallowly I had been able to pry it loose with a thumbnail. It was on the table beside my cup, a small metallic turd dropped by a dwarf robot. I had stuck Saran Wrap across the starred hole in the glass port.

"Let me give it a try," he said.

"You think you can explain why? Come *on!*"

"When I was twelve years old I received on my birthday a single-shot twenty-two rifle chambered for shorts. It was a magical adventure to have a gun. It made a thin and wicked cracking sound, and an exotic smell of burned powder and oil. A tin can would leap into the air at some distance when I had merely moved my index finger a fraction of an inch."

"Meyer, the killer."

He smiled. "You anticipate me. There were good birds and bad birds. One of the bad birds was a grackle. Of the family *Icteridae,* genus *Quiscalus.* I do not recall why it was in such bad repute. Possibly it eats the eggs of other birds. At any rate, it seemed to be acceptable to shoot one, whereas shooting a robin would have been unthinkable. I had watched grackles through my mother's binoculars. A fantastic color scheme, an iridescence over black, as if there were a thin sheen of oil atop a pool of india ink. I had shown enough reliability with the rifle to be allowed to take it into the woodlands behind our place, provided I followed all the rules. There was no rule about grackles. I went out one Saturday afternoon after a rain. A grackle took a busy splashing bath in a puddle and flew up to a limb. I aimed and fired, and it fell right back down into the same puddle and did some frantic thrashing and then was still. I went and looked at it. Its beak was opening and closing, just under the surface of the water. I picked it up with some vague idea of keeping it from drowning. It made a terminal tremorous spasm in my hand and then it was still. Unforgettably, unbearably still. As still as a stone, as a dead branch, as a fence post. I want to say all of this very carefully, Travis. See this scar on the edge of my thumb? I was using a jack-knife to make a hole in a shingle boat for a mast, and the blade of the knife closed. This bled a good deal, and because it sliced into the thumbnail, it hurt. It hurt as much as anything had ever hurt me up until that time. And that had happened about two months before I murdered the grackle. The grackle lay in my hand, and all that fabulous iridescence was gone. It had a dirty look, the feathers all scruffed and wet. I put it down hastily on the damp grass. I could not have endured dropping it. I put it down gently, and there was blood left on my hand. Bird blood. As red as mine. And the pain had been like mine, I knew. Bright and hot and savage."

He was silent so long I said, "You mean that . . ."

"I'm looking for the right way to express the relationships. Travis, the gun was an abstraction, the bullet an abstraction. Death was an abstraction. A tiny movement of a finger. A cracking sound. A smell. I could not comprehend a gun, a bullet, and a death until the bird died. It became all too specific and too concrete. I had engineered this death, and it was dirty. I had given pain. I had blood on my hand. I did not know what to do with myself. I did not know how to escape from myself, to go back to what I had been before I had slain the bird. I wanted to get outside the new experience of being me. I was, in all truth, in all solemnity, filled with horror at the nature of reality. I have never killed another bird, nor will I ever, unless I should come upon one in some kind of hopeless agony. Now here is the meat of my analogy. Those young people in that boat have never killed their grackle. They have not been bloodied by reality. They have shed the make-believe blood of a West that never existed. They have gawped at the gore of the Godfather. They have seen the slow terminal dance of Bonnie and Clyde. They have seen the stain on the front of the shirt of the man who has fallen gracefully into the dust of Marshal Dillon's main street. It is as if . . . I had walked into those woods and seen a picture of a dead grackle. They do not yet know the nature of reality. They do not yet know, and may never learn, what a death is like. What an ugly thing it is. The sphincters let go and there is a rich sickening stink of fecal matter and urine. There is that ugly stillness, black blood caking and clotting and stinking. To them, that gun somebody took out of his fish box is an abstraction. They find no relationship between the movement of the index finger and the first stinking step into eternity. It is emotional poverty, with cause and effect in a state of disassociation. And they . . ."

He had become hesitant, the words coming more slowly, with less certainty. He smiled with strange shyness and shrugged and said, "But that doesn't work, does it?"

"I think it works pretty well."

"No. Because then they could only kill once. But some of them go on and on. Pointlessly."

"Some of them. Weird ones. Whippy ones."

"Theorizing is my disease, Travis. A friend of mine, Albert Eide Parr, has written, 'Whether you get an idea from looking into a sunset or into a beehive has nothing to do with its merits and possibilities.' I seem to get too many of my ideas by looking into my childhood."

"They didn't nail either of us between the eyes this time."

"Ever the realist."

We cleaned up and sacked out early. I lay wakeful in the big bed, resentful of Meyer nearby in the guest stateroom, placidly asleep. When he had been involved in a government study in India, he had learned how to take his mind out of gear and go immediately to sleep. I had known how, without thinking about it, when I had been in the army, but in time I had lost the knack.

Meyer had explained very carefully how he did it. "You imagine a black circle about two inches behind your eyes, and big enough to fill your skull from ear to ear, from crown to jaw hinges. You know that each intrusion of thought is going to make a pattern on that perfect blackness. So you merely concentrate on keeping the blackness perfect, unmarked, and mathematically round. As you do that, you breathe slowly and steadily, and with each exhalation, you feel yourself sinking a tiny bit further into the mattress. And in moments you are asleep."

He was, but I wasn't. Once I had explained Meyer's

system to a very jumpy restless lady, telling her it wouldn't work for me and it wouldn't work for her. I said, "Go ahead. Try it. It's just a lot of nonsense, Judy. Right, Judy? Hey! Judy? Judy!"

Tonight I was too aware of all the world around me. I was a dot on the Waterway chart between the small islands. Above me starlight hit the deck after traveling for years and for trillions of miles. Under the hull, in the ooze and sand and grass of the bottom, small creatures were gagging and strangling on the excreta of civilization. The farthest stars had moved so much since the starlight left them that the long path of light was curved. After the planet was cindered, totally barren of life, that cold starlight would still be taking the long curved path down to bound off black frozen stone. Ripples slapped the hull. I heard a big cruiser go barreling down the Waterway, piloted by some idiot racing to keep his inevitable appointment with floating palm bole or oil drum. Long minutes after the sound had faded, his wash tipped the *Flush,* creaked the lines, clinked something or other in the galley. It disturbed a night bird, which rose from one of the islands, making a single horrid strangled croak. Far off on the north-south highways there was the insect sound of the fast-moving trucks, whining toward warehouses, laden with emergency rush orders of plastic animals, roach tablets, eye shadow, ashtrays, toilet brushes, pottery crocodiles, and all the other items essential to a constantly increasing GNP.

My heart made a slow, solemn ka-thudding sound, and the busy blood raced around, nourishing, repairing, slaying invaders, and carrying secretions. My unruly memory went stumbling and tumbling down the black corridors, through the doors I try to keep closed. A tickle of sweat ran along my throat, and I pushed the single sheet off.

Where had Carrie Milligan gotten the money?

Had she told anyone I had it?

What had the money to do with being in the same clothes too long?

Kidnap?

Smuggling?

Casino?

Robbery?

Let's take it to Nutley and give it all to the little sister and then go fishing, preferably down off Isla de las Mujeres.

But first, friend, let us try to get the hell to sleep. Please? Please? Keep the black circle absolutely round. Sink deeper with each exhalation. Absolutely round.

4

A good marina—and rare they are indeed—is a comfort and a joy. The private channel to Westway Harbor was about six hundred yards long. It was a seminatural basin, dredged to depth, with the entrance narrowed for protection from wash, storm waves, and chop. The gas dock was inside the entrance, tucked over to the south side. Small-boat dockage was on the southern perimeter of the basin. There were an estimated eighty berths for bigger craft dead ahead and to my right as I came through their entrance.

A brown young man in khaki shorts came out of the dockmaster's office, gave me a follow-me wave of his arm, and hopped onto an electric service cart. I eased to starboard and followed him to the indicated slip, then swung out and backed in between the finger piers as Meyer went forward and put loops over the pilings as we eased past. When the young man sliced the edge of his hand across his throat, Meyer made both bow lines fast to the bow cleat, and I killed my little diesels. The young man was polite. He helped with the lines. He asked permission to come aboard. He handed me a neatly printed sheet of rules, rates, and regulations, services available, and hours of availability. I asked him if he was Oliver, and he said Oliver had gone to lunch. He was Jason. Jason had a jock body, a Jesus head, and gold-wire Franklin glasses.

The instructions were clear and precise. I helped him plug me into the dockside electricity. He took a meter reading. I said we'd like phone service, and he said he'd go bring an instrument. I tasted the hose water and told Meyer to top off the water tank while I went to the dockmaster's office to make arrangements.

As I walked, I admired the construction of the docks. Concrete piers and big timbers and oversized galvanized bolts holding them together. The trash cans were in big fiberglass bins. There were safety stations, with life rings and fire extinguishers. The water lines and power lines were slung under the docks, out of sight. They had about thirty empty berths. The fifty boats in sight looked substantial and well kept, especially a row of a half dozen big motor sailers. A calico cat sitting on the bow of a big Chriss stopped washing to stare at me as I walked by.

There was a big tall lady behind the counter in the office. She had very short black hair and strong features. She was barelegged and barefooted and wore yellow shorts and a white T-shirt and a gold wedding ring. She stood about six feet high, and though the face was strong enough to look just a little bit masculine, there was nothing masculine about the legs or the way she filled the T-shirt. And she was almost as tan as I am. It made her cool blue eyes look very vivid, and it made her teeth look very very white.

"Mr. McGee?"

"Yes. You've got a fine-looking marina here."

"Thank you. I'm Mrs. Birdsong. We've been open exactly two years today."

"Congratulations."

"Thank you." Her smile was small and formal. This was an arm's-length girl. With a long arm. Twenty-eight? Hard to guess her age because her face had that Indian shape which doesn't show much erosion from eighteen to forty.

We made the arrangements. I paid cash for three days in advance, saying we might stay longer. I asked about a rental car, and she walked me over to a side window and pointed to a Texaco sign visible above the roof of the next-door motel and said I could get a car there.

Just as we turned away from the window there was a roar, a yelp of rubber, and a heavy thud as someone drove a dusty blue sedan into the side of the building.

A big man struggled out from behind the wheel and walked unsteadily to the doorway and paused there, staring at her and then at me.

"Where have you been? Where—have—you—been?" she asked. Her eyes looked sick.

He was six and a half feet tall, and almost as broad as the doorway. He had a thick tangle of gray-blond hair, a mottled and puffy red face. He wore soiled khakies, with what looked like dried vomit on the front of the shirt. There was a bruise on his forehead and his knuckles were swollen. He wafted a stink of the un-washed into the small office.

He gave her a stupid glaring look and mumbled,

"Peddle your ass anybody comes along, eh, Cindy? Bangin' dock boys, bangin' customers. I know what you are, you cheap hooker."

"Cal! You don't know what you're saying."

He turned ponderously toward me. "Show you not to fool around with somebody's wife, you bas'ard, you rotten suhva bish."

She came trotting toward him from the side, reaching for him, saying, "No, Cal. No, honey. Please."

He swung a backhand blow at her face, a full swing of his left arm. She saw it coming and tried to duck under it, but it caught her high on the head, over the ear. It felled her. She hit and rolled loose, with a thudding of joints and bones and skull against the vinyl tile floor, ending up a-sprawl, face down.

Cal didn't look at her. He came shuffling toward me, big fists waving gently, shoulder hiked up to shield the jaw. If he'd left enough room for me to slide past him and bolt out the doorway, I would have. Dog drunk as he was, he was immense and seemed to know how to move. I did not want to be in the middle of any family quarrel. Or any wife-killing. She was totally out, unmoving.

One thing I was not going to do, and that was stand up and play fisticuffs. Not with this one. I was getting a good flow of adrenaline. I felt edgy and fast and tricky. I put my hands out, palms toward him, as though pleading with him not to hit me. He looked very happy, in a bleary way, and launched a big right fist at the middle of my face. I snapped my open palms onto that thick right wrist and turned it violently clockwise, yanking downward at the same time. The leverage spun him around, and his wrist and fist went up between his shoulder blades. I got him started and, with increasing momentum, ran him into the cement block wall. He smacked it, dropped to his knees, and then spilled sideways and sat up, blood running down into his eye and down his cheek from a new split in his forehead. He smiled in a thoughtful way and struggled up and came hunching toward me again. This time I moved inside a pawing left hand and hit him as fast and as hard as I could, left-right, left-right, to throat and belly. I knew it damaged him, but as I tried to slide past him, once more thinking of the doorway, he hit me squarely in the forehead. It creaked my neck, turned the bright day to a cloudy vagueness, and put me into slow motion. As I was going down, my head cleared. I hooked my left foot around the back of his right ankle and kicked his kneecap with my right foot. He grunted and tried to stomp me as I rolled away.

As I came to my feet I saw he was having trouble making his right leg hold him up. And the blood obscured his vision. And he was gagging and wheezing. But he was coming on, and I wanted no part of him. I had lost the edge of my reflexes. I was halfway aware of the whirling blue lights of the cop car outside, and of men moving smartly through the doorway.

"Cal!" some man yelled. "Cal, damn you!"

Then they walloped the back of his head with a hickory stick. They rang the hard wood off the skull bone. He tottered and turned and pawed at them, and they moved aside and hit him again. He puddled down, slowly, still smiling, with the unbloodied eye turning upward until only the white showed.

One of the officers rolled the limp hulk face down, brought the hands around behind, and pressed the cuffs onto the wrists. He said, "Hoo-wee, Ralph. He do have a stink onto him. We want him riding in with us?"

"Not after the last time we don't."

Jason, who had helped us dock, was kneeling on the floor. He had lifted Mrs. Birdsong into a sitting position. Her head was a little loose on her neck, and her eyes were vacant. He was gentle with her, murmuring comfort to her.

"She okay, Jason?" an officer asked.

"I . . . I guess I'm all right," she said.

"How about you?" he asked me.

I worked my arms, massaged the back of my neck. My head was clearing the rest of the way, taking me out of slow motion. I felt of my forehead. It was beginning to puff. "He hit me one good lick."

"Why?"

"I haven't the faintest idea. I was checking in."

"He brought his boat in a little while ago," Jason said. He helped Cindy Birdsong to her feet. She pulled free of him and walked over to a canvas chair and sat down, looking gray-green under her heavy tan.

"Want to prefer charges?" the officer asked.

I looked at Cindy. She lifted her head and gave a little negative shake.

"I guess not."

The cop named Ralph sighed. He was young and heavy, with a Csonka mustache. "Arthur and me figured he might head back here. We've been trying to catch up with him for two hours, Cindy. We got all the charges we need. He run two cars off the road. He busted up Dewey's Pizza Shack and broke Dewey's arm for him."

"Oh, God."

"Earlier he was out to the Gateway Bar on Route Seven eighty-seven, and he pure beat the living hell out of three truck drivers. They're in the hospital. I'm sorry, Cindy. It's since he got on the sauce so bad. And being on probation from the last time . . . look, he's going to have to spend some time in the county jail. I'm sorry, but that's the way it is."

She closed her eyes. She shuddered. Suddenly Cal Birdsong began to snore. There was a little puddle of blood under his face. The ambulance arrived. The cuffs were removed. The attendants handled him with less difficulty than I expected. Cindy got a sweater and her purse and rode along with the snoring gigantic drunk, after asking Jason to take care of things.

Jason leaned on the counter and said, "He was okay. You know? A nice guy up to about a year ago. I've worked here since they opened. He drank, but like anybody else. Then he started drinking more and more. Now it makes him crazy. She's really a very great person. It's really breaking her heart, you know?"

"Booze sneaks up on people."

"It's made him crazy. The things he yells at her."

"I heard some of them."

The part of his face not covered by the Jesus beard turned redder. "She's not like that at all. I don't know what it is with him."

"Where do they live?"

"Oh, right over there, in this end unit in the motel. They built the motel the same time as the marina, and leased it out, and in the lease they get to use the unit at this end, a little bigger than the others. Cal inherited some money and they bought this piece of waterfront and put up the marina and the motel. But they could lose it if it keeps up this way."

He went and got a mop and a pail and swabbed up the blood. While he was at it he mopped the rest of the floor. A good man.

I stepped around the wet parts and went back to the *Flush*. Meyer was annoyed. Where had I been? What had happened to my forehead? What were we going to do about lunch?

I told him how I'd happened to meet the Birdsongs. Lovely couple.

When we went to get a car and get lunch, I saw a different fellow in the office. This one was beardless and smaller and rounder, but just as muscular.

"Jason here?"

"He went to lunch. Can I help you?"

"I'm McGee. We're in Slip Sixty."

"Oh, sure. We talked on the phone. I'm Oliver Tarbeck. I understand you and Cal went around and around."

"Sort of. If I can get a rental car, where should I park it?"

"In that row over there where it says Marina Only. If it's full, come here to the office and we'll work something out."

"Place to eat?"

"A block to the left, on this side. Gil's Kitchen. It's okay for lunch."

We had lunch first. The place wasn't okay for lunch. Gil had a dirty kitchen. A fried egg sandwich was probably safe. We went from there to Texaco, which had some sort of budget rental deal, and I tested to see if I could get my knees under the wheel of the yellow Gremlin before giving him the Diner's Card. Nobody will take a cash deposit on a car any more. It forces everybody into cards. As the world gets bigger, it gets a lot duller.

I asked him if he could tell me how to find Junction Park. He gave me a city map and marked the route.

The Gremlin did not have air, but it had some big vents. Meyer read the map and called the turns. It was easy to see the shape and history of Bayside, Florida. There had been a little town on the bay shore, a few hundred people, a sleepy downtown with live oaks and Spanish moss. Then International Amalgamated Development had moved in, bought a couple of thousand acres, and put in shopping centers, town houses, condominiums, and rental apartments, just south of town. Next had arrived Consolidated Construction Enterprises and done the same thing north of town. Smaller operators had done the same things on a smaller scale west of town. When downtown decayed, the town fathers widened the streets and cut down the shade trees in an attempt to look just like a shopping center. It didn't work. It never does. This was instant Florida, tacky and stifling and full of ugly and spurious energies. They had every chain food-service outfit known to man, interspersed with used-car lots and furniture stores.

Junction Park was inland and not far from a turnpike interchange. It had been laid out with some thought to system and symmetry. Big steel buildings were placed in herringbone pattern, with big truck docks and parking areas. The tall sign at the entrance said that Superior Building Supplies was the fourth building on the right.

I parked and told Meyer to see what he could pick up at the neighbor establishments, a heating and air-conditioning outfit, a ladder plant, and a boatbuilder.

I went into the front office of Superior Building Supplies. A slender and pretty girl in a dress made of ticking was taking file folders out of a metal file and putting them into a cardboard storage file. She straightened and looked at me and said in a nasal little voice, "It isn't until Monday."

"What isn't?"

"The special sale of everything. They're taking inventory over the weekend. And right now."

"Going out of business?"

She went over to her desk and picked up a can of Coke and drank several swallows. She gave me a long look of appraisal.

"We sure the hell are," she said finally. She shook her gingery hair back and wiped her pretty mouth with the back of her hand, then belched like any boy in the fifth grade.

A man came through the open door that led back to the warehouse portion. He had a clipboard in his hand. He was sweaty and he had a smudge of grease on his forehead. Lots of red-brown hair, carefully sprayed into position. Early thirties. Outdoor look. Western shirt with a lot of snaps and zippers. Whipcord pants. Boots. A nervous harried look and manner.

"We're not open for business, friend. Sorry. Joanna, find me the invoices on that redwood fencing, precut, huh?"

"Cheez, I keep telling you and telling you, it was Carrie knew where all that—"

"Carrie isn't here to help us, goddammit. So shake your ass and start looking."

"Listen, Harry, I don't even know if I'm going to get paid for this time I'm putting in, right?"

"Joanna, honey, of course you'll get your pay. Come on, dear. *Please* find the invoices for me?"

She gave him a long dark stare, underlip protruding. "Buster, you've been talking just a little too much poremouth. Just a little too much. And you've been getting evil with me too often, hear? I think you better go doodle in your hat. I'm going to go get my hair done. I might come back and I might retire. Who knows?"

She slung her big leather purse over her shoulder. He tried to block her way to the door. He was begging, pleading, insisting. She paid no attention to him. There was no expression on her face. When he took hold of her arm she wrenched away and left, and the glass door swung shut.

Harry went over to a big desk and sat in the large red leather chair. He closed his eyes and pinched the bridge of his nose. He sighed and looked at me and frowned. "Friend, we are still not open for business. We are even less open than we were. Let me give you some sound advice. Never hump the help. They get uppity. They take advantage."

"I came by to ask about Carrie Milligan."

"She used to work here. She's dead. What's your interest?"

"I heard she was killed. I'm a friend of hers from Fort Lauderdale."

"Didn't she used to live there?"

A bare-chested young man in jeans came out of the warehouse area and held up two big bolts. "Mr. Hascomb, you want I should count every damn one of these things? There's thousands!"

"Hundreds. Count how many in five pounds and then weigh all we got. That'll be close enough."

The boy left, and Harry Hascomb shook his head and said, "It's hard to believe she's dead. She worked day before yesterday. That's her desk over there. It happened so sudden. She really held this place together. She was a good worker, Carrie was. What did you say you want?"

"She came to see me two weeks ago. In Fort Lauderdale."

He was so still I wondered if he was holding his breath. He licked his lips and swallowed and said, "Two weeks ago?"

"Does that mean anything?"

"Why should it mean anything?"

I did not know where to go from there. The loan of money seemed all at once frail and implausible. I needed to find a better direction. "She came to see me because she was in trouble."

"Trouble? What kind of trouble?"

"She wanted to leave something with me for safekeeping. It happened it wasn't the best time for me to try to take care of anything for anybody. There are times you can, and times you shouldn't. I hated to say I couldn't. I was very fond of Carrie Milligan."

"Everybody was. What did she want you to keep?"

"Some money."

"How much?"

"She didn't say. She said it was a lot. When I heard about her being killed in that accident, I began to wonder if she'd found anybody to hold the money. Would you know anything about anything like that?"

Once again Harry went into his motionless trance, looking over my shoulder and into the faraway distance. It took him a long time. I wondered what he was sorting, weighing, appraising.

At last he shook his head slowly. "My God, I wouldn't have believed it. She must have been in on it."

"In on what?"

He undid a snap and a zipper and fingered a cigarette out of his Western pocket, popped it against a thumbnail, lit it and blew out a long plume of smoke. "Oh, shit, it's an old story. It happens all the time. You never expect it to happen to you."

"What happened?"

"What's your name again?"

"McGee. Travis McGee."

"Don't ever go partners with anybody, McGee. That's my second piece of advice for you today. Jack and I had a good thing going here. My good old partner, Jack Omaha. It wasn't exactly a fantastic gold mine, but we lived very well for quite a few years. And then the ass fell right off the construction business. We had to cut way back. Way way back. Trying to hold out until conditions improve. I think we might have made it. Things are looking a little bit better. I've always been the sales guy and Jack was the office guy. Anyway, he took off two weeks ago last Tuesday. On May fourteenth. Know what he was doing before he took off? Selling off warehouse stock at less than cost. Letting the bills pile up. Turning every damned thing into money. The auditors are trying to come up with the total figure. I'm a bankrupt. Good old Jack. Come to think of it, I guess he had to have Carrie's help to clean the place out. She only worked two days that week. Monday and Friday. Went out sick Monday afternoon. Came back in Friday. That was the day I finally decided Jack hadn't just gone fishing, that maybe he was gone for good. When did you see Carrie?"

"Thursday."

"It figures. I never figured her for anything like that. Even though she and Jack did have something going. No great big thing. It was going on for maybe three years, like ever since she started working for us. Just a little something on the side now and then. An overnighter. What we used to do, we'd send the girls, Carrie and Joanna, on another flight up to Atlanta, and then Jack and me would go up to catch the Falcons and stay in the HJ's next to the stadium. Just some laughs."

"And you think that was the money Carrie wanted me to keep for her?"

"Where else would she get it? Maybe Jack wanted her to run away with him. He was more hooked than she was, you know. Think of it this way. She helps him and gets a nice piece of change, and everybody thinks Jack took it all. When the dust settles, she can get the money and who'd know the difference?"

"Except she's dead."

"Yes, there's that. I want to make one thing clear, McGee. If you come across that money it belongs right here in this business. It was stolen from this business. It was stolen from me, and if you find it, it belongs right here."

"I'll keep that in mind."

He squashed his cigarette out. "None of this had to happen," he said softly. "I wake up in the night and think about it. If I'd had the sense when the money was rolling in, I would have put it in a safe place. Instead I farted it away on boats and cars and houses. If I'd kept it, I could have bought Jack out when things got slow. I could have squeaked through. In the night I think about it and I get sweaty and I feel like my gut was full of sharp rocks."

"What will happen?"

"I have to sell off what we've got left and throw it in the pot. It gets divided up among the creditors. I guess I'll lose the house too, maybe the cars. Then I'll start hitting my friends for a job. That son of a bitch said he was going fishing Tuesday and he'd be in Wednesday, and he said he had some money lined up to tide us over. I wanted to believe him. By Friday I got worried. I got some phone calls about bills I thought were paid. I called Chris. Jack's wife. She didn't know where the hell he was. She thought he was off in the boat somewhere. I phoned the marina and the boat was tied up there, nobody aboard. You know what? I just remembered. I had Carrie check out the bank accounts. She acted like she hated to tell me he had cleaned them out. He'd left ten bucks in each of them. He's a wanted man. I brought charges. I signed papers. It was on the news. I hope they find the son of a bitch, and I hope he has a lot of money left when they find him."

"You never thought Carrie was involved?"

"Not until you told me about her being in Lauderdale when I thought she was sick in bed. Not until you told me she wanted you to hold a lot of money for her. I swear. I mean I thought Jack was smarter than let some girl in on a thing like that. I wouldn't ever give Joanna any kind of leverage. I guess it was just that she kept a close enough eye on the books, he couldn't work it without her help. And, knowing that, she cut herself in pretty good. Maybe she was afraid Jack might come back to her for the money."

"Did you case her as a thief?"

"Her! I thought I was surrounded by friends. I guess they decided that since the business was going to fold no matter what anybody did, the thing to do was grab the goodies and run. Like maybe running into a burning motel and grabbing a wallet. Shit, maybe I would have cleaned the place out first if I'd thought of it before Jack did. And if I knew how. I wonder where Jack is now. Brazil?"

For once Meyer followed my standing instructions. He came in and folded his arms and leaned against the wall beside the door. He didn't say a word.

"We're closed," Harry told him.

I said, "He's with me."

Harry stared at him. Meyer stared back, letting his underlip and his eyelids sag. With all that hair and with that inch of simian forehead he looked so baleful as to be almost subhuman. Of course the effect is ruined if he opens his professorial mouth.

Harry swallowed and said, "Oh. Uh . . . what kind of work are you in, Mr. McGee?"

He rolled a yellow pencil under his palm, the flat sides clicking against the top of the desk. I let him roll it four times before I said, "Oh, I guess you could call it investments."

He smiled too brightly. "Want to buy a nice building-supply business?"

I gave it a slow four count while the smile faded.

"No."

The kid came out of the warehouse again. "For Chrissake, there's supposed to be almost two dozen wheelbarras and I can't find a good goddamn one out there."

"Wait a second," Harry said. He took a sheet of letterhead, turned it over, and with a marking pen printed C L O S E D on it, and put pieces of Scotch tape on the corners. He stood up and said to me, "Nice to have met you, Mr. McGee."

"I'll stay in touch," I said. It didn't seem to make him happy.

After we left I looked back and saw him tape the sign to the inside of the glass door.

Meyer said, "What kind of fantasy were you selling him in there?"

"I was making it up as I went along. I was throwing in stuff to keep him talking. I dropped the loan idea."

As I drove slowly back toward town, I briefed Meyer on what I had learned. Then it was his turn. He gave it such a long dramatic pause, I knew he had done well. Why shouldn't he do well? I have busted my gut to learn how to make people open up. Meyer was born with it. A loving empathy shines out of those little bright-blue eyes. Strangers tell him things they have never told their husband or their priest.

He said that the secretary to the president of the Bayside Ladder Company, Inc., was one Betty Joller and, being Carrie Milligan's best friend, Betty was all racked up over the accident. Once upon a time Betty and Carrie and girls named Flossie Speck and Joanna Freeler had shared a little old frame house on the waterfront, at 28 Mangrove Lane. When Carrie moved out, they had gotten another girl to share rent and expenses. Meyer couldn't recall the new girl's name.

Anyway, Carrie Milligan was at the Rucker Funeral Home on Florida Boulevard, and there was to be a memorial service for her tomorrow, Saturday morning, at eleven o'clock. The sister, Susan Dobrovsky, was down from Nutley. She had arrived late last night. Betty Joller had picked her up at the airport and taken her to the Holiday Inn.

"You did well!" I told him. "Very very well."

It made him beam with pleasure.

I found 1500 Seaway Boulevard. I reminded him that Carrie had lived in 38B. I dropped him off and told him to see what he could get from the neighbors, and then work his own way back to Westway Harbor, and wait for me there if I wasn't back yet.

5

*T*he Omaha house was in a fairly new subdivision called Carolridge. The developer had bulldozed it clean in his attempt to turn it from flatlands to slightly rolling contours. The new trees were all growing as fast as they could. In twenty years, when the block houses were moldering away, the shade would be pleasant and inviting. But in the mid-afternoon heat, all the houses sat baking white in the sun, and the spray heads made rainbows against immature gardenia bushes.

There were two cars in the carport at the Omaha place, and a fairly new cream-colored Oldsmobile in the driveway. A little wrought-iron sign was stuck into the parched grass, spelling out THE OMAHAS.

They give the development houses names. This was probably called The Executive or The Diplomat. It looked like eighty to ninety thousand, the top of the line for the neighborhood. Purchase would guarantee membership in the Carolridge Golf and Country Club. You could read the house from the outside. Three bedrooms, three and a half baths, colonial kitchen, game room, cathedral ceilings, patio pool, fiberglass screening.

I pushed the button and heard the distant chimes inside. Bugs keened in the heat. Some little girls went creaking and grinding past on their Sears ten-speeds, giggling. Somebody was running some kind of lawn machinery three houses away. A cardinal was sitting on a wire, saying *T-bird, T-bird, T-bird—cool, cool, cool*. I pushed the button again. And finally again. Just as I was about to give up, a woman opened the door. She had a broad, coarse, pretty face. She wore fresh lipstick, a sculptured blond wig, tie-dye jeans, and a white sunback blouse with no sleeves.

"Mrs. Omaha?"

"Yes. We were out in the back. I hope you haven't been ringing the doorbell long?"

"Not very long."

"I didn't know you'd come so soon. What happens is I keep getting a dial tone all the time, even when I'm trying to talk to somebody." She had a thin little-girl voice. She had the dazed glazed manner of someone awakened from deep sleep. Her mouth was puffy, her eyes heavy. The fresh lipstick missed its mark at one corner of her mouth. The sculptured wig was slightly off center. There was a red suck mark on the side of her throat, slowly disappearing as I looked at it.

"I'm not from the phone company," I said.

Her gaze sharpened. "Oh, boy, you better not try telling me you're selling something. You just better not try that."

"My name is McGee. Travis McGee from Fort Lauderdale. A friend of Carrie Milligan."

She was puzzled. "So what? What do you want here?"

"Did I come at a bad time?"

"Brother!"

"Suppose I come back later?"

"What for? Carrie is dead, right? Jack took off. Let's say they were very very good friends and I couldn't care less."

"I was talking to Harry over at Junction Park. He says Jack cleaned out the partnership accounts on May fourteenth. Carrie came down to Lauderdale to see me on the sixteenth. She was jumpy. She thought she was being followed. She gave me some money to keep for her."

"How much?"

"Maybe some other time would be . . ."

"Come on in, Mr. Gee. It's real hot this afternoon, isn't it?"

I followed her through the foyer to the long living room. She filled the rear of the stretch jeans abundantly. As she walked she reached up and patted the wig. The draperies were pulled shut. The subdued daylight came from the outdoor terrace area where, through the mesh of the drapery fabric, I could see a screened swimming pool as motionless as lime Jell-O in the white glare.

A tall and slender man stood in front of a mirror, combing his dark hair down with spread fingers. He wore a pair of quiet plaid slacks and a white shirt. His necktie hung untied. Over the back of a nearby chair I saw a dark blazer with silver buttons.

He said, "Honey, I'll get in touch again about the . . ."

He spotted me in the mirror. He whirled and said, "Who the hell are you?"

"This is Mr. Gee, Freddy."

"McGee," I said. "Travis McGee."

"This here is Fred Van Harn, my lawyer," Chris explained.

I put my hand out. He hesitated and then shook hands and gave me a very pleasant smile. "How do you do?"

"Honey, I asked him in because he says he's got some of the money. Maybe he's got all of it. Tell him he has to give it to me, dear. Mr. McGee, it's my money."

I looked at her in astonishment. "I haven't got any money!"

"You said Carrie gave it to you to keep for her!"

"She did, but I gave it right back. I couldn't accept the responsibility."

"How much was it?" Chris Omaha demanded.

"I'm sure I wouldn't have the slightest idea. She said it was a lot. She didn't say how much. What is a lot to one person is not a lot to another person."

Chris said, "Oh, God damn everything." She plumped herself down on a fat hassock which hissed as she sat on it.

Freddy said, "Do you know who did agree to keep the money for her?"

"She didn't say who she was going to try next."

"Where did this happen? And when?"

"On Thursday, May sixteenth, at about three or four in the morning aboard my houseboat moored at Bahia Mar in Fort Lauderdale."

"Why would she come to you?"

"Perhaps because she trusted me. We were old and good friends. I loaned her my houseboat for her honeymoon."

Freddy had long lashes, rather delicate features, olive skin. His eyes were a gentle brown, his manner ingratiating.

"Why did you come here, Mr. McGee?"

"I had a long talk with Mr. Hascomb. I just thought Mrs. Omaha would like to know about Mrs. Milligan coming to me. I thought it might answer some questions about her husband."

"You wouldn't listen to me, would you?" the woman said to Freddy in a whiny and irritating voice. "I told you that Milligan slut had to be in on it somehow, but you wouldn't listen to me. I happen to know as a fact that Jack was screwing her for years, even though he didn't know I knew, and—"

"Be quiet, Chris."

"You can't tell me to be quiet! You know what I think? He cleaned out the business and mortgaged everything in sight, this house and even the boat, and she was going to run off with him, but she probably had some boy friend and they decided it was safer and easier to chunk my husband on the head and throw him into—"

He moved close to her. "Shut *up*, Chris!"

"I can put two and two together even if you can't, Freddy, and let me tell you one thing—"

She didn't tell him one thing. He was one very fast fellow. He had a sinewy hand and a long whippy arm and a very nice clean pivot. He slapped her so fast and so hard I thought for one crazy moment he had shot her with a small-caliber handgun. It knocked her completely off the hassock. She landed on her hip and rolled over onto her shoulder and ended up face down on the carpeting. He got to her quickly, turned her, and pulled her up to a sitting position. Her eyes were crossed. The impact area was white as milk. I knew it would turn pink, then red, and finally purple. She was going to be lopsided for quite a few days. A little trickle of blood ran from the corner of her mouth down her chin.

He sat on his heels, holding her hand, and said, "Darling, when your attorney tells you to be quiet, there might be a very good reason for it. So you have to learn to be still when he tells you to."

"Freddy," she said in a broken voice.

He pulled her up to her feet and turned her toward a doorway and gave her a little push. "Go in and lie down, darling. I'll come in and say good-bye in a few minutes. Close the door, please."

She did as ordered. He turned mildly toward me and said, "Now let's understand where you fit, Mr. McGee. You just wanted to get involved?"

"Doing my duty as a citizen."

"I'm familiar with your type. The smell of money brings people like you out of the woodwork. I can't think of a way you can work any kind of a con in this situation. So give up and go home."

"I'm familiar with your type too. I saw the way you tied that tie. Very quick and neat. Ready Freddy, servicing another client. I bet you're in and out of those clothes as often as a fashion model."

I saw the little flare behind his eyes and hoped he would try me. I tried to look smaller and slower than I am. Finally he smiled and looked at a microthin gold watch gold-clamped to a lean and hairy wrist.

"With a deposition at four o'clock, there's no time for schoolyard games, my friend."

"Nor will there ever be, eh?"

A sudden flush made him look healthier, and then pallor turned him gray-green. "I think you'd better leave, McGee. Now!"

So I left that enchanting place. Pale shag, silk lampshades, velvet wing chairs, brocade, imitation Tiffany stained glass, Japanese lacquer, gilt mirror frames. Somehow like a matinee in a department store. Van Harn looked about thirty, or a shade under. The lady looked well over. They were consenting adults, consenting to afternoon games in the tangly bed under the long exhalation of the air conditioning.

As I backed out a phone truck pulled up. I smiled and waved at him and wondered what kind of reception he'd get. Good luck, fella. Must be an interesting line of work.

It was quarter to four. The yellow Gremlin was hot enough to bake glaze on pottery. The steering wheel was almost, not quite, too hot to touch. I stopped wondering what to do next and ran around for a mile or two trying to get cool in a hot wind.

I found a shopping center and discovered that they had left some giant oaks in the parking lot. This runs counter to the sworn oath of all shopping center developers. One must never deprive thy project of even one parking slot. And, wonder of wonders, there was an empty slot under one tree, in the shade. As I got out of the Gremlin, a cruising granny glowered at me from the air-conditioned, tinted-blue depths of her white Continental.

I found pay phones in a big Eckerd Drug, the phone stations half hidden by huge piles of pitchman's merchandise.

At the Holiday Inn they had a Miss Dobrovsky registered in Room 30, but she did not answer the phone. I looked up Webbel, who had driven the truck. There were about fifteen of them, but no Roderick. I wondered why Susan Dobrovsky would stay in the Holiday Inn instead of in Carrie's apartment. Squeamish, maybe. But sooner or later she would have to decide what to do with Carrie's personal belongings. That made me think of personal arrangements, and so I looked up the number for the Rucker Funeral Home and asked for Miss Susan Dobrovsky. After a long wait the man came back on the line and said that Miss Dobrovsky was busy with Mr. Rucker, Senior. I told him to tell her to wait there for me. Wait for McGee. Right there.

Rucker's Funeral Home was from the orange plaster and glass brick era. It had arches and some fake Moorish curlicues along the edge of the flat roof. A small black man was listlessly rubbing a black hearse parked at the side entrance. There was a large cemented area at the side and in back where doubtless they shaped up the corteges. I saw Carrie's bright orange Datsun in the parking lot on the other side of the building. On one side of the home there was a savings and loan branch, and on the other side a defunct car wash. I stuck my yellow Gremlin beside the orange Datsun, wondering if the industrial abrasive was still in the trunk. The bright colors screamed at each other.

She was sitting on a marble bench in the hallway just inside the front door. She looked enough like Carrie so that I was able to recognize her at once. She was a taller, younger, softer version of Carrie. She had on a dark gray tailored suit, a small round hat. She carried a purse and white gloves. Her eyes were swollen and red. She looked dejected and exhausted. But she was a marvelously handsome lady.

"I'm pleased to meet you, Mr. McGee."

"Did Carrie write you about me?"

"No. It was just . . . she phoned me long distance over a week ago, one night about ten. I was getting ready for bed. She talked a whole hour. It must have cost a fortune. She was funny. She kept laughing and saying silly things. Maybe she was drinking. Anyway, she made me get a pencil and paper and write down how to get in touch with you. She said that if anything happened to her, it was important I should get in touch with you. She said I could trust you. She said you're a nice person."

"She was in a loyal minority, Miss Susan."

"I . . . I don't know what to do about this," she said. She took a sheet of letterhead paper, folded once, out of her dark plastic purse and handed it to me. It was a heavy, creamy bond, and the statement of account had been typed with a carbon ribbon electric, flawlessly. It added up to $1677.90. It contained all manner of processing charges and service charges and mortuary overhead charges. It contained a coffin for $416 including tax, and it included an embalming fee, crematorium fee, death certification fee.

"She wanted to be cremated. It's in her will even. I can't pay all that. He has some kind of installment note he wants me to sign. He seems very nice . . . but . . ."

By being very firm with a chubby sallow fellow I gained an audience with Mr. Rucker, Senior. If you shaved Abe Lincoln and gave him a thick white Caesar hairpiece, and left the eyebrows black, you would have a reasonable duplicate of Rucker, sitting there in perpetual twilight behind his big walnut desk.

His voice was hushed, gentle, personal.

"I should be pleased to go over the billing with you, sir, item by item. Let me say I am glad the little lady has someone to help her in this time of need."

"Shall we discuss the coffin first?"

"Why not, if you wish? It is very inexpensive, as you can see."

"The decedent is to be, or has been, cremated."

"Cremation will take place this evening, I think. I can determine for sure."

"So there's no need for a coffin."

He smiled sweetly and sadly. "Ah, so many people have that misconception. It is a regulation, sir."

"Whose regulation?"

"The State of Florida, sir."

"Then you will be willing to show me the statutes which pertain?"

"Believe me, sir, it is standard practice and . . ."

"The statutes?"

"It may not be specifically spelled out in the law, but . . ."

I reached and took the pen from his desk set and drew a thick black line through the coffin and said, "Now we're down to twelve sixty-one ninety. I see you've charged for embalming."

"Of course. And a great deal of cosmetic attention was required. There were severe facial lacerations which—"

"It wasn't ordered and is not required by law prior to cremation."

He gave me a saintly smile. "I am afraid I cannot accept your judgments on these matters, sir. I must refer them to the sister of the deceased. We must bring her in on this. I must caution you that this is a very difficult situation for her, all this petty squabbling about the account as rendered."

"It's easier on her to just go ahead and pay it?"

"This is a very sad occasion for her."

"Wait right here," I said.

I went and found Susan on the bench in the hallway. I sat beside her and said, "We can cut that bill by a thousand dollars, but he thinks it will be such a rough experience for you to haggle over price, we should go ahead and pay it. What do you think?"

For a moment she was blank. Then I saw the tender jaw clamp into firmness and saw her eyes narrow. "I know what Carrie would say."

Mr. Rucker Senior stood up behind his desk when I walked in with Susan Dobrovsky. "Do sit down, my dear. We'll try to make this as painless as we possibly—"

"What's this crap about you overcharging me a thousand dollars?" she said in a high, strident, demanding voice.

He was taken aback but he recovered quickly. "You don't quite understand. For example, it may not be absolutely legally necessary for you to purchase a casket, my dear, but I think it would be a gross disrespect to your poor sister to have her . . . tumbled into the burning chamber like some kind of . . . debris."

She braced her fists on his desk and leaned closer to him. "That is not my sister! That is a body! That is debris! My sister is not in there any more and there is no reason for you to . . . to try to get me to worship the empty body, damn you, you greedy old man!"

He moved around the side of the desk, his face quiet as any death mask, and said, "Excuse me. I'll have this account recomputed. It will take just a few minutes."

He went out a side door. When it was open I could hear an electric typewriter rattling away. When he closed it behind him, she turned blindly into my arms. She rolled her head against my shoulder and gave three big gulping sobs and then pulled herself together, pushed away from me, honked into a Kleenex, and tried to smile.

"Was I okay?" she asked.

"You were beautiful."

"I was pretending I was Carrie and it was me who was dead. She'd never let him take advantage. I was just so confused when he gave me the bill before."

"Is the memorial service to be here?"

"Oh, no. Betty Joller sort of arranged it. It's going to be on the beach there at Mangrove Lane where she used to live."

Rucker Senior came back into the room and tried to hand her the new billing. I reached across her and took it. It was far more specific. It came to $686.50. I no-

ticed he had included a sixty-dollar urn, sixty-two
forty with tax. I was tempted to strike it but decided it
was best to let him have a minor victory.

"Here are the rings from the deceased," he said,
holding out a small manila envelope. She hesitated, and
I took that also and slipped it into my shirt pocket.

"Satisfactory arrangements for payment will have to
be made," the man said.

I took out my money clip, slipped the currency out
of it, and counted out seven one-hundred-dollar bills
on the front edge of his desk. "We'll need thirteen fifty
in change and your certification on this bill, Mr. Rucker."

He expressed his opinion by looking most carefully
at each bill, back and front. He made change from his
own pocket and receipted the bill. *Paid in Full. B. J.
Rucker, Sr.*

"You may pick up the urn here between one and
two tomorrow afternoon," he said.

I nodded. There were no good-byes. We walked out.

Out in the afternoon sunshine of the parking lot, she
swayed against me, leaned heavily on my arm as we
walked. She shook her head and straightened up and
lengthened her stride.

"He had me go back in there and see her," she said.
"I thought there was some mistake. Her face wasn't the
right shape even. She looked like she was made of wax.
He showed me how the inside of the casket is all quilt-
ed, the kind he was selling me. Would he have really
had it burned up, or would he have saved it for the
next person?"

"I think B.J. would have had it burned up."

The lower angle of the sun had stretched casuarina

shadows across our two bright little cars. Before she unlocked the Datsun she turned to face me and said, "About that money in there, I'll be able to . . ."

"It was your money."

"What do you mean?"

"I owed it to Carrie."

"Is that true? Is that really true?"

"Really true."

"How much did you owe her?"

"It's a long story."

"Well, I'd like to know."

"She told you to trust me."

"Yes . . .?"

"Trust me not to tell you now, and trust me to have good reasons not to tell you. Okay?"

She looked at me for a long moment and then slowly nodded. "Okay, Mr. McGee." Her hair was long, and a couple of shades darker than Carrie's cropped silvery mop. The face was as round as Carrie's, the cheekbones high and heavy, but her eyes had more of a Slavic tilt, and their color was a seagreen-gray.

I made her try calling me Trav, and after three times it came easier and she smiled.

"How long are you going to stay?"

"Well, I guess until the lawyer says it's okay to go back to New Jersey. I've got to sort out all her stuff in that apartment. It's in a terrible mess. Somebody broke in and tore up the furniture and rugs and emptied everything out on the floor."

"When did this happen?"

"So much is happening, I'm getting confused on the dates. She was killed Wednesday night. Betty Joller was in bed and heard it on the eleven o'clock news. Betty, being her best friend, got dressed and drove to the apartment figuring my phone number would be in Carrie's phone index someplace, and I should be told. Betty has a key to the apartment that Carrie gave her. Betty got to the apartment about midnight and found it all in such a mess it took her a half hour to find my phone number. She was crying so hard I couldn't understand what she was trying to tell me. And when she did . . . wow, it was like the sky falling down. Carrie was seven years older, and I saw her just once in the last six years, when she came back to Nutley five years ago for our mother's funeral. I had no idea it would hit me so hard. I guess it's because she was the only close family I had left. There's some cousins I've never seen since I was a baby."

"Did Betty Joller report it to the police?"

"I don't really know. I guess she would have. I mean it would be a normal thing to tell the police about it. I told the lawyer about it, and he asked me if there was any specific thing we could report as being taken in the robbery, and I said maybe Betty could figure out what was missing, that I wouldn't know."

"Who's your lawyer?"

"He's a good friend of a girl that lives at 28 Mangrove Lane. I keep forgetting his name. But I've got his card here. Here. Frederick Van Harn. He just has to straighten out about the will and the car and all that. I guess it will be okay because he is the one who drew up the will for her. After she broke up with Ben she wanted to be sure he didn't get a dime that was hers if anything happened to her. Ben was at the funeral too, five years ago, but I can't remember him at all." She looked at her watch. "Hey, I've got to get going. Betty is coming over to the Inn, and we're going to work it all out about tomorrow. You're coming, aren't you?"

"Of course."

She drove away and I drove back to Westway Harbor.

6

I parked my rental in one of the reserved slots. As I walked past the office toward the docks, Cindy Birdsong came to the door and said, "Can I speak to you a moment, Mr. McGee?"

"Of course."

She had changed to a white sunback dress, and she wore heels, which put her over the six-foot line. A big brown lady with great shoulders and other solid and healthy accessories. And a mighty cool blue eye, and a lot of composure and pride.

"I want to apologize to you for the trouble my husband gave you this noon. I am very sorry it happened."

"It's perfectly all right, Mrs. Birdsong."

"It's not all right. It was a very ugly scene. If they release him on bail, I am sure he will want to apologize personally. I'm going to visit him this evening in the hospital, and I know he will be very ashamed of himself."

"He had a few over the limit."

"A few! He was pig drunk. He never used to get like . . . well, I shouldn't burden you with our personal history. Thank you for giving me the time. If there is anything you need we are . . . always anxious to serve our customers. Oh, and I meant to thank you for not signing a complaint." Her smile was inverted and bitter. "There are enough of those to go around as it is."

"If there's any way I can help . . ."

She blinked rapidly. "Thank you very much. Very much."

Meyer was aboard *The Busted Flush,* dressing after having just gotten back from taking a shoreside shower. I broke open a pair of cold beers and took him one and sat on the guest stateroom bed and watched him put on a fresh white guayabera.

"Fifteen Hundred Seaway's one of those bachelor boys and girls places," Meyer said. "Everybody seems to laugh a lot. It's very depressing. Eighty small apartments. There's a kind of . . . watchful anxiety about those people. It's as if they're all in spring training, trying out for the team, all trying to hit the long ball, trying to be a star. And in a sense, they're all in training. They're pretty trim and brown. Very mod in the clothes and hair departments. They're all delighted that there's a long waiting list for Fifteen Hundred. Pools and saunas and a gym. Four-channel sound systems. Health fads. Copper bracelets. *The Joy of Sex* on each and every coffee table, I would guess. Water beds, biofeedback machines. There doesn't seem to be any kind of murky kinky flavor about them. No group perversion scenes. Just a terrible urgency about finding and maintaining an orgasm batting average acceptable to the peer group. Their environment is making terrible demands upon them. I bet their consumption of vitamins and health foods is extraordinary."

We went up onto the sun deck and sat in the shade of the big canopy over the topside controls. "It doesn't sound like the kind of place where Carrie would want to live."

"No. It doesn't. It isn't. I didn't say why I was asking about her. I imagine they assumed I'm some kind of relative of hers. There was a coolness toward her. They thought she was standoffish, too much of a private person. She didn't get into the swing of things. I guess the pun is intentional."

"An outcast in Swingleville, eh?"

"Not exactly. More like a special friend of the management. The management is Walter J. Demos. He owns it and manages it and is sort of a den mother to all. He lives there, in the biggest apartment. He personally approves or disapproves of every applicant. He won't accept tenants who are too young or too old. He settles quarrels and disputes. He collects the rents, repairs plumbing, plants flowers, and he laughs a lot."

"How old a man?"

"I wouldn't want to guess. He looks like a broader, browner version of Kojak. He has a deep voice and a huge laugh. He is a very charming and likable man. He is very popular with his tenants. He is Uncle Walter. I think Uncle Walter is a smart businessman. The rents start at three hundred and seventy-five a month, and his occupancy rate is one hundred percent. By the way, he told me about Carrie's apartment being burglarized the same night she—"

"I heard about it. Was the door forced?"

"No. The layout is arranged for maximum privacy. If you go from your apartment to visit somebody, there's very little chance of your being seen. And it seems to be local custom to have a batch of keys made and hand them out to your friends."

"How long had she lived there?"

"Four months only. I picked up the rumor that Uncle Walter had moved her to the top of the list. They all seemed miffed about it. Jealous, almost. They don't want Uncle Walter to have a special girl."

"Did you get the feeling from him that she was special to him?"

"He seemed very upset about it, about her being killed. He said all the usual things. She had the best years of her life ahead of her. A pointless tragedy. And so forth."

"Seems like high rent for Carrie to pay."

"That's something that kept cropping up in conversation. Those tenants seem to feel they have to give a continual sales talk about the joys of living in Fifteen Hundred. They claim that because they don't have any urge to go out at night or away for vacations, it really saves money to live there. The little shopping center is so close you can walk over and wheel the stuff home. The ones who work close, some of them at least, have given up cars and use bikes. It's fascinating, in a way. A village culture. Maybe it's part of the shape of the world to come, Travis."

"Let us hope not."

"You seem a bit sour."

I stretched and sighed. "Carrie is in an upholstered box at Rucker's, her face reassembled with wax and invisible stitching. Tonight they will tote her off to the electric furnace and turn her into a very small pile of dry gray powder. So I am depressed."

"I don't think I can add anything of interest. Carrie didn't make any close friends there."

"Pun intended?"

"Not that time. Maybe you're not as sour as you act?"

"I'll tell you my adventures," I said. And did.

When I had finished he said, "I suppose we'll learn that young Mr. Van Harn is the attorney for Superior Building Supplies, which would account for his doing Carrie's will and being recommended to the sister, and being with Mrs. Omaha."

"I had the same feeling."

"What next?"

"We have a drink with a little more authority, and then we find a place to eat."

"Please don't give Gil's Kitchen another chance."

"And you call yourself fair?"

"You wouldn't!"

"You are right. I wouldn't. But between the drinking and the eating, let's go see where Carrie was killed."

By seven o'clock we had found the approximate place where it had happened. County Road 858 was called Avenida de Flores. It was an old concrete road, the slabs cracked and canted. Weeds stood tall on the shoulders. The shoulders slanted down into overgrown drainage ditches. There were a few old frame houses, spaced far apart, on the west side of the road. On the east side was a grove, with high rusty hurricane fencing installed on the other side of the drainage ditch. I went on out past the city limits sign and turned around in the parking area of a large new shopping plaza and came back, driving slowly.

I pulled off into the weeds of the shoulder, car at a big list to starboard, and stopped.

"For what?" Meyer asked.

I nodded toward the house two hundred feet ahead. An old man was riding a little blue power mower back and forth across the big expanse of front yard. "We just get out and start looking up and down the shoulder, and he'll come over and tell us all."

That is one of the few bonuses when looking into a fatal accident. People do love to talk about it.

In a few minutes I heard the mower cough, sputter, and die. Cars whooshed by, whipping the weeds around, blasting the hot wind against us. I looked up and saw the old man fifteen feet away, walking smartly, his face aglow with the terrible delight of someone loaded down with ghastly details.

"Hey, you wouldn't be looking for the spot where that there Mulligan woman got killed Wednesday night, would you?"

I straightened up and said, "Milligan. The name was Milligan. Carolyn Dobrovsky Milligan, Fifteen Hundred Seaway Boulevard, Bayside, tag number Twenty-four D, thirteen thirteen. Her name was not Mulligan, it was Milligan."

I used the voice and manner of the small-bore bureaucrat, petulant, precise, and patronizing. I needed no further identification as far as he was concerned. I was one of Them.

"Milligan, Mulligan, Malligan. Shoot, you're looking on the wrong side of the road is what you're doing."

"I doubt that," I said. "I doubt that very much."

He peered up at me. "Well, by Jesus H. Sufferin' Christ, you are something, you are! You may know her name right, but you don't know the first goddamn thing about the rest of it."

"I think he might be able to give us a little help," Meyer said, right on cue.

"Your partner here has got a little bit of sense," the old man said. "My name is Sherman Howe, and I've lived in that house there twelve years now, and you wouldn't believe the number of idiots get smashed up and killed on this straight piece of road in the night-time. One drunk son of a bitch about six months ago—see over there where that fence by the grove is fixed up new?—he come off the road and went through that fence, and he went weaving amongst the trees until he zigged instead of zagged and hit one dead center and mushed his skull on the windshield, dead as a fried mule. I keep my clothes on a chair by my bed and I keep a big flashlight handy, and when I hear that crunching in the night, I dress fast and come see what help I can give because that's the Christian thing to do. If it's bad, I blink the light back at the house here, and Mabel is watching for it, and she phones for the ambulance, and that's exactly what happened Wednesday night, and I was down here before that poor boy had even found the body, so don't tell me what side of the road it was on, mister. I know what side. Come with me. Watch out, now, you don't get yourself killed. Nobody slows down. Nobody gives a shit anymore what happens to anybody else in the world. Let me see now. . . . Sure. Here's where her car was. She was heading north, out of town, when she ran out of gas and pulled

over onto the shoulder right here. See where she drove
in? See the tracks? And the grass is still matted where
the wheels set. It happened at twelve minutes after ten
by my digital clock on my bed stand, and I'd just
turned out the light to go to sleep. Mabel was in the
living room watching the teevee. She still likes it, but
it's got to the point where all that slop looks alike to
me. I think the dead woman was . . . wait, follow me
and I'll show you where the body was. I'm the one
found it. That Webbel kid didn't have a flashlight at all.
It was right about here I seen her arm kind of laying up
against the side of the ditch in the grass, and the grass
sort of hid the rest of her. She was right here, down in
this dry ditch, her head aimed that way and her feet
this way, neat as you please. Would have played hell
finding her if that arm hadn't been up like it was and
bare, so it caught the light from my flashlight. Sixty-
five feet from the point of impact. I paced it off. Lordy,
she was a mess. That whole left side of her face and
head. . . . Anyway, I put the light on her and that boy
fainted dead away. He fell like his spine had give way
on him. I put my fingers on that girl's neck and thought
I felt something, but I couldn't be sure. I ran and
flashed my light three times at the window where
Mabel was waiting, and she phoned it in. Then there
was a terrible screeching and nearly another accident
on account of that Webbel kid had parked half on
the road and half off, being so shocked by hitting her
the way he did. His motor was still running, so I run the
truck off all the way onto the shoulder and turned it
off. He was sitting up by then, moaning to himself.
Pretty soon I heard the sirens coming from way off.
The cops got here first. Those blue lights tamed traffic

down. They took flash pictures of the two cars and the body, and they measured the skid marks, which didn't start until he was right at or a little past the point where he hit her. Any fool could see it wasn't the kid's fault."

"Would you care to explain your . . . theory, Mister Howe?"

"Theory! Goddammit, it's fact! Now you look and see that she was parked real close, too close, to the pavement. Maybe it was as far as she could get, running out of gas like that. The car lights were off. That's supposed to be what you ought to do if you are over on the grass at night, because, you leave taillights on, some dumb stupid drunken son of a bitch is going to aim right for those taillights thinking he's following you. Now the Webbel boy was driving one of those big Dodge pickups that's built like a van in the front, where the driver sits high, right over the wheels. You can see that this road is two lane and pretty narrow lanes at that. They talk about widening it, but all they do is talk. I heard them question the boy. There was a car coming the other way. He couldn't swing out around that girl's car. No room. He had to cut it pretty close. Now she must have slid across and got out the passenger side so as not to open her car door into traffic. Then she walked around the front of the car and stepped right in front of that farm truck. It sort of dented in the front right corner of that truck. Busted the right headlight, dented the metal, and so on. You could see where the post hit her head. She didn't realize a car would be so close. He said he saw her out of the corner of his eyes just as he hit her. He said there wasn't anything he could have done about it, and that kid is absolutely right. He was on his way home, and my guess is she was on her way to that gas station up across from the plaza, that stays open way late. When the ambulance came the medical fellow said she was dead. Massive skull fractures, he said. But he said it would be declared a DOA and the certificate would be made out at the hospital. Let me see. They took her away, no need for sirens. They'd got her ID from her purse in the car. The keys were in the ignition. It wouldn't start. When the wrecker came, the fellow looked at the gas gauge on the woman's car, and he had a can of gas on the back of the wrecker. He put some in and it started right up. I forget who drove it away. They took it down to the City Police Station. By that time the television truck was here, but there was nothing to take pictures of. So they just got the facts and used their radio to call them in. There was no cause to hold the Webbel boy. He was too shook to drive, but by then his father and his brother had arrived, and the brother drove the truck on back home. Their place is in the northwest part of the county. I guess that's all of it. You got any other . . . theory, mister?"

"When all the facts are in, all the *pertinent* facts, Mister Howe, I'll be able to summarize."

He turned toward Meyer. "Summarize, winterize, I feel sorry for you, friend, having to work with this sorry son of a bitch." He marched away without a backward glance. When I heard the mower start up again, I looked and saw him riding solemnly back and forth in the fading light of day.

Meyer said, "You couldn't have gotten any more under hypnotherapy. What are you looking at?"

I was down on one knee in the weeds, between the

matted places where the rear wheels had rested. I pointed to the place where the weeds and grass were withered and blackened. It began at a point midway between the wheels and slightly behind them. There was an area six inches in diameter and a random line half that width leading down the slope into the dry ditch, getting narrower and less evident as it approached the ditch.

"Gasoline spill will do this," I said. I dug down into the dirt with thumb and finger and pinched some of it up and sniffed it. It had a faint odor of gasoline. "I think her car fills on the left corner, aft of the wheel. But if it fills there or in the rear center, no matter how clumsy the man was who dumped gas into it, he could hardly manage to spill this much way under here without getting a lot right under where he was pouring."

"It soaked in before it got to the ditch," Meyer said.

"There had to be a lot of spill for it to run down the slope at all. It's been dry lately."

Meyer nodded. "And so she didn't stop because she ran out of gas. But it had to look as if she had a good reason for stopping. Is there some kind of drain under there, on the underside of the gas tank?"

"We'll be able to check that out. For now let's say yes."

"Am I following your scenario, Travis? X is in the car with Carrie. X is driving, let's say. He pulls off the road and stops. He picks a place a long way from any house. No street lights. He strikes her on the head with the traditional blunt object. He leans across her and opens the door. He pushes her out. The weeds are tall enough so that she would not be picked up in the lights of any passing car. He wiggles under the car with a

wrench and a flashlight and opens the drain valve.
When all the gas has run out, he closes the valve. He
pulls her around to the front of the car, waits until he
gets the right traffic situation and the right kind of oncoming vehicle, then boosts her up and walks her into
the front corner of it. Then he takes off. Isn't that a little bit too much to get out of some weeds and grasses
killed by gasoline? Isn't that too much of a dreadful
risk?"

"Maybe it's too much. If X wears dark clothing, that
would diminish the risk. He could stretch out flat beside her just ahead of the front bumper. He could look
under the car for oncoming traffic heading the same
way."

We went to where the front of the Datsun had been
and looked at the weeds. It is too easy to let your
imagination interpret the patterns.

"If so," Meyer said, "he didn't have much time to
get out of sight. Too risky to go across the highway.
Over the fence?"

I studied the fence line. "Under it. Where it's washed
out. I think this was one very cool cat who checked his
escape route first."

"Would your scenario include some telltale dark
threads caught on the wire at the bottom?"

"There could have been, until you mentioned it."

I slid under the fence, on my back. Meyer stayed
outside. There were inches to spare. I searched a
quarter-acre area and came up with the startling conclusion that it was a very well-maintained grove.
Nothing more. He could heave her into the front of the
Webbel truck and spin and hit the hole before the truck
could stop. Then, in dark clothing, he could melt back

into the black shadows of the night and walk parallel to the fence line until it was safe to go over or under the fence.

Or, I thought as I went back under the fence, another vehicle had stopped there. Maybe a wife got nervous about a can of gas in the trunk of the family car. Dump it out this minute, dearest. Or maybe a can started leaking and somebody abandoned it there, and later somebody picked up the can, thinking it usable. Many false structures have been built from the flawed assumption of the simultaneity of seemingly related events.

As we got into the rental car, Meyer said, "We have no way of knowing that the gasoline was spilled—"

"At the same time. I just went through that."

"There are certain concepts which offend emotional logic. You have stopped beside a two-lane road at night. Traffic is light but fast. You walk to the front of your car, after sliding out on the passenger side. What are you going to do? Cross the road? Hitchhike? Open the door on the driver's side? Assume there is a good reason, do you step out, or do you look first?"

"If you are smashed, maybe you step out."

"If you are drunk, you would have opened the door on the driver's side, wouldn't you?"

"I don't know. But what the hell was she trying to do? Walk to one of those houses and phone? If so, Meyer, would she leave her purse and car keys?"

"Nice point. Now what?"

The wrecker stood beside the large gas station across from the entrance to the shopping center. It was a very muscular beast. It was painted bright red. It had warn-

ing lights, emergency lights, floodlights, and blinkers
affixed to all available surfaces. The big tires stood
chest high. The array of winches and cables and reels
on the back end of it looked capable of hoisting a small
tank up the side of an office building.

"Something I can do for you?" the bald sunburned
man said.

"I didn't know they were making them so big."

"Mister, when you get a tractor trailer rig totaled
across three lanes of an Interstate, you need something
big to get it out of the way fast."

"Did that go out Wednesday night when that woman
got killed just down the road there?"

His face twisted in pain. He spat and sighed. "Oh,
Jesus, yes, it went out. Ray took it out. I had two guys
out with flu. That goddamn Ray. You know what the
payments run on this brute son of a bitch?" He kicked
a high tire.

"No idea."

"Four hundred a month. A *month*. And Ray, the
dummy, has to diagnose. Is he some kind of mechanic
already? Hey, he says, no gas. So he puts some in. So
what does that cost me? Thirty bucks' tow charge.
Jesus!"

"Is he around?"

"Look, what's your interest in this thing, mister?"

"It's a case study project for the Traffic Advisory
Council for the State Department of Transportation."

"Oh. Well, that's him at the far island there, checking the oil on the green Cadillac. Just don't hold him
up on working the island, okay? It's money out of my
pocket."

Ray was a stumpy nineteen with blue eyes empty of guile and with a face ravaged by acne.

"Gassy smell? Well, yeah. The way it was, see, I leaned inside to check the gear it was in and the brake. I was glad to see the keys there because it was in park, you know, and I was moving it to N when on account of the gassy smell inside it I looked at the gauge and seen it was empty. I turned the lights on. It's best at night, a short tow, keep the lights on, all the lights you got. I put gas in, figuring if it would run what's the sense towing it. I didn't know the boss would get his ass in such a big uproar about it, see. And I didn't even think who is going to pay for the couple gallons I put in, or the service call. That made it worse. Jesus, he's been all over me all the time since Wednesday. I'm about ready to tell him to shove his job."

I went to the boss and thanked him and said, "I have to interview the dead woman's sister. I can give her the bill for the gas and service, if you want."

He brightened up. We went into the office. He made out the bill. I looked at it and shook my head and handed it back. "Not like that, friend. Two gallons, not five. Five dollars' charge, not ten."

"So what are you, her brother? Look, the dead lady is in no shape to care what the bills are."

"Do you want to take a dead loss or fix the bill?"

"Everybody is all of a sudden getting weird," he muttered, and made out a new bill.

At ten o'clock we were back aboard the *Flush,* up on the sun deck under hazy stars, in two unfolded deck chairs like old tourists on a cruise ship. The events of the long day had been more abrasive than I had realized while they were happening. I felt a leaden weariness of bone and spirit.

I whapped a mosquito which tasted the side of my neck and rolled him into a tiny moist gobbet of meat and dropped him out of his life onto the deck. In many ways the Hindu is right. All life in all forms is so terribly transient there is an innocence about all acts and functions of life. Death, icy and irrevocable, is the genuine definition of reality. In my unthinking reflex I was doubtless improving the mosquito breed. If, over a millennium, man whapped every side-of-the-neck biter, maybe the mosquito race would bite only neck napes.

"Mr. McGee?" the polite voice said from the dock. I got up and walked aft to look down. There was Jason with the Jesus face and wire glasses standing under the dock light in a T-shirt with the short sleeves torn off, ragged blue-jean shorts, and a pair of boat shoes so exquisitely and totally worn out it looked as though he had wrapped his feet neatly in rags.

"Hi, Jason."

"Permission to come aboard?"

"Come on."

He came up the side ladderway like a big swift cat. He accepted a can of beer from the cooler. He had something to say, but he seemed to be puzzling out how to say it. He sat on his heels, on those brown legs bulging with big muscles.

I finally had to give him some help. "Something bothering you?"

"Sort of. I mean maybe it isn't any of my business.

What I wouldn't want is her having a worse time than she's having already. Okay?"

"Her being Mrs. Birdsong."

"She's really a great person. If I could have got to the office quicker, maybe the two of us, you and me, we could have grabbed onto Cal and quieted him down. I know how he could get. Did you hit him with anything? Did you pick up anything and hit him on the head?"

"I sort of hurried him into the wall once. Ralph or Arthur rapped him on the head with a hickory stick, a couple of good licks."

"Hey! That's *right*. I forgot that part. Then maybe it was from them. Look, can you tell—not you but medical doctors—can they tell which knock on the head did the most damage?"

Meyer answered. "I don't think so. Provided, of course, there's no depressed fracture or anything like that. The brain is a jelly suspended in a lot of protection, and oftentimes the greatest damage happens in the area directly opposite the point of impact. This could be in the form of a subdural hematoma, a bleeding which gradually creates enough pressure inside the brain to suppress the vital functions."

"Well, she visited him and then went out and got something to eat and went back and found a half dozen people working on him, but he was dead. There's going to be an autopsy. She came back in terrible shape. They gave her some pills. She's asleep now. A girl friend of Oliver's is sitting with her. Bet you it was a heart attack, or maybe a stroke that didn't have anything to do with getting hit on the head."

My neck was still sprained from being popped on the forehead. I hadn't enjoyed meeting the fellow, but had not wished him dead.

"Thanks for letting me know," I said.

"It's okay. I've been here the whole two years, you know. He was a pretty great person until he got to boozing real bad. And until just a little while ago, even though he got too drunk when he got drunk, he wouldn't drink when there was something he had to do that was best done sober. Like when Jack Omaha would hire him to captain."

"Jack Omaha!"

He turned toward me. He was slowly and carefully folding his empty beer can the way somebody might fold a Dixie cup, turning it into a smaller and smaller wad. "You knew Jack?" he said.

"No. But I heard he took off with a lot of money."

"That's what they say."

"You don't believe he did it?"

"No. But that's because somebody told me he didn't."

"Who would that be?"

"Somebody that knew him better than I did."

"Carrie?" I said.

I heard the air whoosh out of him. He stood up. "Who the hell *are* you?"

"Carrie's friend. When she married Ben Milligan she honeymooned aboard this old barge."

"Hey! I remember something about that. Sure. Have you got a great big shower stall aboard, and a big tub? And . . . uh . . ."

"A big bed? All three."

He leaned his rear against the rail and stood with ankles crossed and arms folded.

"Cheez. That Ben came by a year ago. She was still living at the cottage then. She and Betty Joller and Joanna Freeler and some bird name of Flossie. How come she ever married him, I wouldn't know."

"Nor anybody else. It happens."

"Mister America. Mister Biceps. He was in some kind of movie deal they were making up in Jax, probably an X movie. He came down to con some money off of Carrie. He'd done it before. She didn't have any. He said he would hang around until she got some. Betty came over and got me. It was a Sunday afternoon. Mangrove Lane is right down the shoreline to the south of us. I got there and he was sprawled out in the living room. I told him it was time for him to get on his Yamaha and into his helmet and head north. So we went out into the side yard and he began jumping back and forth and yelling 'Hah! Hah!' and making chopping motions. He came toward me and I kept moving back. I picked up the rhythm of the way he was hopping, and when he was up in the air, or starting up, I stepped into him and hit him in the mouth so hard it pushed this middle knuckle back in, and the first thing that hit the sod was the nape of his neck. He jumped up with both hands on his mouth, yelling, 'Not in the mouth. My God, not my mouth. Oh, God, my career!' So the girls babied him a little and I stood around until he got on his bike and roared away. I haven't seen him since. I don't think Carrie saw him either before she got killed. Are you coming to the service tomorrow morning?"

"At eleven? Yes. The sister asked me."

"She seems nice, that Susan. Carrie was too old for me. Maybe she wasn't, but she thought she was, which is the same thing. We had some laughs. She was making it with Jack Omaha. I told her that was dead end, and she said, What the hell, everything is. And there's not much answer to that, I guess."

"Where did Omaha keep his boat?"

"Right here. There it is, tied up to that shoreline dock at the end there, past the office, over beyond the lights."

I stood up. It was hard to see. "Bertram?"

"Right. Forty-six-foot with all the high-speed diesel you can use. All the extras. One hell of a lot of boat."

"I can believe it. It's one hell of a lot of price too."

"You can get that one at a pretty good price right now. The bank wants off the hook on it. I understand they'll take ninety-five cash."

"They ought to get that with no trouble if it's been maintained."

"Two years old and clean."

"Do you mean Omaha couldn't run it himself?"

"No. He could run it. But you can't fish and run it at the same time. When he got an urge to go billfishing, he'd get Cal lined up. He liked the edge of the Stream up beyond Grand Bahama. That's a good run, so they'd take off way before daylight and come back in by midnight or later. It makes a long day. Sometimes Carrie would go along."

"When was the last time?" Meyer asked. "Do you remember?"

"Only on account of the cops being here asking us. It was on a Tuesday, the fourteenth of . . . this month? Is it still May? Yes, the thirty-first. May is one of the months I always think should have thirty days. Yes, Jack Omaha took off with Cal about three in the morning, and they didn't come back in until after midnight. They questioned Cal about it. Just the two of them alone? Where had they fished? How had Jack acted? What time did they get back? How was Jack dressed? What was he driving? And so on and so on."

He stood up, shrugged, moved toward the ladder-way.

"What time is it?" he asked. "I've got to go help Oliver lock the place. Anything you want, just ask either one of us."

After he was gone I strolled over and looked at the Bertram. It was called *Christina III*. It looked very fit and very husky. When I went back, Meyer was in the lounge. He was tilted back in a chair, hands laced behind his thick neck, staring at the overhead and frowning.

"Now what?" I asked.

"Do you know how they locate invisible planets?"

"No. How do they do that, Professor?"

"Because the visible ones act in erratic and inexplicable fashion. Their orbits are . . . warped. So you apply gravitational theory and a little geometry of moving spheres and you say, Aha, if there is a planetary body right *there* of such and such a mass and such and such an orbit, then all the random movements of the other planets become logical, even imperative."

I sat on the yellow couch. "So what kind of mass and orbit are we looking for?"

"Something large, important, illegal, and profitable."

"Involving a fast cruiser?"

"Possibly."

"Okay. Sunken treasure or Jamaican grass, routed via the Bahamas."

"Isn't there a lot of cannabis coming into Florida?"

"All the way from Jax around to Fort Walton Beach. Yes. Based on what they've intercepted and what they think they've probably missed, it would be at least ten tons a week. From Colombia, Mexico, Jamaica, and maybe some other BIWI islands."

"Big money?"

"Not as big as you read in the papers. Street value doesn't mean a hell of a lot. It passes through a lot of hands. The biggest bite is in getting it into the country and into the hands of a distributor. That's where you double your money, or a little better. Five thousand worth of good-quality, nicely cured Jamaican marijuana will go here for possibly twelve thousand. But if it is intercepted, they'll call it a quarter-million street value. It has to go from distributor to big dealer to little dealer to pusher-user to user. Everybody bites."

"How do you know all this?"

"What I don't know, I make up."

"Seriously, Travis."

"Boo Brodey wanted me to come in with him on a run last year. He laid it all out, including the comparison with Prohibition and so on. I said, Thanks but no thanks."

"Didn't he get picked up?"

"He's out again."

"Did you disapprove?"

"Can't you read me on that?"

Meyer chuckled. "I guess I can. You don't like partnership ventures and middleman status. You don't like large investments. You don't like coming to the notice

and attention of the law. You wouldn't want anybody
to have the kind of hold over you that Boo would have
had. It's not your idea of high adventure. It's what the
British would call a hole-and-corner affair. Tawdry. A
gesture of defiance for the very young."

"So why ask questions you can answer?"

"I guess I meant, Do you disapprove of a person
using the weed?"

"Me? I think people should do whatever they want
to do, provided they go to the trouble of informing
themselves first of any possible problems. Once they
know, then they can solve their own risk-reward ratios.
Suppose somebody proved it does some kind of permanent damage. Okay. So the user has to figure it out
if there is any point in his remaining in optimum condition for a minimum kind of existence. For me, it was
relaxing, in a way, the couple of times I've had enough
to feel it. But it gave me the giggles, warped my time
sense, and made things too bright and hard-edged.
Also it bent dimensions somehow. Buildings leaned just
a little bit the wrong way. Rooms were not perfectly
oblong any more. It's a kind of sensual relaxation, but
it gave me the uneasy feeling somebody could come up
behind me and kill me and I would die distantly
amused instead of scared witless."

"I am trying to imagine you giggling."

"I can still hear it."

"What about it being sunken treasure, Travis?"

"I am thinking back to the money. How it was
packaged. Hundreds on the bottom, then fifties, twen-
ties, tens. Some had fives on top. Tied with white cotton string, in both directions. With an adding-machine
tape tucked under the string. Bricks of ten thousand.

Somebody very neat. It smacks of retail business, my friend. Think of it this way. Suppose you are taking in a lot of cash from various sources, and you use that cash to buy from several other sources, after removing your own share. Assume you do not want to change little ones into big ones at your friendly bank. Okay, if you put all the hundreds together, you have some thin little bricks to buy with. But at the other end you've got some great big stacks of little bills to add up to the same kind of round number. So you mix them up, and you have fairly manageable sizes."

"Sounds less and less like doubloons," Meyer said.

"Yes, it does."

"When I get this pain right between my eyes it means I've done enough thinking for now—on a conscious level. Now the subconscious can go to work. Do you have the gut feeling Jack Omaha is dead?"

"Yes."

"Then that makes the *Christina III* a very unlucky vessel."

"Jack Omaha, Carrie Milligan, and Cal Birdsong."

"And," he said, "the invisible planetary body which warped the other orbits. Good night."

After I had puttered around aimlessly and had at last gone to bed, I found myself reliving the memory of Boo Brodey when he tried to recruit me. He's big and red and abraded by life—by hard work and hard living, by small mercenary wars and thin predatory women. Yet there is something childlike about him.

He paced up and down in front of me, his face knotted with anxiety and appeal, chunking his fist into his palm, saying, "Jesus, Trav, you know how I am. Somebody tells me what to do and when, it gets done. I work something out myself and it's a disaster. Trav, we're talking about the money tree. Honest to Christ, you wouldn't believe it, the kind of money. Kids, weird little kids, are bringing in bags of grass right and left. Anything that'll fly, that's the way to do it. You can lease an airplane to fly up to Atlanta and back. Okay, you put it down on the deck and go to Jamaica and buy ten thousand worth and come back, and you got thirty thousand before the day is over. It's coming in on boats and ships and everything, Trav. Come *on!* The narcs aren't all that hard-nose about grass. They know they can't keep it out, and a lot of them, they don't know for sure it hurts anybody anyway, right? Come on in with me and help set it up. You know, the contacts and all. Help me out, dammit!"

When I told him I didn't want in, he wanted me to set it all up for him. I could stay outside and get a piece of it in exchange for management skills. I said no, I didn't want to go down that particular road. If you make it with grass, you find out that hash and coke are more portable and profitable. You kid yourself into the next step, and by the time they pick you up, your picture in the paper looks like some kind of degenerate, fangs and all. And all you can say is, Gee, the other guys were doing it too.

If I were really going to do it, I would refit the *Muñequita* for long-range work. Tune her for lowest gas consumption and put in bigger tanks. She's already braced to bang through seas most runabouts can't handle. Then I would . . .

Whoa, McGee. There is larceny in every heart, and you have more than your share. So forget how far it is across the Yucatan Straits, leaving from Key West.

7

I T was an overcast morning with almost no wind at all. The wide bay was glassy calm, the outlying headlands misted, looking farther away than they were.

There was a narrow, scrabbly, oyster-shell beach beside the cottage at 28 Mangrove Lane where Carrie Milligan had once lived. A narrow wooden dock extended twenty feet into the bay. It was still solid, just beginning to lean. It was good, I guessed, for another couple of years. Two old skiffs were high on the beach, overturned, nosing into the sea grapes.

Jason sat on the end of one of the skiffs. He wore a white shirt and white trousers. He had a big plantation straw hat shadowing his face. He was playing chords quite softly on a big guitar with a lot of ornate fretwork against the dark wood. The chords were related but did not become any recognizable song. They were in slow cadence, major and minor.

Meyer and I joined the group, standing a bit north of most of them, in the shade of a small gnarled water oak. I saw Harry Hascomb and the young man who had been counting stock in the warehouse. I saw Mrs.

Jack Omaha, Gil from Gil's Kitchen, Susan Dobrovsky, Frederick Van Harn, Oliver from the marina, Joanna from Superior Building Supplies, and a man it took me a few moments to place. He was Arthur, the younger of the two cops who had subdued Cal Birdsong.

There were seven young ladies in long pastel dresses. The dresses were not in any sense a matched set. They were all of different cut and style, but all long and all pastel. Susan wore a long white dress which was just enough too big so that I suspected it was borrowed. Susan and the other girls all had armfuls of the lush Florida flowers of late springtime.

A young man stepped out of the group and turned and faced us. He had red hair to his shoulders and a curly red beard. He wore a sports jacket and plaid slacks.

In a resonant and penetrating voice he said, "We are here today to say good-bye to our sister, Carrie." The guitar music softened but continued. "She lived among us for a time. She touched our lives. She was an open person. She was not afraid of life or of herself. She was at home being Carrie, our sister. And we were at home with her, in love and trust and understanding. In her memory, each one of us here now most solemnly vows to be more sensitive to the needs of those who share our lives, to be more compassionate, to give that kind of understanding which does not concern itself with blame and guilt and retribution. In token of this pledge, and in symbol of our loss, we consign these flowers to the sea."

He moved to the side. The guitar became louder. One by one the pastel girls walked out to the end of the dock and flung the armloads of blooms onto the gray

and glassy bay. There were tear marks on their cheeks.
The flowers spread and began, very slowly, to move
outward and in a southerly direction with the current.
It was a very simple and moving thing. I had the feeling of a greater loss for having so undervalued Carrie. I
excused myself by saying I had really not known her
very well. But that was what Red-beard had said, that
we should be more sensitive to the needs of others—
and more sensitive, I added, to their identities as well.
If she had meant this much to these people, then I had
slighted her value as a person.

The music trailed off and stopped. Jason stood up
and bobbed his head to indicate that was all. The mur-
mur of voices began. Susan went a little way down the
beach and stood, watching the floating flowers.

I looked at the twenty or so people I did not know,
and I realized anew that there is a new subculture in
the world. These were mostly young working people.
Their work was their concession to the necessities.
Their off-work identities were contra-establishment.
Perhaps this was the only effective answer to all the
malaise and the restlessness and the disbelief in institu-
tionalized life, to conform for the sake of earning the
bread and then to step from the job into almost as
much personal freedom as the commune person.

I realized Meyer was no longer at my elbow. I
looked around and did not see him. Jason nodded to
me and said, "Was it okay?"

"It was beautiful."

"I figured if I just noodled around it would be better.
If you play something, people start making the lyrics in
their heads and they miss the other words. Robby did

fine, I thought. He's an architect. Cindy wanted to make it to the service here, but she's still too shook."

"She shouldn't have even thought about it."

"Well, she thought a lot of Carrie. When Cindy was sick last year, Carrie came over and straightened out the books. It took her a whole weekend to do it, the way Cal had screwed things up. Look, I think I ought to talk to Susan. You think it would be okay?"

"I think it would be fine."

He moved off down the beach. Meyer came up to me and said, "There's a hex nut on the bottom of the gas tank. The undercoat is off it on one of the surfaces, and the metal is shiny where the undercoat flaked off."

I stared at him in disbelief. "With all these people around, you were damn fool enough to—"

"I was flipping my lucky silver dollar and catching it, like this. I dropped it and it hit the toe of my shoe and rolled under the Datsun. I didn't get a good look or a long look."

"Don't try to be cute about these things."

"Don't try to be McGee, you mean?"

"Don't get huffy. If you want to travel with the team, learn the ground rules. I've told you before. Don't *ever* take a risk you don't have to take, just to save time or inflate your ego."

"Now wait a minute—"

"There are a lot of things you can tell me that I would never know or guess unless you told me. You have a lot of special information in your head. So have I in mine. My information can make you live longer. And better."

"Better than what?" a girl asked. I turned. Joanna.

Miss Freeler, recently of Superior Building Supplies. Dear friend of Harry Hascomb. Ex-friend. Slender girl with a delicate and lovely face, long fall of ginger-colored hair. Green eyes, slightly protruding and very challenging. The girl challenge, old as time.

"Live better than Harry is going to live for a while."

"That wouldn't be hard," she said. "Bet your ass. Harry is going to have to give up a lot of goodies. I know you from the office yesterday, when I quit. I remember you because you've got weird eyes. And for other reasons too, I might add. I bet you hear that from all the girls. You know, you got eyes the color of gin. What's your name?"

"McGee. And this is Meyer. Joanna Freeler."

"Hello, Meyer," she said. "Hello, McGee. What are you two dudes doing here at the memorial?"

"Friends of the deceased," I said. "From Lauderdale."

"Sure. That's where she married that muscle bum. Why didn't she marry you? Weren't you available, McGee?"

"Weren't. Aren't. Won't be."

"Now you're singing my song," she said.

She was wearing a long orange dress. The color was not good with her coloring. She had thrown her flowers farther and spread them wider than any of the others.

"You seem to be in good spirits," I said.

She clenched her jaw and glared up at me. "That's a shitty thing to say, friend. I miss her like hell. And in one way or another, I'll always miss her. Okay?"

"I didn't mean anything by what I said."

"Then apologize for letting your mouth run with your head turned off, McGee."

"I do so hereby apologize."

She hugged my arm and smiled and said to Meyer, "You run along, dearie. I have to ask this man something."

Meyer said, "I'll walk back to the boat."

"You've got a boat here? At Westway? Hmm. A fast boat?"

"If you really really press her, she'll do seven or eight knots."

"You a pilot? Like in an airplane?"

"No."

"Come along. I just don't like to say some kinds of things in front of two people. All right?"

She led me well away from the others, over to the far edge of the lot. One water oak had sent out a huge limb, parallel to the ground, the top of it almost as high as my shirt pocket. Joanna gave a little bounce and put her palms on the limb and floated up, turning in air to sit lightly. She patted the limb beside her. "Come into my tree, friend."

I sat beside her. She took my hand and inspected it carefully, back and front.

"Hmm. You've had an active past."

"You could have said that in front of Meyer."

"It's hard to say what I want to say in front of just one person. I mean it's so easy for you to get the wrong idea. I'll miss Carrie. But she *is* dead, right? And the world goes on. One thing I know from all this, maybe the same thing Carrie figured out, there's got to be

more to living than sitting on your butt forty hours a
week in an office and getting laid once in a while by the
joker who signs your paycheck. I could retire, maybe.
If I play it right. But what I want is more interesting
work. Like what Carrie was doing."

"What was she doing?"

"Don't try to get cute, McGee. Listen, I *knew* that
girl. There's four of us in the cottage now. Me and
Betty Joller and Nat Weiss and Flossie Speck. So before she moved out and since, Carrie was supplying the
cottage with free grass for her friends, like a paper bag
this big half full. We must have two pounds left. Do I
have to spell it out? What I wasn't told, I can guess. So
it all fell apart for you people. She went to Lauderdale. .
Now you are here to put it back together again, right?
So this is a job application. I'm very smart and I know
how to keep my mouth shut."

"I wouldn't say you know how to keep your mouth
shut."

"This one time I have to take the chance, or where
am I? Outside, as usual."

"Who do you think I represent?"

"You are sitting in my tree playing stupid. You look
smart and rough. You're in distribution after the crazy
people bring it in. I want to be a crazy people because
I need something weird to do, and the money is nice. I
told Carrie she shouldn't be involved, and here am I
asking to get involved. What did happen to Jack?"

"Didn't Carrie tell you that?"

"She said he got scared and probably grabbed his
share and ran. But that doesn't . . . ."

"Doesn't what?"

"Never mind. Skip it."

"Did Harry know what was going on?"

"Cowboy Harry? He's a jerk. How could he know what was going on? It takes him both hands to find his ass. Why did you come to see him anyway?"

"To talk to him about Carrie."

"Why would you want to talk to him about Carrie?"

"You can keep your mouth shut?"

"You know it!"

"Just trying to get a line on who pushed Carrie in front of that truck."

The color drained out of her face. She wiped her mouth and shuddered. "Come on, now!"

"She was killed. I guess you could call it an occupational hazard, right? If you want to accept that kind of risk, maybe we can find something for you."

"But who . . . who . . ."

"The competition, probably."

She looked down and plucked the orange dress away from her body. "I'm getting all hot and sticky. I better change. Don't go away, huh? I want to think this over, okay?"

Joanna dropped lightly from the limb and went to the cottage, striding long, and disappeared inside. A lot of the people had left. Some had gone into the cottage. Others were talking, by twos and threes. I saw Susan walking toward the Datsun, so I dropped down and got to the car just as she did. Her eyes were red, but she managed a smile.

"I think Carrie would have liked it," she said.

"I'm sure she would. Yesterday I walked off with her rings. I forgot to give them to you. And I left them on the boat. We could go get them now."

She frowned and shook her head. "There's no hurry.

I have to be here a few days anyway, Fred . . . Mr. Van Harn says."

"Do you want me to go and pick up that package from Mr. Rucker?"

"Oh, no, thanks. I already talked to Betty about it, and she's coming with me now and we'll go over there before two o'clock. It's perfectly all right, really. But thank you."

A sturdy girl in a yellow dress came hurrying to the car, saying, "Sorry, Sue. I got to talking to somebody."

"Betty, this is Travis McGee. Betty Joller."

She had one of those plump pretty faces which go with wooden shoes and beer festivals. Her eyes were Dutch blue, and her smile was totally friendly and not the least bit provocative. "When I saw you standing with Meyer, I figured it had to be you," she said. "Carrie told me once that the only really happy time she could remember was when you loaned her and Ben your houseboat for their honeymoon. We're all going to miss her so much around here."

They got in, and Susan hitched her white dress up above her knees and then backed smartly around and they left. At my elbow Joanna said, "Now that Susan is some kind of great package."

"And Jason has his eyes on it."

"I noticed that. She's too young for you, chief."

"So are you."

She laughed so hard it bent her over. The laugh was silver bright under the shade trees, unfitting for the occasion. "Me? Me?" she gasped. "I'm the oldest person around anywhere." She wore little salmon shorts and a soft gray top. She had wound her ginger hair into a pile atop her head and pinned it in place casually. Ends were escaping. It made her throat look very slender and vulnerable.

She looked around. "Where did you leave your wheels?"

"We walked over from the marina."

"So I'll walk back with you, okay?"

"Okay, Joanna."

"We haven't made our deal yet."

"Deal?"

She carried a small white canvas beach bag. She twirled it by its draw cord. "Keep playing dumb and I'll brain you, honey."

So we went out to the sidewalk and walked through sun and shade, past little frame houses and new little stores, to the marina. Jason was back at work. He was in his khaki shorts standing on the bow deck of a big Chris, hosing it down, washing off the salt, and the new arrivals, a pair of small round white-haired people in bright boat clothes, stood sourly watching his every move. "Get that cleat too," the man yelled. "The cleat!"

"Yessir," said Jason the musician. "Yessir, sir."

Joanna was loudly enthusiastic about the below-decks spaces of *The Busted Flush*. While she was trotting around, oh-ing and ah-ing, Meyer told me he had some errands. I gave him the car keys. I did not know if he had errands or a sudden attack of discretion.

I caught up with her in the head, standing in front of the big mirror, touching her hair, turning and looking back at herself over her shoulder. She saw me in the mirror and said, "This is really some kind of floating playpen. It's funny. I keep feeling left out. I keep thinking that it isn't right that all this has been going on without me. After all, I'm the best in the world. You didn't know?"

"You hadn't mentioned it before."

"Don't tell me you designed all this?"

"No. It was as is when I won this barge in a poker game."

"Ah. Hence the name."

"There was a Brazilian lady that went with it, but I wouldn't let him bet her."

"Are Brazilians so great?"

"I wouldn't know. Anyway, I kept the decor."

She was smiling. Then suddenly she slumped her shoulders, shook her head, her face somber. "It's so great to kid around, isn't it? I guess the real reason I'm quitting the job is because it wouldn't be the same there without Carrie. Can I have a beer?"

"Of course."

We sat in the galley booth, facing each other across the Formica top. She was pensive, silent, unreadable.

Finally she said, "So it isn't any game. So I don't want in, thanks just the same. Sorry I bothered you."

So I told her the truth about my relationship to Carrie. And why I was here with Meyer. She turned beet red and had to get up and pace around to control her restless embarrassment. It took me about five minutes to get the record straight. I left out the part about the money.

"You must have thought I'd lost my mind!"

"I decided you weren't too tightly wrapped, kid."

"You encouraged me, damn you!"

Finally she calmed down and sat down, sipped her beer, and said, "Okay, I can see why you think she was killed. The purse and the gas and so on. But why? She wasn't into anything *that* rough. Everybody and his brother is hustling grass into Florida. There's absolute tons of it coming in all the time. It's about as risky as running a stop sign."

"Did she tell you how it worked?"

"Not in so many words. It was no secret they used Jack's cruiser. There is no way this coast can be policed. Too many small boats and little airplanes and all."

"Didn't anybody at the cottage ask Carrie where she got it?"

"Betty always did, and Carrie would say something different every time. Like she'd say they had a special on it at Quik-Chek. It was top quality, cured right. Jason says it's the best he's ever run into. It was fun, the four of us, Betty and me, Carrie and Floss. Betty got a little machine and made cigarettes. And we had the cookbook, too, and made those hash puppies. Like on an evening, there'd be eight or ten of us sitting around, and maybe Jason making music, and we'd get onto a real nice level. And there'd be good relaxed talk that made sense, not like when everybody is drinking and people get ugly or silly. They say now it can mess up having babies, and it can lower your resistance to colds and flu and infection and so on. So? Automobiles can kill you, and people don't stop driving."

"The imperatives aren't the same."

"The what aren't what?"

"Excuse me. Let's not get into a hard sell."

"Are you opposed?"

"Joanna, I don't know. A fellow who was pretty

handy with a boat once said that anything you feel
good after is moral. But that implies that the deed is
unchanging and the doer is unchanging. What you feel
good after one time, you feel rotten after the next. And
it is difficult to know in advance. And morality
shouldn't be experimental, I don't think. I find that the
world is full of things which are unavoidable and which
cloud my mind. When my mind is clouded, I am ex-
periencing less. I may think it is more, if the mind is
warped, but it is less, really. The mind looks inward,
not outward. So I just . . . try to make sure there's always somebody in the control room, somebody standing watch."

"Somehow it sounds dull."

"It isn't."

She wrapped her fingers around my wrist. "Okay,
smart-ass. Do you think you'd feel good after me?"

"If the reasons are right, sure."

"Is there more than one reason, friend?"

"The biggest and most important reason in the world
is to be together with someone in a way that makes life
a little less bleak and solitary and lonesome. To exchange the I for the We. In the biggest sense of the
word, it's cold outside. And kindness and affection and
gentleness build a nice warm fire inside. That's okay.
But if you want to set some new international screwing
record, or if you want to show off the busiest fastest
hips in town, forget it."

The fingers slackened their hold on my wrist and she
pulled her hand back. Tears stood in her eyes. She
smiled and shook her head and said, "No way, McGee.
Whatever it is you're selling, I can't afford it. I went

that route once, and it stung. It stung a lot. If that's the kind of dressing you want on the salad, eat elsewhere. I am a very good lay for the Harry Hascombs of the world, and I always feel good afterward, thanks."

"Always?"

"Go to hell!" she said and got up. "All I am is your garden-variety man-eater. I like it. Go to hell!"

"To each his dagnab blue-eyed own."

She smiled. "And I'll always miss Walt Kelly too." She held her hand out to me. "Friends? I didn't exactly come here to set up a friendship. But it'll have to do. God! I am starving. What have you got here?" She had opened the refrigerator. "Is this corned beef? Cheese. Where's the bread? I have this terrible food engine inside me. I eat enough for three truck drivers and I'm always hungry and I never gain one little ounce. I could give you bone bruises, dear."

I sat and watched her make sandwiches. She was very deft, and she made a lot of them. She ate about twice as much as I ate. She ate with such enthusiasm it made her sweaty, even in the air conditioning. She ate with such a lusty, bright-eyed joy that I had the wistful wish to have played her game and bundled her into the sack five minutes after Meyer stepped off the boat. She was intensely alive, as vital and immediate as anyone I had met in a long time.

"How often did she bring the samples?"

"What? Oh, when we were about to run out. Her moving to that Fifteen Hundred place had something to do with the deal. She told me she was getting a free ride on the apartment. But she missed us."

The phone rang. It startled both of us. I went into

the lounge and answered it. It was Meyer. "About the autopsy on Birdsong, it was heart. Some kind of aneurysm. Thought you'd like to know. I hope I . . . haven't disturbed you by phoning."

"You can come back aboard any time."

"Oh."

"What's this with the Oh?"

"Just Oh. Nothing complicated. Oh."

She sauntered into the lounge and stretched out on the yellow couch, placing her second mug of milk on the coffee table. "This is truly some great boat."

"What is Chris Omaha like?"

"Nobody can ever figure out how come Jack stayed with her so long. She's dumb, loud, and greedy. Rotten to him and rotten to the kids. Ever since the kids got old enough to be sent off to school, they've been away. She likes to be alone in the house in case something wearing pants comes by to make a delivery or fix something. Jack caught her a couple of times. But leave her? No. Carrie thought for quite a while maybe he would leave Chris and marry her. I don't know what the hold is. It was a kid marriage for them. Seventeen and eighteen they were. It finally got to be an arrangement, I guess. He could have Carrie, and she could have anybody who happened to come along."

"Like Ready Freddy Van Harn?"

"Ready Freddy? Wow, you read him right. I'll have to tell Floss what you called him. No, Fred is the lawyer for the business, and he's Jack and Harry's personal lawyer, and he'll be handling the estate, what's left, but he wouldn't boff around with old Chris, not when he can tag the best there is."

I recounted my reasons for contradicting her. She
looked astonished. "What *about* that! What do you
know? I guess old Chris snuck up on his blind side or
something."

"He was Carrie's lawyer?"

"From being the lawyer for the business. When she
wanted to make out a will so that Ben couldn't get her
savings or her car or anything like that, she asked Fred
one day when he was in to see Harry about something,
and he made some notes and drew up a will and had
her come into the office and sign it. I guess he made
himself the executor. That would be okay by Carrie.
And Betty told me she'd warned Susan about Fred.
Susan seems like such a nice kid. Fred even got to
Betty one time. I guess it was sort of a challenge to
him. Betty is sort of sexless, you know? She has all the
equipment and she's pretty, but something's left out.
Fred got her a little bit bombed on wine and then he
took her. It wasn't exactly rape, but it was as close as it
could get and still not be. She hates him. He really hurt
her, because she's built small, and that Fred has . . .
well, all I can say is that you'd never know, looking at
him, so kind of slender and girlish almost. And pretty.
But he's a bull. He's huge. He's so huge he's sort of
scary. And . . . he likes to hurt. I don't like kinky
things. I like it, you know, for fun. It doesn't seem to
be fun for him. Oh, he knows a lot of tricks and so
forth. But it's more like he read up on it in engineering
school. Once was enough for me. He's with you but he
isn't. He's . . . I don't know how to say it."

"Remote?"

"Ri-i-ght! I think Fred is trying to score every girl in

Bayside and surrounding area. He's real hell on wives. Maybe that's why he put Chris on his list. Men have tried to beat up on him for messing around, but he is just as quick and just as mean as a snake. He's a good lawyer, but he's not a very nice person. I don't know how marriage is going to work out for him. He's going to get married. It was in the paper. Jane Schermer. Very social and very very rich. It's grove money from way back. He has some ranchland out near all her groves, lots of it, but nowhere near as big. The Van Harn family used to have money, but about the time Fred was in Stetson Law, his daddy shot himself and it turned out he was almost totally busted. It was something to do with letter stock. I don't even know what that is. But that's what they say. Something about pledging letter stock for bank loans, and him being the lawyer for the bank. Fred works hard. I think he's maybe made back a lot of money. Everybody says he does a good job. But I think that way down deep he's a creepy person."

"Bayside seems like a busy place."

"It's okay, I guess. I really don't know whether I'll stay around. I left once before and came back. Maybe I'll come to Lauderdale and live on this boat with you for a while. Okay?"

"We'll keep your name on file, Miss Freeler."

"You are so nice to me."

My alarm bell bonged as Meyer stepped aboard, onto the mat on the stern deck. He knocked and came in and smiled at pretty Joanna on the yellow couch. "I like to see healthy young girls drinking milk," he said. She had set aside a couple of sandwiches for him, neatly packaged in Saran. She stirred herself and got up, yawning, and said she was going back to the cottage for a nap. I took her by the shoulders and turned her around and gave her a little push toward the state-rooms. She trudged off, scuffing her heels, and when I looked in on her she was snoring, a large snare-drum sound for such a small lady.

I sat with Meyer while he ate at the booth in the galley.

"I tracked it down," he said. "The place Carrie had her car serviced. It's a big Shell station right across from the entrance to Junction Park. It was handy for her because she could leave her car there while she was working. It was in last Tuesday. They looked up the ticket. They changed the oil and the filter and put on new wiper blades—and filled the tank."

"And if it was filled Tuesday, and she didn't go on any trips . . ."

"She worked all day Tuesday and Wednesday."

"Very nice work, Meyer."

"Thank you."

"About that planet theory of yours, how they find the invisible one by seeing what it does to the orbits of the others, I have a candidate for planet. One attorney by the name of Frederick Van Harn. He impinges on the lives of too many of the people we're interested in."

"Including Mrs. Birdsong."

"Huh?"

"He was coming out of her motel unit when I drove in."

"Oh, that's just great. Anyway, he's top priority. All we can find out. Right?"

"Yessir, sir."

And despite my protestations that it wasn't all that urgent, he headed on out again after reborrowing the car keys.

8

JOANNA woke up at four and said a sleepy farewell and went tottering off. I wrote a note to Meyer and left it where he would see it. I locked the *Flush* and walked all the way to 1500 Seaway Boulevard, estimating it at a little less than two miles south of the marina. At first it was very hot, but then a quick thunderstorm came slamming in. I stepped over a hedge and took refuge under a tremendous old banyan. A small white dog yapped at me from a screened porch, some of his yapping drowned by thunder. A pale woman came out onto the porch to see why he was making such a fuss. Over the rain sound I yelled, "I'm trespassing!"

"You can trespass on the porch here if you want."

"I'm terrified of the savage dog. Thanks anyway."

She smiled and went back into the house. When the rain stopped, mist rose from the pavement. The air was washed clean and was much cooler. I stepped along faster than before.

Fifteen Hundred was a jumble of villas and town houses, of joined and separate structures interconnected by arcades and roofed walkways. The layout established small courtyards of various sizes. It did allow for a maximum privacy of approach and departure, but at the expense of security. In a world where violence is ever less comprehensible and avoidable, people—especially the middleaged and the old—settle more comfortably behind barred gates, locked lobbies, roving guard dogs. They seek to die in bed, of something gentle and merciful.

I roamed, looking for Walter J. Demos. His was number 60, the ground floor of a town house near the back of the property, looking out at the pool area. A pretty lady in jeans and work shirt and tousled hairdo opened the door and said, liltingly, "No vacancies, none at all; so sorry." She started to close the door.

"I want to talk to Mr. Demos."

"He isn't even adding any names to the list, it's so long now." She had sweat beads of exertion on her forehead and upper lip. Behind her I could see a mop pail with a wringer fastened to it.

"I don't want to live here."

"Then you must be out of your tree. If it's about something else, well, let me think. Mary Ferris was after him to do something about her disposer. I think he'll be there by now. That's Twenty-one. Go past the pool and through that arch at the right and it will be . . . the second? No, the third doorway to your right. Go up the stairs and come back toward the front of the building."

Walter J. Demos wore gray coveralls and an engineer cap. The coveralls were wet-dark around his middle in a wide irregular band. He did indeed look something like a shorter broader Kojak, his face and jaw massive, almost acromegalic.

He showed me what he had in his hand. It looked like a tangled ball of dirty string.

"Do you know what this is? Can you guess?" he asked.

The woman giggled. She was plump and coy and underdressed.

"I wouldn't know."

"Miss Mary here had a lovely artichoke yesterday, and she put all the inedible parts of it into her disposer. Artichoke leaves, my friend, are made of string. And in a little while the string wound itself into a tangled mess and stopped the machinery."

Mary giggled again and switched back and forth, chewing a knuckle, scuffing her sandaled foot.

She thanked him and he gave her the string to dispose of in a less damaging manner. He picked up his tin toolbox, and we left to walk slowly back toward his apartment.

"I could tell them all to call the repair people. I could spend all my time in the pool. But it would drive me quite mad, I think. I have to keep busy. That's the way I am, Mr. McGee. And it saves my people money, which is increasingly important these days. Everyone chips in and helps whenever and wherever they can. We're a family here, helping and protecting each other."

"Meyer told me he got that impression."

"Oh, then *you* must be the friend he mentioned. I chatted with him for just a few minutes, but he struck me as charming and highly intelligent. I like intelligent people. That's the way I am."

"Have you found out who trashed Carrie's apartment?"

"What? Oh, no, we haven't. And I doubt we ever will. No one resident here would ever do a thing like that."

"Even though she was resented by the other . . . members of the family?"

He stopped and peered at me. "What would give you that idea?"

I was tempted to remind him of Meyer's intelligence, but I thought I could make a little more mileage by using the dead lady, so I said, "Mrs. Milligan was quite aware of it."

He grunted and we walked on, right to his door. The lady had stopped sweating. He took her hand in both of his. "Thank you so *very* much, Lillian. You know how much I appreciate it."

She went smiling off, purse in hand. He closed the door and looked around. "Nice job," he said to himself. "Very nice." He turned to me and made a wry grimace. "I have to be so very careful. If one of them cleans up for me too often, the others get jealous. Please sit down. You were telling me that Carrie had some fantasy about resentment."

"Purely a paranoid fantasy. She thought that because you put her at the head of the list and gave her the first empty apartment, the others resented her. She thought that because she was getting a rent-free ride, they resented her. She thought that because she didn't care to mingle, they resented her. She would rather have stayed with her friends in the cottage at Mangrove Lane. Maybe you should have told the whole family that Carrie wasn't a very special and dear friend, but just part of the pot distribution system. Jack Omaha, Cal Birdsong, Carrie Milligan, and you."

He was good. He stared at me. At first he chuckled and then he laughed and then he roared. He slapped his thighs and rocked back and forth and lost his breath. Finally he held his wrists out and, still choking, said, "Okay, officer. I'll go quietly. You've got me."

"Why the special treatment she got from you? Tell me so we can all laugh."

He lost all traces of mirth. "You're beginning to annoy me. It's no business of yours, but I'll tell you anyway. A friend of mine asked me to make the apartment available to Mrs. Milligan. Jack Omaha asked me. My books show the rent paid every month. She may have had a free ride, but it wasn't from me. Probably Jack felt that it would be more pleasant to have ... more privacy and more access to the lady."

I lifted eyebrows and looked at him politely. "I'm beginning to annoy you, Mr. Demos?"

"Frankly, yes."

There are a lot of choices in every instance. And it is easy to make a bad choice. A man will react badly to the promise of some unthinkable punishment. The musician will buckle at the thought of smashed hands. The choice cannot be made with the thought of taking any pleasure in the choice. It has to be businesslike, or it will not be convincing. This man was the benign daddy, the solid meaty big-skulled patriarch, full of such amiable wisdom and helpfulness that he would appeal to the little girl in any woman who might be still searching for poppa. A gregarious man. A sensualist. A skilled, successful, and unlikely womanizer who had built himself a profitable world teeming with prey. He was pleased with himself, and evidently still greedy.

"I'm thinking of alternate ways of annoying you, Mr. Demos."

"What do you mean?"

"We have a specialist we could import. His nickname is Sixteen Weeks. He's very bright about guessing just how much punishment a given person can endure and still recover. He can guarantee you sixteen weeks in the hospital, Walter. At your age you might not ever get about as well as you do now."

His attempt at a smile was abortive. "That's grotesque."

"Or, if we decide to head in another direction, I'd turn the problem of dispositon over to Meyer. He works things out so there isn't any fuss. As you noted, he's highly intelligent. We gave him the problems of Mr. Omaha, Mr. Birdsong, and Mrs. Milligan. He'd find something plausible for you. They could find you on the bottom of the pool some morning."

I think he tried to smile again. It gave his mouth an odd look. "Are you quite mad? Why are you saying such terrible things? What do you *want* from me?"

Rhetoric, all by itself, is too abstract. It needs punctuation. Show and tell. I stood up, smiling. I moved slowly. He watched me with some agitation. I walked slowly around to the back of his chair. He leaned forward and craned his neck around to watch me. I knew he was wondering whether or not to get up out of the chair.

It takes a reasonable amount of precision. In the

clavicle area, where the muscle webs of the trapezius and deltoid are thinned out, the descending brachial plexus, which includes the big ulnar and radial nerves to the arm, is close to the bone. I chopped down, a short swift smashing blow, and hit him just as he started to move, hit him on target, mashing the nerves against bone with the bone ridge of my knuckles.

Walter J. Demos screamed in a very aspirated hissy way and came floundering up out of the chair. His right arm hung dead. He clasped his right shoulder in his big left hand. He stared at me with bulging eyes and roared with pain. Tears ran down his face.

There was a flurried rapping at the door. "Walter?" a woman cried. "Are you all right? Walter?"

"Tell her to call the cops," I suggested. "We can all sit around and talk about how much pot you moved out of this place."

"Walter?" she yelled.

"Everything is fine, Edith," he called. "Go away!" He sat down again and said, "You broke my shoulder!"

"It isn't broken. It will be okay again in a week."

"But I can't move my arm. It's numb."

"The feeling will come back, Wally."

"Nobody ever calls me Wally."

"Except me. I can call you Wally, can't I?"

"What do you want of me? Were they really killed? Really?"

"What we want is an established outlet in Bayside. Your previous source has dried up, Wally. Now tell me how you got into it and how you've been operating."

He found a hanky with his left hand and patted his

eyes and blew his nose. He rubbed his numb arm. He talked and talked and talked.

He had always purchased supplies for apartment repairs and redecorating from Superior. He became friendly with Jack Omaha and they would have coffee together at a diner near the industrial park, within walking distance. One day he told Omaha that a lot of his tenants had become ill from smoking grass adulterated with some unknown compound. Jack said that his personal supplier, his milkman, had recently been busted, and he was buying it at a gas station and paying too much. Omaha had taken a lot of his vacation time in Jamaica. Half joking, he had told Demos he was tempted to go get his own, but it wasn't worth the risk unless he arranged to have a lot of it brought in, and he couldn't see himself peddling it. Demos told Omaha that quite a bit could be absorbed at 1500 Seaway Boulevard, and some of his tenants could probably get rid of a lot more at the offices where they worked.

It wasn't long before they had talked themselves into it. Omaha came back from Jamaica with guarantees, having talked to local hustlers named Little Bamboo, Popeye, Hitler, John Wayne, and so on.

At that point it was decided that Walter would be better off if he did not know any of the details of the smuggling operation, and if Omaha did not know a thing about his wholesale operation. The first shipments were small. As they got bigger, Demos brought in his most trusted tenants and it became a cottage industry, taking the bulk and weighing, measuring, and bagging it for the smaller wholesalers and the retail trade.

"We thought we'd be able to avoid getting mixed up with any—excuse the expression—hoodlums. We didn't see that there was anything terribly sinister about it. We were filling a demand at a fair price. We tried to cut our risks. Bringing Carrie here to live was part of the risk-cutting. She'd tip me in advance as to when a shipment would be coming in. I'd get my people ready. On those nights she'd be driving one of the little panel trucks from Superior instead of her own car. When it was unloaded, checked, and weighed, I'd give her the money. We'd work all night. I wanted it all out of here by the following morning. Except personal supplies, of course."

"When was the last shipment?"

He looked dispirited. He nursed his shoulder. He sighed. I could feel a certain satisfaction in having diagnosed him so precisely. But with satisfaction there was also regret. Demos had been full of himself, full of a big-bellied confidence, sure of his place in his world. But in had come the pale-eyed stranger who had said terrifying things and who had sickened him with pain. His world had become fragile all of a sudden. His heart was heavy. He was not a bad man, everything considered. He had been a jolly sly man, a manipulator, a greedy chap, overconfident. He had changed.

"Do you want me to annoy you some more, Wally?"

"No! No, I was trying to remember exactly. A Tuesday night. That would make it May fourteenth. Yes. I can't remember the exact time, but it was before midnight."

"How much was there?"

"An average shipment. Ten sacks, I think. Forty

kilos each. Over eight hundred and fifty pounds. I think I gave her about ninety thousand dollars."

He described, by request, the way the money was wrapped. It fit the way it had been packaged when Carrie gave it to me. The adding-machine tape was from his office machine. He handled the money, figuring the commissions to his peddlers.

I pressed him to find out how well he had done. He was evasive. In the beginning he had plowed everything back into increasing the shipments. He guessed Jack Omaha was doing the same. They were on a cash-and-carry basis with each other. When they got to maximum weight coming in, he had started to skim, and he guessed that Omaha had started too. He said he was having a problem legitimizing the cash, trying to work it out in such a way that he could apply it to the outstanding mortgages on Fifteen Hundred. He guessed that probably Jack Omaha was having the same problem, but he hadn't discussed it with him. He started to ask me about Jack Omaha and changed his mind. He didn't want to know anything about Omaha. Or Carrie.

I asked to see Carrie's apartment. He said that a Miss Joller and a Miss Dobrovsky, Carrie's sister, had gone through everything and packed up some things for shipment to New Jersey, and had called Goodwill to come pick up the rest. It had been cleaned and the new tenant was moving in tomorrow morning. So there was nothing to see.

He said he had a headache and would like to lie down. I told him we had some more ground to cover first. I asked him what Carrie did with the money.

He said he had the impression she took it down to

Superior and put it in the safe. It seemed logical that she would have some safe place to put it.

"What do you want from me?" he asked again.

"You have a nice operation, Wally. It's cleaner than some loft or old warehouse or a trailer parked in the woods. And you have those nice clean little clerks and bank people doing the pushing and being very careful because they don't want to mess up this great life-style you created for them. I don't have to put you out of business because you're already retired. You've got no supply, right? Do you know what I'm going to recommend? I'm going to say you should be our exclusive distributor in Bayside. How *about* that?"

I couldn't detect any genuine enthusiasm in his response.

"What does . . . it entail?"

"We'll guarantee top quality. We'll guarantee no hassling by the law. We'll expect you to absorb, say, a ton a month, cash on the line, half again what you were paying Omaha. In time we'll have you broaden the line. Coke and hash."

"Oh, I just couldn't handle that, Mr. McGee. I really couldn't. That quantity and price. . . . This has been just a small operation. An amateur thing. You know. I just couldn't. . . ."

I stood up, smiling at him. "It's all settled."

"Don't I have any choice?"

"Choice? Of course! You stay right here and hang onto that cash, because when we make a delivery, you have to be able to pay. You have to accept what we send you. Don't try to look for another supply source. You just wait. If you want to fuss and bob and weave and make trouble, that's your choice. If so we'll kill you and make our deal with whoever takes over this place. It might be a couple of months before we set you up as a distributor, Wally. Hang in there."

He didn't move. I let myself out. I was a little depressed by my own childishness. It was a fair assumption it could work exactly as I had outlined it to Demos. The contact would probably be a lot less melodramatic than I had made it. Actually the setup would probably not appeal. It was too unusual. Hoodlums are the true conservatives. When you are winning, never change the dice. Distribution would be limited to the candy-store, horse-room, bartender, cocktail-waitress, coin-machine, call-girl circuits. Demos's arrangement was too fancy and made too much sense.

I took a small detour to go around by the pool. The after-work residents crowded the pool area. They made a youngish, attractive throng in their brown hides and resort colors. The scene looked like a commercial for swimming pools.

They made gay little cries of glee and fun. A game of water tag was in progress.

Wally's Paradise. There was one thing wrong with it, and that was what probably created the slightly frantic gaiety. They all loved it here. They were all going to stay. They were going to obey all the rules, and pay the rent, and stay and stay and stay.

It was a life-style designed for the young. Twenty years from now it was going to look a lot less graceful and productive. Unless all leases were canceled at age thirty-five, and your family throws you out. It was a pretty problem for Wally, and a dreadful one for his tenants.

I skirted the jolly crowd and walked back to the marina. I needed the long walk in order to sort out everything I had learned from Walter Demos and fit it into the facts and inferences I had acquired before chatting with him.

9

*T*HE day was darkening prematurely by the time I got back to the marina. As I passed the office there was a bright blue click of lightning, a white dazzle, and an enormous crash of thunder. I ran through the first heavy drops and boarded the *Flush.* . . .

It was still locked, the security system still operative. Meyer was not back yet. My note to him was still where I had left it. He arrived, soaking wet, ten minutes later.

After he had changed, we sat in the lounge and exchanged information.

"Frederick Van Harn is a very impressive young man," Meyer told me. "In a very short time he has built up a very wide-ranging and profitable practice of law. He has been pulling together the shattered remnants of the Democratic Party in this county. He will very probably run for the state legislature and very probably make it, after he marries Jane Schermer. Her Uncle Jake is the power and money behind the party. Van Harn can speak very persuasively in public. A lot of people don't care for him personally, but they have a grudging respect for the way he came back and started building a career right on the top of the ruin his father made of his life. About two years ago Van Harn bought the Carpenter ranch twelve miles west of town. The Schermers live out that way. Jane has extensive grove land out there."

"From what Joanna said, I'd think his reputation as a womanizer would get in the way of his electioneering."

"The general feeling around the area seems to be that he has a way with the ladies, but he'll settle down after he marries Jane. It isn't doing him any harm that I could see. And I spent my time drinking beer in a place across from the courthouse. Bail bondsmen. An investigator for the state's attorney. Bartender. A lady from the tax office. There was just one questionable area that turned up."

"Such as."

"Gossip. About money. It just seems to the spectators that Freddy has bought too much too fast. They wonder if maybe Freddy's father killed himself because he couldn't avoid being caught, but left a stash of cash around somewhere. They say the ranch he bought is twelve hundred acres, high and dry. It had to be at least a million one, even without the ranch house and the man-made lake and the airstrip and hangar. So even if he made out well in the law, how could he pay his taxes and still have enough left over for his lifestyle? He's about thirty years old, and he's been at it here just six years, but he started slow and small."

"Did you get any information on how well his father lived?"

"Oh, very well, apparently. Cars, boats, hunting lodges. women."

"You've come back with a lot."

Meyer smiled. "It's a cozy bar. The conversation was general. Everybody joined in. Freddy has charisma. He's one of the people that other people like to talk about. So it was easy. Besides, due to constant pressure from you, I'm getting better at being a sneak."

"That isn't a word I would have chosen."

"Once you face up to reality, everything is easier."

From time to time the rain came down with such a roar we couldn't hear each other. Wind buffeted the *Flush,* thudding her against the fenders I had put out and made fast to the pilings. Then the rain steadied down into a hard, continuing downpour. I opened two cans of chili, and Meyer doctored the brew with some chopped hot pickled peppers and some pepper seeds. He does not approve of chili unless the tears are running down his cheeks while he eats. His specialty, Meyer's Superior Cocktail Dip, is made with dry Chinese mustard moistened to the proper consistency with Tabasco sauce. The unsuspecting have been known to leap four feet straight up into the air after scooping up a tiny portion on a potato chip. Strong men have come down running and gone right through the wall when they missed the open doorway.

It was a good night to stay aboard. It was a good night to conjecture, to try various possible patterns of human behavior and see how well they fit, much like kids in the attic trying on old uniforms, wearing old medals.

I got out charts of the Caribbean and worked out alternate routes from Bayside to Kingston and to Montego Bay. It was easier to route back in pre-Castro days. (Maybe everything was easier.) I made it 650, if you were a straight crow. But avoiding Fidel's air space with enough of a margin of comfort made it 1,000 miles. No great problem for the huskier variety of private aircraft, provided fuel was available at the Jamaica end.

So add in the Bertram. From predawn to after dark would give you, say, sixteen hours. Allowing for variations in wind and weather and the size of the seas, call it an outside distance of 120 or 130 out and the same back. That would also allow some time at the far end, for rendezvous.

As I had to start somewhere, I picked 220 mph for the aircraft cruising speed. Give it an hour at the far end for gassing and loading. Ten hours would do it. Leave in daylight, return by daylight. Okay, so why push the boat so hard? Probably two reasons. First, because the seas close to Florida are so full of small craft, you have to go a long way to get out of the traffic. Second, once you are in open empty water, you are too hard to find from the air. So you have to head for some distinctive land mass that the aircraft can find without too much trouble.

I drew a 130-mile half circle on the chart, with the point of the compass at Bayside. Of the areas included, I was willing to vote for the north side of Grand Bahama, over away from the folks and the casinos, where the water is tricky. Big stuff goes way north to come around into the Tongue of the Ocean. Little stuff stays inside, south of Grand Bahama. If they picked a tiny island off the north shore, a pilot could orient himself by the configuration of Grand Bahama, head for the tiny island, and the rendezvous point could be, for example, a mile north of that crumb of land.

If they had a source in the Bahamas for the Jamaican weed, then I was wrong. But that was not likely. Too much risk and too low a margin.

And our Freddy Van Harn had an airstrip and a hangar. And he was Jack Omaha's lawyer. Chris Omaha's lawyer. Lawyer for Superior. Lawyer for Carrie, and Susan, and the marina.

"The invisible mass," Meyer said, "distorting the orbits."

"Distorting the orbits, or removing the planets?"

"But why?" Meyer asked.

"You know, that's really a rotten question."

"It has to be answered. Otherwise there's nothing."

"Let's find out first if he has an airplane."

"How?"

"The direct approach. Let's go look. Very very early tomorrow."

Somebody came hurrying out of the rain and boarded the *Flush*. We both heard the warning bell. I snapped on the aft floods, and through the rain curtain we saw Joanna scuttle close to the door for shelter. She was holding a package.

I let her in. She was one very damp lady.

"Hey!" she said. "This is such a rotten Saturday night, all things considered, I decided we ought to have some kind of celebration. Okay?" She turned and put her package on the table, her back to me. "And it just so happens—"

There was a huge white ringing crash, blinding light, deafening sound, and I was spun and dropped into darkness, hands out to break the fall that never ended. . . .

I opened my eyes and looked up at a white ceiling. There was an annoying whining ringing sound going on which made it difficult to think clearly. I looked back up over my head and saw the familiar white tubular headboard of your average hospital bed and thought, Oh, Christ, not again! A quarter millimeter at a time I rolled my head to the left and saw a narrow solitary window with the venetian blinds almost but not quite closed. A white floor lamp beside the window was turned on. The chair in front of the window was empty. My head made a funny sound against the pillow as I rolled it back into place. I brought up from beneath the covers a slow brown enormous hand and willed it to feel of my head. It felt bandage and then moved dumbly back to lie inert against my chest. So. The other arm worked. Both legs worked. I wished somebody would turn off the ringing. I rolled my head to the right and saw a closed door. A long sigh ended in sleep.

I woke up. The ringing was not quite as loud. There was night instead of sunshine between the slats of the blind. I thought nothing had changed until I found I couldn't move my right arm. I turned my head and studied the arm. It was strapped to a board. There was a needle in the vein inside my elbow. The needle was taped in place. I saw a rubber tube that went up to a bottle hanging over me. It seemed to be about half empty. The stuff in it was gray-white and semitransparent. I reached around in my head for the nurse word: I.V. Meaning . . . intravenous. Meaning I was having dinner.

After considerable fumbling around I found a push button safety-pinned where I was least likely to be able to reach it with my left hand. But I managed, and I thumbed it down.

After a few minutes the door was slung open and a dainty little white-haired nurse about fifty years old came trotting in. "Oh, hey!" she said. "Oh, good!" Then she said something I couldn't hear because of the ringing.

"What? Somebody turn off the damn bell."

She leaned close. She laughed. "Bell? It's in your ears, sweetie. From the bomb."

"Bomb?"

She checked the I.V. and said, "You're doing okay here. They're not going to have to go into your skull, sweetie. Now be patient. I'm supposed to get Dr. Owings to check you."

"Where am I?"

"Ask your doctor, sweetie." And she was gone, the door hissing slowly shut behind her.

Dr. Owings really took his time. I found out later that he was out of the hospital. And I found out that one Harry Max Scorf wanted to be present when I came out of it, if I came out of it.

After an hour, Dr. Hubert Owings came in, wearing that familiar look of the distracted, overworked professional. If you ordered a doctor type from central casting, they wouldn't have sent Hubert. He looked like a cowhand in a cigarette ad, even to the lock of hair falling forward across the hero forehead. The man who followed him in was small and spare and old. He wore a thick ugly gray suit, a frayed and soiled shirt in a faded candy stripe. It was buttoned at the throat, but he wore no tie. He wore a gleaming white ranch hat, the Harry Truman model, and, as I found out later, gleaming black boots. His face was small, withered, and colorless.

"Mr. McGee," said my doctor irritably, "Captain Scorf may want to read you your rights."

"Now, Hube," Scorf said in a plaintive voice, "it's nothing like that. Son, I'm Harry Max Scorf, and I just want to know if you'll freely and willingly answer any questions I might have about the death of Miss Freeler."

I stared at him. "Miss Freeler?"

"Captain, if you would just sit over there and let me handle the usual questions?"

"Sure, Hube. Sure thing."

Hube shone a sharp little light into my eyes, first one and then the other. "Your name?"

I gave it at once. He straightened up and stared down at me in perplexity. I didn't know what was wrong, and then like an echo, I heard my voice giving my name, rank, and serial number.

"I don't know why I did that," I said.

"What do you remember doing last?"

"While waiting for you, doctor, I've been trying to remember. The last thing I know is that I was standing in a very heavy rain under a banyan tree, and a little white dog on a screened porch was barking at me. I was on my way to see . . . someone at Fifteen Hundred Seaway Boulevard, and I don't know if I ever got there. I don't know how I got here, or why. This *is* Bayside?"

"It is. You were brought in unconscious with a severe concussion and a deep laceration on the back of your head, triangular, with a flap of scalp dangling."

"What about Meyer?"

"At the time you were brought in—"

"What about Meyer!"

"He's jes' fine," Harry Max Scorf said.

"Thanks, Captain."

Looking annoyed, Hube said, "If you'd remained unconscious any longer we were going to have to—"

"What day is this?"

"Thursday evening. Nine thirty on Thursday evening, Mr. McGee. The sixth day of June."

"For the love of—"

"Hold still, please. I'm trying to check you."

I became aware for the first time of the catheter. He sent Scorf out of the room for no good reason while he uncoupled me from the input and output tubes. He asked me if I thought I could stand up, as if I felt like trying to stand up. I did, in the ridiculous hospital long bib, and walked carefully and shakily around the bed and got back in, sweating with the effort it had taken.

He left me with Scorf, saying, "If you feel you are getting too tired, just say so, and the captain will leave."

After the door closed, Scorf said, "Now just why did you and your friend come up here from Lauderdale, McGee?"

"No answers at all, Captain. Not until the blanks are filled in. What happened? I remember now that Joanna's last name was Freeling."

"Freeler. Now what I know about the bomb comes from the two experts we had come in and check it all over. You and Meyer were on your houseboat Saturday night. It was raining hard. That girl came aboard with a package. She put it on the table and bent over it to unwrap it. It went off. You and your friend were lucky because you were both standing behind her and not too far apart, so her body took the major force of the explosion. It blew the girl practically into two halves. She never knew what happened. It knocked both of you down, you and Meyer. You hit your head and he didn't. He's lost the hearing in one ear, but they think it's coming back."

"What did it do to the boat?"

"Blew out all the glass. Blew a small hole in the deck, and blew a great big hole in the overhead, like ten feet by ten feet. Then it rained into the hole all night long. It's a mess. They're working on it now."

"They?"

"At that Westway Harbor Marina. Jason and Oliver and a friend of theirs. With Meyer helping."

"Where's Meyer?"

"Waiting for me to get out of here. He got called the first thing. Anyway, it was what they call a primitive-type bomb."

"Primitive?"

"No timing device or anything like that. They explained it to me after they found enough to know how it probably worked. The package was about so big, tied with string. There were four sticks of dynamite in there, taped together and taped into place. There was a battery and a cap and a little switch, a contact switch. What the fella who made it did, he stuck a thick piece of cardboard between the switch terminals. Then he tied string to the cardboard and led the string out a

hole in the side of the box and fastened it to the string
he tied around the box. So anybody unties it and pulls
the string off, they pull that cardboard out and contact
is made and it all goes *bam*. It went off about eight
inches from the middle of that girl. Bombs are so
damned ugly and messy. I can't get inside the head of a
fella who'd use a bomb."

"Who are you, anyway?"

"Harry Max Scorf."

"I mean your official capacity."

"Oh, I should have said. I'm with the City and
County of Bayside. Used to be just with the County.
What I am, I'm kind of a special investigator. Odds
and ends of this and that. I work when I please and
how I please."

"Must be nice."

"It's worse than having hours. A man works longer.
Then again, there isn't anything I'd rather be doing. No
family. No hobbies. Tuesday I drove on down to Fort
Lauderdale and I walked around that Bahia Mar
Marina and asked questions about you and Meyer.
You don't seem to have much visible means of support,
McGee."

"Salvage work. Here and there. It's spotty."

"I combed every dang inch of what's left of your
houseboat."

"What's left of it!"

"Steady there. It floats. I came to a conclusion."

"Which is?"

"I don't really think you came up here to straighten
out the distribution of pot in Bayside County."

"Thanks, Scorf."

"Somebody will come along soon. No place along

the coast can stay amateur. They'll take in the ones who'll play along and kill those that won't, and turn it from nickels and dimes into big money, like it is other places. I thought they were already here. Maybe they are. But it's not you and Meyer."

"Why not?"

"Because the job calls for running the hard stuff, and running women, and selling to everybody, grannies and little kids. It calls for buying the law and buying the courts, and you and Meyer are quick enough in your own way and hard enough in your own way, but you got stopping places that are way short of what it takes. If you got a stubborn bartender and you bust both his arms and change his face, the replacement bartender is willing to do business with you. Bars are a nice distribution point for off-premises use."

"Are you working on a book?"

"Don't get snotty with an old man. I could write one."

"Why *are* we here?"

"Well, Harry Hascomb has one story, and that Miss Dobrovsky, she's got another, and Jack Omaha's wife has another. They add up to Carolyn Milligan having been a friend of yours. But if you thought that girl was killed, and you came here to find out who did it and why, and you didn't check in with us and show credentials—which you haven't got—then you're in trouble, aren't you?"

"I know she was killed and so do you. I just wonder if it was entirely an accidental death. That's all."

"And you wanted to attend the service?"

"Right!"

"Now you lunged at that like a bass, boy."

"Remember, I hit my head when somebody killed Joanna."

"We can set here and josh each other from now till the end of time. And you can duck and bob and weave all you want. The thing I've got the most of is time. If somebody did kill Carolyn on purpose, who is your guess?"

"Shouldn't this be some kind of a trade?"

"It is. You've been busy. You've been lying to people. Maybe you've been obstructing justice, or concealing the evidence of a crime, or impersonating an officer. Things like that. I won't act on any of that, at least right now. That's the trade."

"Take me in, officer. Read me my rights."

He sighed and shoved his white hat farther back on his head. "Well, let's see now. What have I got to trade? How about this? So far we've kept a lid on that autopsy on Cal Birdsong. It was heart, all right. But Doc Stanyard didn't like the way it looked, that big soft clot in the pleural cavity and no real sign of any aneurysm. He checked it slow and small and found that something went into there on Cal's left side, between the ribs, smaller than a knitting needle or an ice pick. It could have been a piece of stiff piano wire, sharpened to a needle point. A person could roll it between thumb and forefinger like one of those Chinese needles, to make it go in easy. The heart really hops around in there when it beats. Run that needle in there back and forth a couple of times, and you'd probably pick an artery open or puncture the sac around the heart or mess up a valve somehow. Doc found the entrance track and laid it open and took slides. I saw them this morning, all developed. The track shows up nice."

"And what was Birdsong doing?"

"Seems he was dog tired. They tried to keep him awake on account of his being hit on the head. They don't like people sleeping with head injuries. But he was pooped and he slept hard. And forever. It wouldn't probably wake him, just that little prickle when it went through the skin."

"Does his wife know this?"

"She was one of the ones with him. We're keeping the lid on while we watch how people act."

"One of the ones with him?"

"That's all the trading material you get for now. Your turn."

"You probably know everything I could tell you."

"Try me."

"Well. . . . Adding two and two, the *Christina* came in on May fourteenth, on Tuesday night, with over eight hundred pounds of marijuana aboard. Just two people went out before dawn Tuesday: Jack Omaha and Cal Birdsong. Sometimes Carrie Milligan went, but she didn't go that day because she was sick and said she would be in when she felt well enough. I would guess that Carrie went to Westway Harbor that night in a panel delivery truck owned by Superior Building Supplies. The boat is docked in a good area for privacy. It's beyond the range of the dock lights, but you can drive up close to it. The grass was loaded onto the truck, and Carrie took it to Fifteen Hundred Seaway Boulevard. After it was off-loaded, Mr. Walter Demos took over, and he paid Carrie in cash for the delivery at the rate of a hundred dollars a pound. My guess is that she drove down to Superior and parked the truck where she had picked it up. She had left her own car there. Standard procedure was for her to put the money from Demos into the office safe. She and Jack Omaha had the combination. End of trade. Anything new?"

"Here and there," he said comfortably. "Here and there. Of course you spoiled any chance of us finding anything at all by scragging Demos in his big love nest. There won't be a scrap anywhere."

"He's anxious to . . . wait a second. It fades in and out, like a bad projection bulb. Sorry. My memory quits when it comes to Demos. Your turn," I added.

"Let me see. Oh, here's something you wouldn't know. In that rain Saturday night somebody had left off a package on the porch of the cottage, well back under the overhang, for Joanna Freeler. Betty Joller told me that when Joanna came home she knew what was in the package. She said it was some wine and cheese and like that, for a snack, a present from somebody who couldn't keep a date that night. Now there was just going to be the three of them in the cottage that night. Joanna and Betty Joller and Natalie Weiss. I think it was intended for the package to be opened with the three of them there. Instead, on an impulse, that girl came running through the rain with it. She was a girl who'd rather be with men than girls any time. Your turn, McGee."

I thought it over and then I decided, What the hell, why not? I went through the whole Carrie Milligan death item by item, stressing the illogic of her supposed behavior, the gassing of her car the previous day, and the signs of fresh tampering with the gas tank drain cock.

He glared down at a freckled fist and said, "Even after years, you miss the damnedest things. You know,

I decided that what she was going to do was cross the road and walk to a lighted house and ask to use the phone. With her purse setting there on the front seat in an unlocked car? Nonsense! It was right there and I missed it cold." He thought it over, and finally said, "That would do for now."

"You owe me one."

"I don't have any more to trade." He was distracted by the conjectures swarming in his head. He wanted to be up and off and away. I had put him onto the possibility of a new pattern.

He stood up. I said, "When do you lock me up?"

He focused on me completely and silently. Harry Max Scorf was no figure of fun. He was one hard and determined little man.

"I'll do whatever needs to be done," he said, and turned and left, tugging his hat to the correct angle as he went through the doorway. Before the door had wheezed entirely shut, Meyer came bursting in, grinning.

10

"WELCOME back!" said Meyer.

"Thanks. What about the *Flush?*"

"It floats."

"Really, how is it?"

"There's nothing that about ten thousand dollars can't fix. Don't worry about it."

"Good God, what's left of it?"

"Don't *worry* about it. You do a lot of talking about the way possessions hold us all in thrall. Pretty things are chains and shackles."

It made me gloomy. I could see a listing hulk with huge holes, with wisps of smoke rising from the interior debris. And it worried me that I should care that much. The important loss was the death of that lively girl. Blown in half. Into two girl parts. Such a great and bitter waste.

I realized that if the *Flush* were entirely gone, if it had burned to the waterline and sunk, I would be able to adjust more easily than to the uncertainty. Baubles and toys should disappear, not become broken litter.

Meyer sat beside the bed. He looked like an apprehensive owl as he said, "I kept wondering what the hell to do if you didn't wake up. People stay in a coma for years. They seem to have families to look after them."

"And you could see yourself stuck?"

"I could see myself tottering down to the drugstore saying, Yep, he's still asleep. Been nineteen year now. Gimme some more of that goo for bedsores."

"Look, I blank out during my walk that Saturday afternoon. Tell me about Joanna."

He told me. I could not make it seem real. It was easier to make the service seem real. They did the same thing for her as they did for Carrie. One less girl in a long dress to throw flowers. Good-bye, my sister Joanna. Her widower father attended, full of indignation and stiffness at such an informal heathen ceremony. But, Meyer said, it melted him quickly and he wept with the rest. It loosened the adhesions in his heart, freeing him from other rituals.

"We're losing too many girls," I told Meyer.

"You've added a new one."

"Hmm. The spry nurse lady?"

"No. Cindy Birdsong. She's spent a lot of time here, so someone would be with you when you woke up. She was sure you would. Then she missed by a few minutes. She left a little while before you came out of it, apparently. She's out there now, waiting her turn."

"Why the devotion?"

"I don't know. It's some kind of penance, maybe. Or maybe she is the kind of person who has to have somebody to fret about. Cal is gone. You were at her marina when we got blown up."

"What did it do to you?"

"Gave my back a little wrench and gave me a sore shoulder and one deaf ear."

"So this is Thursday, everybody keeps telling me, June sixth, they keep saying, and it is five days gone out of my life, and what useful thing have you done with those days? I don't like it any more around here, Meyer. I want to go home. Every time I get blown up by a bomb I get that same feeling. Let's go home."

"That wrapped head makes you look strange. It's like a turban. Lawrence of Arabia, or some damned mercenary. You're dark enough for an Arab, but the pale eyes make you look very savage somehow."

"Meyer, what did you find out?"

"Oh. While you were unconscious? Let me think. Oh, yes. That's quite a nice hangar out there at the ranch. Quonset-type construction. That's where ranch equipment gets repaired and maintained too. There's a slow charger for batteries, and a battery cart to boost the aircraft batteries when starting the aircraft up cold. There's a fifteen-hundred-gallon gas tank and a pump to service the aircraft and the ranch vehicles. There's about six employees out there, which means a pretty good payroll, wouldn't you say?"

"Meyer!"

"Are you supposed to sit up like that? There, that's better. Okay. Travis, he has . . ." Meyer paused and took out his little pocket notebook and flipped through the pages, grunting from time to time.

"Meyer!"

"He has a Beechcraft Baron, designation B fifty-five. It has two two-hundred-and-sixty-horsepower Continental engines, designation Ten four-seventy L.

The fuselage is twenty-nine feet long, and the wing-span is thirty-seven feet ten inches. At ten thousand five hundred feet, at a long-range cruising speed of two hundred and twenty miles per hour, with optional fuel capacity of a hundred and thirty-six gallons, he can carry two people and over eight hundred pounds of cargo for sixteen hundred miles, less ten percent safety factor, which gives us fourteen hundred and forty miles. It has an automatic pilot and a lot of other things which I didn't write down here. He bought it used a year ago for sixty-five thousand. He financed it. It can carry four people. It is white with a blue stripe."

I stared at him. "And you went out there and went in the hangar!"

He stared back. "I wish I could say yes."

"What did you do?"

"You reminded me to be cautious when I looked under that Datsun."

"What did you do?"

"I did what all economists do. I went to the library. And after a two-hour search I found an article about him and his place in a magazine called *Florida Ranchorama*. It had a picture of the hangar, with airplane inside. Then I went to the airport, over to the private airplane area, and talked with some mechanics there about airplanes. I asked some questions and then I did a lot of listening. I found out more about airplanes than I care to know."

"You did very well, old friend."

"Shall I blush and simper?"

"If you don't keep it up for long. I hate blushing and simpering in a grown man when it goes on and on."

"You seem to be doing a lot of yawning."

"I am dead tired for some unknown reason, and I am starving. I've never been so empty."

We got hold of the sprightly little old nurse, who said the kitchen was closed and who then went off and checked with Dr. Owings to see if it was all right for Meyer to bring food in. He said fine, and he would approve it because I had a private room.

When Meyer left on his errand it was after eleven, and I did not expect Mrs. Birdsong to be waiting that late. But she was. She came in, and her face went from somber to beautiful in the glow of her smile. She came around and sat on the chair and then stood up again. Awkward moment.

"Please sit down," I said.

"I am so used to sitting right here without . . ."

"You don't need any invitation, really. Meyer told me how faithful you've been."

She had seated herself again, on the edge of the chair. She wore khaki slacks, fitted and faded almost white. She wore a tan shirt with silver buttons. She clutched a brown leather purse with both hands. She wore a trace of lipstick, nothing more. When she looked down the dark glossy hair would have swung forward, would have softened her face, had she not worn it cropped so desperately short. In manner and looks it was almost as if she were trying to deny her femininity, or perhaps she was so shrewdly aware of herself, she knew that any attempt to deny it merely emphasized it.

"Faithful," she said, giving the word a bitter emphasis. "Sure, I guess so. I . . . didn't want you to wake up and not have anyone close by to tell you what happened. But I missed out on that . . . too."

"I appreciate it. Maybe it was good to have someone nearby. I think that people are never totally completely one hundred percent unconscious. I think that they are always aware to some degree of what is going on around them. I think I knew you were here."

"How could you know it was me?"

"Maybe just that someone was here who cared."

"Cared. Yes, that word is okay, Mister McGee. Cared if you lived or died. I'll buy that word."

"I'll give it to you free."

She smiled and again that transformation, but the smile did not last long enough. She flushed visibly and said, "I didn't think about it being hard to talk to you when you woke up."

"Is it hard?"

"Well, I don't know what to say. We buried my husband Monday. I've hired another person. With Jason, Oliver, and the new man, Ritchie, everything can go on . . . as before. After the insurance people told Meyer that you're not covered, he said it was okay if I told the boys to work on your houseboat whenever they have the time."

I sat up. "I'm covered!"

"For lots of things, yes. If your tanks had blown up, yes. Or sinkings or collisions or fire or running aground. But not for people bringing a bomb on board, you're not covered. Should you be sitting up like that?"

I settled down again. She reached and gave a quick shy pat on my arm.

"It's sort of in their spare time, so I'm only billing you for supplies."

"It wasn't your fault."

"I don't know. Sometimes things happen that maybe a person could have stopped."

"And people can take too much onto themselves. If I had done this . . . or that . . . or the other, then maybe this or that or the other would never have happened. The world-mother syndrome."

She thought it over. "I guess I am sort of that way."

She looked down and away, lost to me, wandering in the backwoods of her mind. It was a strong clear face, clean and dark and timeless, like the face of a young monk seen in an old drawing. It was somber and passionate, withdrawn yet intensely involved. The curve of the lips, shape of the throat, set of the eyes, all spoke of fire and of need carefully suppressed, held down in merciless discipline.

Meyer came back. She stirred to leave, but he had brought food for her too. He said it had not been easy at that time of night. Quarter-pounders with cheese, in square cartons, still hot. He had brought six of them, and a container of milk and two containers of coffee. Meyer sat on the foot of my bed. I was certain I could eat three of them. I was famished. Yet it was all I could do to finish the first one. I drank the milk. I sagged back. I thought I would close my eyes for just a moment. I heard them talking, and their voices sounded strange to me, as if I were a child again, half asleep in the back seat while the parents talked together in the front seat. When the little white-haired nurse woke me up to find out if I wanted a sleeping pill, Meyer and Cindy were gone and the room was darkened. I heard a siren far away. I turned back into my sleep, wormed my way back to dreaming.

On Friday at eleven thirty Dr. Hubert Owings changed the dressing on my head, making it much smaller, getting away from the turban effect. He checked me over and approved me for release. I phoned the marina and got hold of Jason, who got hold of Meyer. Meyer said he would be along to pick me up in a half hour. I told him to bring money. And clothes. The clothes I had been wearing when I arrived were too badly dappled with the blood of Joanna to ever consider wearing again.

I borrowed a shower cap and took a shower. Meyer arrived and said he had stopped at the cashier's office and bought me out, and given the release ticket to the nurse at the floor station. I got up too quickly and felt dizzy. I had to sit down for a minute before I could get dressed. Meyer was worried about me.

"Hube said I'm fine. A heavy concussion. No fracture. I came out of it okay, he says. If I start to have fainting spells, come back in for observation. They are short of beds or they'd keep me longer."

The world looked strange. There were little halos around the edges of every tree and building. I did very deep breathing. It is strange to sleep for five days and five nights and have the world go rolling along without you. Just like it will keep on after you're dead. The wide busy world of tire balancing, diaper changing, window washing, barn dancing, bike racing, nose picking, and bug swatting will go merrily merrily along. If they were never aware of your presence, they won't be overwhelmed by your absence.

On the way back Meyer told me that Cindy Birdsong had made arrangements for me to have a unit at the motel, next to hers. I could not get any rest aboard the *Flush* because of all the sawing and hammering. I was supposed to get a lot of rest. The prescription would make me drowsy. I said it was a lot of nonsense.

But when I got out of the car I gave up all hope of walking out to look at my boat. I saved everything I had left for the immense feat of tottering over to the motel and collapsing onto the bed which Cindy and Meyer guided me to.

I slept through lunch and woke up at five o'clock. I put my shoes on and latched my belt and went on the long walk out to the *Flush*. The sun was still high and hot. I heard the power saw long before I recognized who was running it. Jason was brown and sweaty, and he was cutting some heavy-duty marine plywood to size. He let go of the trigger on the saw and put it on the uncut sheet and stuck his hand out. "You don't look so bad, Mr. McGee."

"Neither does my vessel."

"Not so bad on the outside until you notice it blew all the ports out of the lounge. It isn't so great in there."

"Do you know how to do . . . what you're doing?"

"Does it make you nervous? I can cut plywood to fit, for God's sake. The thing is to get it sealed before it rains again. We're into the rainy season now. I fixed the two broken cross members, those beam things. They were splintered. I cut out the bad parts and bolted in new pieces. It's okay now. Stronger than before."

"In case I get another gift bomb?"

"Nobody around here makes any jokes about that."

"I'm sorry."

"Joanna was an okay person. Not like Carrie, but

okay. I mean there was no need for anybody to blow her into pieces."

I climbed aboard and up the side ladderway. There was one hole left, a neat rectangle about two feet by five feet. There was new plywood over an area at least sixteen by thirty feet, the major portion of the sun deck. Jason came up with the last piece and laid it in place. It fit so snugly he had to stomp it into place with his bare heels. He knelt on it and took the nails from his canvas apron and smartly whacked the nails home. He threw one to me. It had a twist like a screw, and it was heavy-duty galvanized.

"These won't let go," he said.

"You're doing a good job."

"Ollie and I both think we are. He did part of this. What I plan on doing is caulk all these seams with a resin compound before I lay the new vinyl decking. It doesn't exactly match this stuff but it's close. Here's a sample. Close enough?"

"Nobody will ever notice. What about the ports?"

"That's another story. I got a guy coming to make an estimate tomorrow morning. At ten, if you want to be in on it."

I left him to his hammering and went below and went down into the forward bilge area. It took thirty seconds to make certain nobody had located my hiding place between the fake double hull, not even the impressive Harry Max Scorf himself. I checked out three weapons. If he found them, he had had the sense to leave them where they were, entirely legal.

The lounge was a sorry mess. It was damp as a swamp and already sour with mildew, a gray-green scum spreading across the carpeting. The yellow couch lay with its feet in the air, a dead mammoth from earlier times. Shards and splinters of coffee table and chairs lay here and there in profusion. A large splinter protruded from the precise center of a stereo speaker. Another had pierced a painting I was fond of, right between the Syd and the Solomon of the painter's lower-right-corner signature. There were thick brown stains of dried blood. There was a chemical smell, like cap pistols and ammonia.

Meyer came hurrying in. "Hello! Should you be roaming around like this?"

"I'm roaming around crying."

"I know. I know."

"Is the wiring messed up? Would the air conditioning work?"

"It kept blowing circuits at first, and I found out that it was the lamp that used to be on this bracket over here. It smashed the inside of it. But now things work."

"Then instead of letting the place rot, let's get some sheet Pliofilm and staple it over the ports and get the air conditioning going to start to dry it out in here. And let's pull up this carpeting and get it trucked away."

"All right. But spare me the 'us' part of it. Go back and rest."

"Is there any ice?"

There was. I assembled a flagon of Plymouth and carried it topside and sat at the controls and sipped and watched the sun sliding down the sky on the other side of Florida. That drink really slugged me. I had to pay special attention to every shift of weight and balance as I walked back to the motel. Every footfall was an engineering problem. My ears had started ringing again.

Cindy heard me and opened the interconnecting

door and stood staring at me. I realized that I was visibly smashed, and I realized she'd had all too much of that in her marriage.

She shook her head. "Travis, good God. Sit down before you fall down."

"Thank you very much indeed."

"Are you going to be sick?"

"I don't think so. Thank you very much indeed."

"Here. Let's swing your legs up. Let me get your shoes."

"Thank you very much indeed."

11

I opened my eyes. It was night. There was a small lamp with an opaque shade on a table in a corner. Cindy Birdsong slept in the wing chair beside the table, long legs extended, ankles crossed, head tilted way over to rest on her shoulder, mouth slightly agape. I spied upon the privacy of her sleep. She rifled the closets and drawers of memory while her body lay a-sprawl, clad in gray cardigan, pink blouse, dark blue slacks.

I looked at my watch. I pressed the button. No display. The batteries had died. I had such an evil taste in my mouth I knew I had been asleep a long time. I felt as if I could eat a bison. Raw. With a dull fork.

I tiptoed to the small bathroom and eased the door shut before I turned the light on. I looked at a gaunt, weathered, and most unfamiliar face. I brushed my teeth with foaming energy and drank four glasses of water. My tan looked yellowed, as if I had jaundice. The white scar tissue in the left eyebrow seemed more visible than usual, the nose more askew. The eyes looked shifty and uncertain. Some kind of hero. Some kind of chronic girl-loser. Some kind of person on the edge of life, unwilling and/or unable to wedge himself into the heartlands.

When I turned the light off and opened the door, Cindy was sitting bolt upright on the edge of the chair, knees together. She hugged herself, rubbing her left shoulder, and said, "I must have dozed off. I'm sorry."

"Why be sorry? What time is it?"

She gave a little start as she looked at her watch. "Good grief, it's a quarter to four! I . . . I really haven't been sleeping well lately. Until now. I guess you were so deep in sleep it was contagious. How do you feel?"

"I'm starving. You asked. I have to tell you I'm going to faint from hunger. I'll fall heavily."

At her invitation I followed her into the larger unit she had shared with Cal. There was a kitchenette arrangement behind folding doors, scrubbed to a high shine. We inventoried the possibilities, and I opted for Polish sausage and lots of eggs. She went into the bathroom and came out with minty breath and brushed hair.

She made an ample quantity and served herself a substantial helping. It was not a meal where conversation was encouraged. It was a meal which required more eggs, and she hopped up and scrambled more. She served good coffee in big mugs.

At last I felt comfortable. I felt cozy. I leaned back. She caught my eye and flushed slightly and said, "I haven't been eating hardly anything. Until now. I've lost about six pounds in the past week or so. I want to keep it off."

"You seemed about the right size and shape when I checked into your marina, lady."

"I get hippy. That's where it all goes."

The silence between us was comfortable—and then uncomfortable. The awareness grew, tangible as that ringing in the ears. She looked down, flushing again. When she got up I reached for her and caught her wrist, then tugged her gently around the corner of the table toward me. She came with an unwillingness, looking away, murmuring "Please." I pulled her to stand by me, against my thigh, and slid my hand to her waist, slid it under the edge of the pink blouse to clasp the smooth warm flesh where the waist was slimmest.

"No," she said in a soft dragging voice, far away.

"I have been losing girls," I said. "It has to stop."

"I'm not a girl. Not any more, I'm not."

I stood up and put my hands on her shoulders, felt a gentle shuddering that was awareness, not revulsion.

"Cindy, I could say an awful lot of dumb things. What it would boil down to is, I'm alive, glad to be alive, and I want you."

"I . . . I just can't quite . . ."

And I steered her slowly and gently to the relative darkness of my connecting unit, through the door ahead of me, arm around her waist, blundering together to the bed.

At the bed, after she sat and I began to undo the buttons of her blouse, she pushed me away and said, "I have to say something first. Before anything happens. Listen to me. Wait. Please. When I heard he was dead there was . . . some kind of dirty joy in me. I cried and carried on because people expected me to."

"It's like that sometimes."

"I don't want it to be like that for me." Her voice was uneven. "I know what they think: It was all just dandy great until he got on the booze. Well, it wasn't all that great. It wasn't even half good between us. He wanted it to be great. I couldn't really love him. I tried to imitate loving him, but he knew it had all gone away for me. He knew I felt empty. That's why he started drinking like that. People got it all backward. And I feel so . . . so rotten. So sick. So really terrible about . . . what I did to him."

It was all the confession she could handle. Guilt broke the dam inside her. I held her and she rocked herself back and forth in her inner agony. Guilt is the most merciless disease of man. It stains all the other areas of living. It darkens all skies.

I held her and eased her and soothed her. When she was nearly quiet, except for the occasional hiccup sob, I wondered if she was too spent for love. I peeled her gently and quietly out of her clothes. When we were naked and enclasped, facing each other on the motel bed, there seemed to be a great deal of her, long and firm and rich, with a body heat degrees above mine.

We were the wounded, she from all the trauma of her tears, me from the concussion and the five lost days. So it was not a physical, sexual greed that motored us.

It was an affirmation, a way to be less alone. In fact for quite a long time it seemed as if it would be love-making without climax, with only slowness, tenderness, and affection.

With the first of morning light she found a slow and lasting release and faded from that crest into the downslope of sleep. I eased out of the bed to close the slats of the blinds and shut out the increasing brightness. As I went back to bed I carried an uneasy afterimage of something, some shadow or substance, flickering swiftly away from the space under the window, out of sight.

On Saturday afternoon I left Meyer and Oliver to finish stapling the Pliofilm over the ports and over the smashed doorway, and went back to the motel, feeling pleasantly tired, and curious as to how she would accommodate herself to this new fact of her life.

She wore a brief yellow sun dress. She came toward me and looked cautiously beyond me to see if we were observed. Then she kissed me quickly on the lips and pulled me inside her quarters for a more emphatic kiss after the door was shut.

She was smiling. She said, "I don't know what I ought to say. But what I want to say is, Thanks for a lovely evening, for a lovely late date."

"You are most very certainly absolutely welcome, ma'am."

"Can you eat beef stew?"

"Indefinitely."

"I want you to keep your strength up."

"That's the best invitation I've had today. You're blushing."

"The stew is canned, dammit. I had to spell Ritchie at the office and didn't have time to fix anything special. But I added a couple of things to make it taste better."

It was excellent stew. We sat across the table from each other, by the window. We could see most of the marina from the window.

I said, "Cindy, my darling, I want to ask you some things. You might wonder why I have to ask them. But it would be a very long story, and I will tell you that long story some day but not right now. Okay?"

"Questions about what?"

"About a lot of things. First question: When Cal went off before dawn on those boat trips with Jack Omaha, where were they going?"

She tilted her head, frowning. "Off Grand Bahama Island after billfish, dear. Sometimes little Carrie Milligan went too. Jack's secretary and . . . well, playmate. I think it was a chance for them to play while Cal ran the boat. The other times they were after tuna and marlin and so on."

"Was Cal getting any extra money from anywhere, in large amounts?"

"Cal? God, no! He was good at spending it, not making it."

"Did you think those trips were strange in any way?"

"Listen, darling. I didn't much care if they were strange or not. I didn't think very much about what Cal did or didn't do. There was very limited communication between us. Before I met him I had been going with someone and I was in love with him, very deeply in love. We had the most horrible fight ever, and he went off and got married. So I went off and got married. He showed me and I showed him. I married Cal, and it was a lousy reason to get married. It was sort of okay in a limited way. The physical part was okay at first, and then it didn't hold up very well, especially not when he was drinking. About his trips, if I thought about them at all, it was to wish they'd happen oftener and last longer. And there was no extra money from anywhere. I guess I ought to tell you that these are almost the same questions our lawyer asked me."

"Fred Van Harn?"

"Yes. He was very solemn and insistent. He said that he wanted to make certain I wasn't mixed up in anything that Cal might have been doing that was against the law. I told him exactly what I've been telling you. He said that he couldn't protect me unless I was frank and open with him. He said that anything I told him was privileged information. I had to say I just didn't know anything, and that it had been a long time since Cal and I had talked much about anything. It wasn't exactly the friendliest conversation in the world."

"What do you mean by that?"

"Oh, it's just that Fred is . . . well, constantly horny. About a year ago he made a pretty startling pass at me. It was in his office. He came up behind me and hugged himself up against me and had both hands roaming all over me. I'm a very strong person."

"I noticed."

"Hush. I picked his hand up and set my teeth in his thumb. He screamed. He had to have a tetanus shot. He got over his problem very quickly. So we haven't been very chummy with each other."

"I wouldn't think so."

"Men like that have an instinct about wives, when they might be vulnerable. Something must show, somehow. For one little instant when he was doing what he was doing, I thought, Well, why not, what the hell? But then I realized that if I was going to say what the hell with somebody, it wouldn't be with Freddy. He's too conscious of those long black eyelashes of his. So I bit him to the bone."

"That pleases me."

"What *was* Cal doing on those trips?"

"Smuggling narcotics."

She stared at me. "You've got to be kidding! You really have got to be kidding!"

"Jamaican marijuana."

"Oh. Just grass. Well . . . "

"What's the matter?"

"That's where he got that stuff. He insisted I try it. A sloppy cigarette, twisted at the ends. A toke, he called it. A joint. He showed me how you're supposed to do it. Then we made love after he knew I was feeling it a lot. Love was strange and dreamy. I could hear the sound his hand made on my skin, a little brushing sound. Things went on forever, and I knew every part of it while it was going on. And I started crying and couldn't stop. It was so sweet and sad I couldn't stop crying. That made him angry and he went storming out. That was the last time we ever made love together, and that was . . . months ago. I guess that was part of what he was smuggling, he and Jack?"

"Probably."

"I liked it and I didn't like it. I would like to try it with somebody I really love sometime, but not until I'd tried everything else first with that person."

She got up and took the dishes to the sink.

I watched her, appreciating the way the brief yellow dress made her legs look uncommonly tan and uncommonly long.

Yet I had the curious feeling that I had not really made love to her. We could make small bawdy jokes together. We could kiss in excellent imitation of new-found lovers. I could look upon her in happy memory of the last time and steamy anticipation of the next time, but at the same time feel as if we were theater people, trained to give a convincing imitation of desire. We were close. We knew all the motions. Yet in a way I could not define we were insulated from each other, not quite touching in some deep and important way.

As a test I went up behind her and put my arms around her and pulled her close. She tilted her head back and said, "You risk a tetanus shot, sir."

"Worth it, ma'am."

"Listen. Where did the money go? If he was taking risks like that, where is the money?"

"I don't know. Maybe he hid it in some safe place, or somebody was holding it for him."

As I turned her around she said, "He used to worry so much about the money we owe on the marina. He used to fret and fume. Hey! What are we doing now?"

"It's siesta time. This is called getting you ready for your three o'clock nap."

"Don't you think you better move back onto your houseboat?"

"Right now?"

"Well . . . not exactly right now, okay?"

By Sunday afternoon the air conditioning was making good headway against the dampness aboard the *Flush*. A milky light and blurred outlines of nearby boats shone through the Pliofilm. The carpeting had been jettisoned, and Meyer had samples to study, before rendering advice.

The ninth day of June. I hadn't adjusted to the five-day gap in my memory. I was being hustled along too fast into the time stream. Ears ringing. A sweet and greedy lady to be with.

"Make some sense of things," I asked Meyer.

He stopped playing solitaire with his carpet samples. "I cannot come up with an overview," he said. "I can sense no paradigm that later events will prove out. I can construct no model from what we have."

"Thanks."

"Believe me, it's nothing."

"I know. I know."

"How about this blue? Indoor-outdoor. Won't fade."

"It's truly lovely, Meyer."

"Come on. Don't you care how it's going to look?"

"Intensely."

"All things considered, you should be jollier, Travis."

"Than whom?"

"Than whom has not such a handsome lady tending his convalescence."

"I feel disoriented. I have a dull ache in the back of my head, and I live in a motel."

Further discussion of my melancholy was terminated by the arrival of Jason-Jesus with Susan Dobrovsky. She looked sallow and subdued, with smudges under her eyes and a listless manner. Jason was being very firm and forthright. The protector. No social strokes. No discussion of the weather. He planted his feet and got right into it.

"Susan and I have been developing a useful dialogue about her situation here. We've decided that it is more important for her to get away, to get back to Nutley, than it is to hang around while Van Harn takes care of the last little legal details regarding Carrie's death."

She sat on the edge of the yellow couch which was going to have to be re-covered. "I want to leave," she said, in a very small voice. "Everything here has been so rotten."

"Mr. McGee, Susan told me that you told her that you owed Carrie some money. You paid off the funeral home in cash. Is there more money Susan should have?"

"Yes."

"How much?"

"What's your special interest in this, Jason?"

"Somebody has to care about situations like this. People have to take care of people."

"Granted. Let me talk to Susan alone. Meyer, why don't you go topside with Jason?"

When they had left and the Pliofilm curtain had fallen back into place, I went over and sat beside her on the couch. She became very still, quite rigid. It seemed a curious reaction. I touched her arm and she made a huge flinching motion, ending up two feet farther away from me.

"Hey," I said. "Whoa. Settle down."

"I'm sorry. I'm sorry. It's just that I'm not reacting to things . . . normally. To being touched by anybody. I can't help it."

"What happened to you?"

She gave me a wide, bright, terrible smile. "Happened? Oh, I was a guest at the V-H Ranch yesterday and the day before. That's all. Mr. Van Harn raises Black Angus and breeds horses. He has twelve hundred acres out there, and the old Carpenter ranch house was built out of hard pine in nineteen twenty-one and it's still as solid as a rock. I . . . nothing . . . can't. . . ."

She bent abruptly forward, face in her hands, hands resting on her knees. I reached to touch her and pulled my hand back in time.

"Were you forced?"

Her voice was muffled. "Yes. No. I don't know. I don't know what to say. He kept after me and after me and after me. It went on and on. I got so tired. So I thought . . . I don't know what I thought. Just that if I let him that would be the end of it."

"Susan, I have to know something. Did he ask you anything about Carrie?"

"There wasn't much talking."

"Did he ask you anything at all about Carrie?"

"Well, he wanted to know the last time I'd talked to her, and so I told him about the long phone call, the one I told you about too. He made me remember everything she said. One part that I told him was about you. You know. Carrie said to me that if a person named Travis McGee got in touch with me I was to trust him all the way."

"Did he seem interested in that?"

"Not any more than in any of the rest of it. He just kept me going over it and over it until he saw there wasn't any part of it I hadn't told him. That was the only talking there was, mostly."

"When did this conversation take place?"

"Yesterday, I think. Yes, yesterday. Early in the morning, I think. I remember the sounds the birds were making. Early sounds."

"How did you get back?"

"He drove me in and let me off at the Inn. He had a meeting. Maybe it was three o'clock yesterday afternoon. Jason came over this morning. I . . . told him about it. I wanted to tell somebody about how damned dumb I was."

"How did Jason react?"

"He wants to go kill him. What good would that do anybody? I shouldn't have gone out there with him. Joanna told me enough about him so I should have been careful, more careful. Mr. McGee, is there any more money? And you still have Carrie's rings. I remember Mr. Rucker giving them to you. He tried to give them to me and I couldn't take them then. I can now. Is there any money?"

"A lot of money."

"A lot?"

"Ninety-four thousand dollars in cash."

Her face went quite blank as she stared at me. She rubbed the palms of her hands on her forearms, one and then the other. "What?"

"Ninety-four thousand two hundred, less six hundred and eighty-six fifty that I paid Rucker. Ninety-three thousand something."

She rubbed the palms of her hands together. She narrowed those tilted gray-green eyes. She swung her hair back with a toss of her head. "Where would . . . Carrie get that?"

"From something she was involved in."

"From smuggling marijuana?"

"Did someone suggest that to you?"

"Betty Joller. It had something to do with why she left the cottage and went to live at that Fifteen Hundred place, Betty said. Would she make that much all for herself?"

"It's possible."

"She always wanted to have a lot of money."

"On the other hand, maybe the money is Van Harn's."

Her sallow round face looked stricken. "Would she be mixed up with him in anything? I wonder if he ever . . . made love to my sister. Jesus! That word doesn't fit. Love!"

"I wouldn't know."

She looked thoughtful. "She was always a stronger type person than me. I mean she could probably handle that kind of a man better than I could. Being older and married and so on. I never knew about men like that. He just kept confusing me. I guess I want that money now. Where is it?"

"In a very safe place."

"Can you get it for me?"

"Do you want to travel with that much in cash?"

"Oh. No, I guess not."

"I can get it to you later. What are you going to do with it when you get it?"

"I don't know. Put it in a deposit box, I guess. I don't know about taxes and so on. And her estate. On the phone something she said made me think she gave you some money too."

"She did. I hope it's going to be enough to get my houseboat fixed up. It was a fee for services. I am trying to find out who killed her."

"Who killed her! You're confusing me."

"Fly out of here. Fly home. I'll bring the money."

"When?"

"When I find out what went on here."

"And you'll tell me? Did somebody actually kill Carrie?"

"It's a possibility."

"Because of what she was doing? Because of the smuggling?"

"I would think so. In the meanwhile, Susan, not one word to anybody. Not even Jason."

"But I am very—"

"Not even Jason. Damn it, she told you to trust me. So trust me. Don't stand around dragging your feet."

"Well, then. Not even Jason."

As I went out onto the side deck with her, I saw Oliver trotting toward the *Flush*. He looked solemn. "Judge Schermer wants to talk to you, Mr. McGee."

"Send him along then."

"Oh, no. He wants you at his car. He's up there by the office."

12

IT was a spanking new Cadillac limousine, black as a crow's wing. It had tinted glass. I saw the black chauffeur walking offstage toward a shady bench.

A young woman stood beside the car. She put her hand out. "I'm Jane Schermer, Mr. McGee. Sorry to disturb you like this, but my uncle is anxious to talk to you."

She was a young woman with a sunburned flavor of ranchlands, cattle, and horses. She had a prematurely middle-aged face, doughy and slightly heavy in the jowls. She was oddly built, tall and broad, with vestigial breasts and very little indentation at the waist. The accent was expensive finishing school, possibly in Pennsylvania.

Jane opened the rear door and said, "Mr. McGee, Uncle Jake."

"How do you do, Judge Schermer," I said politely.

"Jane, you go take a little walk for yourself. This is man talk. Give us fifteen minutes. McGee, come on in here, but don't sit beside me. You can't talk to a man sitting beside you, damn it. Open up that jump seat and sit facing me. That's fine. Please don't smoke."

"I had no intention of so doing."

He chuckled. "No intention of so doing. You ever read for the law? Can't get the stink out of the upholstery."

He looked ludicrously like Harry Max Scorf. He looked as if somebody had taken Harry Max and inflated him until his skin was shiny-tight and then had spray-painted him pink. His round stomach rested on his round thighs. He wore khakis and a straw ranch hat. The motor purred almost soundlessly. The compressor for the air conditioning clicked on and off.

"You're one sizable son of a bitch, aren't you?" he said. "That's some goddamn pair of wrists on you. You go about two twenty-five?"

"Few people guess it that close."

"I guess a lot of things close. It's been a help over the years."

"Do you want to get to some kind of point?"

"Saving us both time, eh? I have a protégé."

"Named Freddy Van Harn, who is engaged to be married to your niece, Jane Schermer. People think he has a political future. Then there could be those who don't think he has any future at all."

"You are a quick one, all right. You surely are. Frederick and I discuss his future and his current problems from time to time. You came up as one of his current problems."

"Me?"

"Pure bug-eyed astonishment, eh? Frederick is a lively young man. It's entirely possible for a fellow like him to become involved in something foolish out of a sense of risk and adventure. At his age—he's only twenty-nine—a single man can do some foolish things, never quite realizing that he might be destroying his whole future and destroying the dreams of the people depending on him. A man can have his sense of values warped by expediency sometimes, McGee. In Frederick's case, he's wanted to make money fast and make it big to wipe out the local memories of his father, a man who made a terrible mistake and took his life. Frederick became overextended, and he took a foolish risk in an effort to make some quick money. I've been very severe with him about that."

"What kind of risk?"

"We don't have to go into that here."

"Then let's say he was flying in grass, dropping it to a friend in a power boat. That would be profitable and foolish enough, don't you think?"

"Out of the goodness of my heart, I would advise you not to get too smart-mouth and high-ass around me. It makes me irritable, and when I get irritable, I'm harder to deal with."

"I'm not after a deal."

"You might be sooner than you know."

"Whatever that might mean."

"Frederick Van Harn is a very talented attorney, and he has that special kind of charisma which means he can go far in public service. It's past time that me and my little group had somebody in Tallahassee speaking up for this county and our special problems here. We've all he'ped him along ever' way we could, ever since he got out of Stetson and set up practice here. Once he's married to Janie he won't have any more money problems to fret about and do foolish things trying to solve them. You get what I mean. Janie inherited ten thousand acres of the most profitable grove lands in this whole state."

"How nice for her."

"McGee, we're talking about image here. We're building an image people are going to trust. You ought to hear that boy give a speech. Make you tingle all over. What I wouldn't want to happen, I wouldn't want anybody to come here, some stranger, and try to make a big fuss based entirely on the word of some dead thieving slut."

"You wouldn't?"

"Especially when it would be bad timing for Frederick in his career. A man shouldn't lose his whole future on account of one foolish act. It wouldn't be fair, would it?"

"To whom?"

"To those of us working hard to see dreams come true."

I shook my head. "Judge, you picked the wrong protégé. You picked a bad one."

"What are you talking about?"

"This Ready Freddy is kinky, Judge. He's all twisted in the sex areas."

"By God, there's nothing twisted about a man liking his pussy and going after it any danged place he can find it. When I was that boy's age I was ranging three counties on the moonlight nights."

"He likes it to hurt them, Judge. He likes to force them. He likes to scare them. He likes to humiliate them. He leaves them with bad memories and a bad case of the shakes."

"I'd say you've been listening to some foolish woman

with too many inhibitions to be any damn good in bed. I'd stake my life that boy is normal. And when he's got a wife and career he'll be too busy to go tomcatting."

"That sexy wife ought to keep him at home, all right."

"Watch yourself! You got a lot more mouth than you need."

"Judge, we have arrived at the end of our discussion. Weird as it may seem to you, I think your protégé is a murderous, spooky fellow. I think he has been going around killing people. I think he killed two friends of mine. Tell him that."

I reached behind me for the door handle. "Wait!" he said sharply. "What are you trying to pull? You can't believe that shit!"

"But I do!"

We locked stares for ten long seconds. And then he looked down and away, lips pursed. "We couldn't be that far wrong," he said softly, wonderingly. He shook himself and glowered at me. "You want to raise the ante. All right. Here is your deal. Twenty-five thousand dollars cash to get out of this county and stay out."

"Not for ten times the offer, Judge."

"You are dead wrong about Frederick. Believe me."

"I'll have to prove that to myself in my own way."

"Stop reaching back of you for that door handle. Set a minute. Everybody wants something bad. What is it you want?"

"It isn't nice to go around killing people."

"Frederick wouldn't kill anybody. Have you got some romantical notion about getting even for Carrie Milligan? My God, McGee, these people that get into drugs, they've got the life expectancy of a mayfly. That girl probably didn't know where she was or what she was doing. She walked into traffic."

"Like Joanna."

"A bomb? Frederick Van Harn fooling around with bombs? That's ridiculous. What do you want? What are you after?"

"Nothing you'd understand, Judge."

"I understand a lot of things. I understand the world is too full of people and half a billion of 'em are starving this year. I understand there's a few million tons of phosphate under the ranchlands down in the southeast corner of this county, and the ecology freaks have kept National Minerals Industries from strip-mining it, and there's a group of us thinks if we put Fred in the State Senate, that might get changed around and a lot of people might make out pretty good. I understand that we're not going to stand for anybody coming in here and messing up our plans. People are starving because of the shortage of fertilizer. Phosphate is high priority, McGee. Now who's going to do the most good in the world, Van Harn or you?"

"It's nice to know why you're so interested in me."

"You know what I'm going to do for you? I'm going to set up a little session between you and Frederick, and I'll let him tell you just what his involvement was."

"Are you sure you want to do that?"

"What's the matter? Afraid he'll shoot your theories full of holes?"

"I met him once. He didn't impress me, Judge."

"You caught him at a bad time. He told me about it."

"Why should he tell you?"

"I asked him if he'd ever met you."

"I'll talk to him, sure. Send this car back with him in it, and I'll talk to him right here. Like this. Alone. If he's willing."

"He's willing to do what we want him to do."

"Let's make it tomorrow. There isn't enough of today left. I seem to get tired easily."

"Tomorrow morning."

I got out. Jane Schermer was strolling slowly toward the limousine. When she saw me holding the door for her, she quickened her step. The Judge kicked the jump seat back into its niche. I handed her in and closed the door. The driver climbed in and chunked his door shut, and the car moved off through the late heat of the day, with barely audible hum of gears and engine.

Cindy was in the office. A man from Virginia was settling up, preparatory to leaving in the early morning on Monday. He was signing travelers' checks. He wore red-white-and-blue shorts and a yellow shirt, funny shoes, and a funny hat. He had narrow little shoulders and a yard of rump. He was telling Cindy how great it had been, except when the bomb went off. She said she was sorry about that bomb. He said he didn't know what people were thinking of these days. Like in Ireland.

He went out with his receipt and with Cindy's wishes for a good cruise back to Virginia. The door swung shut and she said, "You look practically gray. What is it, dear?"

"The Judge wore me down. I'm going to go lie down."

"Before you fall down."

"I'm going to swim in that motel pool first."

"Should you?"

"If I don't get the dressing wet."

"Somebody ought to be with you."

The new fellow came in. Ritchie. A little older than Ollie and Jason, a lot less hairy. He said Jason was out on the docks and sure, he'd take the desk.

I went to the *Flush* and got swim trunks. Meyer wasn't aboard. I changed in the motel, and by the time I got to the pool Cindy was there, taking long sweeping strokes, a fast crawl from end to end, using kick turns. The dusk light was turning orange, making the world look odd, as though awaiting thunder. I sat on the edge of the pool and admired the smooth flexing of the muscles of her back and hips and thighs as she made those turns. Then I lowered myself into the pool and paddled lethargically around, keeping my head high. She wore a white suit, white swim cap.

When I clambered out, refreshed and relaxed, she was still swimming hard, but she was beginning to labor, beginning that side to side roll of exhaustion. At last she came to the edge and clung, panting audibly. I went and took her wrists and hoisted her out. She stumbled against me and recoiled, turning away from me.

"What was that all about?"

"What was what all about?" She walked over to her towel and mopped her face, tugged the cap off, shook her dark hair out, and sat on an aluminum chaise and closed her eyes.

I sat on the concrete beside the chaise and took hold of her hand. It was brown and boneless, without response. "What was the compulsive swimming all about?"

"Exercise. That's all."

"All?"

"Well. I guess I was fighting us. Working off anger."

"Why?"

"It just seems too pat. Just too damned easy, that's all. Nothing comes for free. Everything costs. I walk around all day wanting to be in bed with you. Knowing I will be. But maybe I won't be."

"Why not?"

"Weren't you listening? I said it was too easy for us."

"And that makes it bad? That makes it ugly?"

"I didn't *say* that."

"Meyer is the one with the erudition. Meyer is the one with all the smarts. I can give you something secondhand from Meyer which might help. It comes from a smart tough old Greek by the name of Homer. I'll tell you what he said . . . if you'll use it."

"I'll try."

"He said, 'Dear to us ever is the banquet and the harp and the dance and changes of raiment and the warm bath and love and sleep.' "

She kept her eyes closed and her face told me nothing. Finally she said, "Dear to us ever. Yes." She turned her head toward me and opened her eyes and linked her fingers in mine. "Maybe that old Greek meant that a thing in and of itself is okay, without deadlines or promissory notes or anything. Just in and of itself alone."

"In and of itself together."

"Well, sure."

And so we went into the motel where there was a last pink tinge of sunlight dimly reflected on a far wall. Out of the wet suits our bodies were enclasped clammy cool, but swiftly heating. There was no constraint in her, only a merging and changing energy, quite swift and certain of itself, strong and searching.

When I awoke she was gone. There was a rusty old projector in the back of my mind, showing underexposed film on a mildewed screen. The projection bulb kept burning out and the film kept jamming in the gate, but by watching closely I could make most of it out. Memory was healing itself, taking me from banyan shelter in the rain to Fifteen Hundred to my talk with the bald man. It was all of a piece, but with murky places which I hoped would become more clear to me as time went on.

It was four in the morning. I was on the edge of sleep, beginning to hallucinate back into my dreams, when the creak of the interconnecting door brought me awake. I smelled her perfume. Her groping hand touched my shoulder. She whispered my name.

I turned the sheet back for her and she came shivering in beside me, chattering her teeth. She wore something gauzy and hip-length.

"What's the matter?"

"I dreamed you were d-d-dead too, darling."

"I'm not."

"I just had to come in and hold you. That's all I want."

"Everything is all right. It's all right.'

"I'll be okay in a little wh-while."

I held her, close and safe. She felt restless for quite a

long time, and then gradually her breathing slowed and deepened. I tried to visualize her face but could not, and at the edge of sleep I had the nightmare vision of face without features, of a rounded, tanned expanse of flesh, anonymous as the back of her shoulder.

When I awoke at dawn she was still with me. I thought I was aboard the *Flush,* and for a time I did not know who she was. Her leg jumped twice and she made a whining sound before turning back into heavy sleep.

As once again she became restless, I tried to find the answer to my feeling that I could not seem to get truly close to her. I did not know enough about her. Had she fallen out of apple trees, ridden a red bike, built castles in a sandbox, scabbed her knees, worshiped her daddy, sung in a choir, written poetry, walked in the rain? She did not tell me enough. I wanted to know all of the complex of experience which had finally brought her to this place and time, to this moment with her dark hair fragrant and pressed against the edge of my chin. A widow, now indulging herself in the delights of the flesh, so long denied by the hulking drunken husband, and feeling guilt for such indulgence. I was being used, and wanted a deeper and truer contact. I wondered if I wanted her to be in love with me, as a sop to my ego, perhaps.

There was a change in the feel of her, in the textures of her, that told me she was now awake. Gently, gently, she disengaged herself as I feigned sleep. She sat on the edge of the bed and groped for the short nightgown, then stood and put it on. Through slitted eyes I saw her put a fist in front of a wide yawn, a yawn so huge it made her shudder. She moved silently across the room and slipped through the interconnecting door. I heard the soft click of the latch and the second metallic sound that meant she had locked the door behind her. A gesture for the motel maid? A disavowal? Or the end of the episode?

13

FREDERICK Van Harn sat in the same rear corner
of the limousine as had the Judge. The black chauffeur
sat upon a different bench because the shade patterns
were different at ten o'clock on that Monday morning.
The engine ran as quietly as before, the compressor
clicking on and off.

I sat on the same jump seat, turned to face him. I
wore boat pants, sandals, a faded old shirt from Gua-
temala. He wore a beige business suit, white shirt, tie of
dark green silk, dark brown loafers polished to satin
gloss. As he looked directly at me I saw that his side-
burns were precisely even. The sideburn hair was long,
brushed back to cover the ears. Neat little ears, I imag-
ined. Maybe a bit pointed on the top. Olive skin, delicate features, long dark eyelashes, brown liquid eyes.

I had been an annoyance to him when we had met at
Jack Omaha's house. He studied me quietly, very much
at ease, not the least bit uncomfortable. His hands were
long and sinewy, and he clasped his fingers around a
slightly upraised knee.

"Mr. McGee, you got under my skin pretty good when we met at Chris's place."

"You went into a massive tizzy."

He smiled. "Are you trying to do it again?"

"I don't know. What are *you* trying to do?"

It was an engaging smile. Very direct. "I'm trying to get you off my back. Uncle Jake thinks you could hurt me."

"Don't you?"

The smile faded. He looked earnest. "I really don't see how. Oh, if you were politically inclined you could give me some static by bringing up the dumb-ass bit about flying marijuana in, but you'd have no proof of that, and I think I could deny it convincingly. Besides, I don't think people are as dead set against it as they used to be. The use of it is too prevalent. I hear that a long time ago the rumrunners were folk heroes along this coast. It's getting to be much the same with grass. I'm not sure you could hurt me."

"What if somebody got notarized statements from Betty Joller and Susan Dobrovsky? Do you think your kinky love life could hurt you any if it came out?"

He colored but recovered quickly. "People must find it remarkably easy to talk to you, McGee. I don't think there's anything kinky about enjoying the hard sell. Reluctance stimulates me. Maybe in retrospect they see it differently than it was. But in both those cases there were plenty of squeals of girlish joy."

"Joanna thought you were tiresome."

"Please stop trying to bait me. Let's try to get along at least a little bit. Try to understand each other."

"What do you want me to understand?"

He shrugged. "How I was such a damned fool. I'd

flown to most of the islands. I'm a good pilot. I've got a
good airplane and I keep it in first-class condition. As
lawyer for Superior Building Supplies, I knew Jack and
Harry were in bad shape and things were getting worse.
I think it was Jack who brought it up, like a joke. I had
said something about falling behind on the ranch payments and trying to get an extension on the loan. He
said we ought to work out a way to bring grass in. He
said he could find a nice outlet for us. We met again
and planned how we could do it, still treating it as a
joke. Finally I went down and lined up a source in Jamaica and then we . . . went ahead. We couldn't afford
much the first time. But it all worked out okay."

"Tell me about it."

He shrugged again. "We'd rendezvous off the north
shore of Grand Bahama. The coast was always clear
because it's difficult water. I'd circle and drop the stuff.
We would have put the big bags inside plastic bags
from Omaha's stock and tied the neck so they'd float
and the seawater couldn't get to the grass. They'd
gather them in with a boat hook. Very simple."

"How about the last trip?"

"What about it?"

"Who was involved?"

"Just the four of us. Carrie went with me. Jack and
Cal were aboard the boat. I had headwinds and I was a
little late coming to the rendezvous point. At about five
fifteen Carrie started horsing those sacks out the door.
She was a strong person. They picked them up. Nine, I
believe there were. So I put my ship right down on the
deck and crossed the coast north of here and came
down to the ranch and landed. She got in the little
truck and went to the marina late that night, and they

loaded the stuff into the truck. She drove it to the outlet and got paid off and took the money down and put it in the safe at Superior."

"What happened to Jack Omaha?"

"I have a theory."

"Such as?"

"I think some professionals were moving in on us. It was too easy to score. I think they got to Jack and scared him badly. I think that he stayed with Carrie and they went down and emptied the safe and went their separate ways. A lot of that money was supposed to be mine. It would have helped me a lot to have it. As it was I had to arrange to . . . borrow it."

"From Uncle Jake Schermer?"

His smile was ironic. "And a lot of advice went along with the money. He was upset about the whole thing. I couldn't make him understand that it wasn't as important as he was making out. It was . . . a caper. It was fun, damn it. Everybody in the group got along all right. Low risk and good money. We were planning on making one or two more trips and then splitting the money and calling it a day. I wanted to come out of it with two hundred thousand clear. And that's what Jack Omaha felt he needed to save the business."

"Harry Hascomb wasn't in on it?"

"Harry talks to make himself important. He talks in bars. And bedrooms. Harry is a jerk. I'm talking to you now, McGee, but there is no part of this you can prove. There is no basis for indictment by anybody."

"And the Judge and his group are going to make certain you have a nice clean record because you are going to make them all rich and happy."

After a flash of anger he spoke slowly and judiciously. "I don't know how much good I'm going to do them. I really don't. The timing is right. I can get elected. The campaign will be well financed. The incumbent is senile. I've built a good base here. I plan to announce right after the wedding. I love this part of Florida. I'm not at all certain I'd be in favor of a new deepwater port and a lot of phosphate mining and processing. It's a dirty industry. The port will bring in other industries. Maybe a refinery. But those are low-employment prospects. They won't keep young people from leaving the Bayside area. And they will pollute the water and the air. On a risk-reward basis I can't make it add up. I have the feeling I want to work in the best interests of the people who will vote me into office, not the few men who have been grooming me for office."

He was impressively convincing. He emanated a total sincerity. Right at that moment he had my vote. I could see what it was about him that made the Judge label him charismatic. He talked to me as if I were the most interesting person he would meet this year.

"What do you think I ought to do?" he asked me.

"Do what you think is right."

"That sounds so easy. Right and wrong. Black and white. Up and down. It divides the substances of life unrealistically. The world is often gray and sideways. According to the game plan, if I go to Tallahassee I ought to be able to move the situation along in five to six years. If there is world famine by then, it will be the thing I should do."

He sighed and shrugged.

"Well, it's my problem and I will have to make the decision. I know I'm going to run for the office. I'll just

have to take one step at a time. McGee, I want to
thank you for listening to me. I haven't killed anybody.
I don't know where the money went. I got into a foolish situation because I didn't weigh all the conse-
quences. And I'm glad now that it's over. I know that
the chemistry between us is not good. I can't help that.
I don't expect everybody to like me. I'll depend on
your sense of fair play."

I found myself shaking hands with him. I got out of
the car hastily, and after it drove away I wiped my
hand on the side of my trousers. I felt dazed. He had
focused a compelling personality upon me the way
somebody might focus a big spotlight. He had that in-
definable thing called presence, and he had it in large
measure. I tried to superimpose the new image upon
the fellow I had met in Jack Omaha's house, listlessly
tying his tie after a session in Jack Omaha's bed. That
fellow's anger had been pettish, slightly shrill. I could
overlap my two images of the man. I wondered if my
previous image had somehow been warped by the great
blow on the back of the head when the explosion had
hurled me off my feet.

This man had been engaging, plausible, completely
at ease. He made me feel as if it were very nice indeed
to be taken into his confidence. There were dozens of
things I wanted to ask him, but the chance was gone.
The chance had driven away in a gleaming limousine,
cool in the heat of the morning.

Yes, if he could project all that to a group, he could
be elected. No sweat.

Yet where were you, Van Harn, when big Cal Birdsong was dying in the hospital, with a thin wire sticking
him in the heart? Were you beside the bed, charismatic

and relaxed? When your men clear new ranchland, do they blow the pine stumps with dynamite? Did those lean sinewy hands hoist Carrie into the front corner of the Dodge truck? Exactly how did you make Susan look so sick at heart, so defeated and sad?

I had been trying to make it all a single interrelated series of acts of violence. But his convincing presence was making it all come unstuck, turning it all into unrelated episodes.

Harry Max Scorf said, "Have a nice chat?"

Usually I can sense people who move up close behind me. Something gives me warning. Not this time. I leapt into the air.

"Jesus!"

"Nope. Only me. Harry Max Scorf."

"Of the City and County of Bayside. I know. I know."

"Your nerves aren't real good, son."

"Yes, I had a nice chat. What else is new?"

"Let's set," he said, leading the way to a shady bench.

I sat beside him, leaning back, squinting from the shady place out at the white dazzle of boats at the marina. I could see a brown lady in lavender bikini prone on the foredeck of a Chris, her head near the gray bulk of a big Danforth. Nearby was the silent gleaming bulk of Jack Omaha's muscular Bertram. Was it beginning to look slightly dingy? The unused boat so quickly acquires that abandoned, unloved, uncherished look. Chrome gets foggy. Bronze turns green. Aluminum pits and flakes. The lines get whiskery and the fenders get dirty. By looking to my right I could see into the office to where Cindy Birdsong stood working

on a ledger, elbow on the counter, fingers clenched in
her hair, tongue sticking out of the corner of her
mouth. Looking beyond the Bertram, beyond the
bikini, I could see Meyer and Jason working, sweat-
shiny on the sun deck of the *Flush,* setting and cement-
ing the vinyl sheets. Behind me was the traffic roar of
the busy Monday streets and highways. Florida no
longer slows down for June. A pity.

Harry Max Scorf produced a blue bandanna and
flicked a shadow of dust off the toes of his gleaming
boots. He took off his white Truman hat with care,
wiped the sweatband, and placed it between us on the
weathered wood of the bench. He seemed to doff force
and authority along with the hat. His head was oddly
pointy.

"What is new," he said, "is that the special task
force hit Fifteen Hundred Seaway Boulevard at first
light this morning. And some sight it was. Nine cars.
Twenty-five men. Feds and state people. I was local li-
aison, sort of observing. They tested me out long ago
and know I can keep my mouth shut. I went along
with the four who hit Walter J. Demos's apartment.
He'd been entertaining a little schoolteacher person in
his bed. They found about thirty pounds of cannabis in
a plastic bag hanging on a hook about three feet up inside his fireplace. I can tell you it was sorry shit, my
friend. Weak and dusty, a lot of big lower leaves cured
bad, powdery as senna leaves. Well, those two had got
some clothes on and they stood in the living room, both
of them crying. The little schoolteacher was crying because she was ashamed and scared for her job, which
she will lose. And that ball-headed Demos was crying
because he was so goddamn mad at himself he couldn't

hardly stand it. All the other men were going through the other apartments. There was one crazy scramble of folks trying to get back to their own beds. I think I've got the figure right. They made fifteen arrests for possession, not counting Demos and the teacher. Of course with Demos with that quantity, it will be for dealing, and that is heavier. You want to put it together for me?"

"You already have."

"I know. I know. But you tickle me. You've got cop sense."

"I can't remember a word of my little talk with him."

"What do you think you might have said?"

"Oh, something to open him up. Come on very very heavy, like somebody from the Office taking over the operation. An amateur like Demos would buy an act that wasn't exactly plausible. Then I suppose I would have told him to hold onto his money and wait for a delivery and not get impatient."

"You just suppose you might have said all that?"

"And left him a posture he couldn't maintain. He is big jolly old Uncle Walter, head of the family. He is supposed to take care of everything and provide everything to make life juicy for his tenants. So when somebody showed up with some product, Uncle Wally bought it, and then they turned him in. I'd say that he was put out of business by the real professionals, easily, quietly, no fuss. He was buying enough for Fifteen Hundred, to maintain the life-style there. The squire of swingleville. The professionals wouldn't bother to work him over. The professionals use the law to weed out the amateurs."

"Did they weed out that girl, that Carolyn Milligan?"

I didn't have to think long. "You don't like that any better than I do, Captain. Makes no sense. I could never believe that."

He sighed and said, "Neither can I. I tried to figure they'd wipe out the supply group: Omaha, Birdsong, Milligan. Then go after distribution. The trouble is, they wouldn't get into that much trouble for the sake of one channel of supply in Bayside County. There's three or four other groups. It isn't all that big. It's all businesslike. Nobody kills anybody unless there is absolutely no other way at all. This whole thing won't hang together because I don't know some things I ought to know. That's always the way it is. When you know enough, all of a sudden you know it all."

"What about Carrie? Did you look into that?"

"I got with Doc Stanyard on that. We went over his autopsy notes. Her left arm was badly abraded on the outside of the forearm and upper arm, with some paint fragments driven into the skin. See what that means?"

"No."

"Use your thick head, McGee."

It took about twenty seconds before light dawned. "Okay, if she was sober enough to pull her car off the road, then she was alert enough to have the normal instinct of lifting her arm to ward off the truck bearing down on her. She would step out and try to ward it off and dodge back. Her arm was hanging at her side when she was hit, so the assumption is that she was unconscious."

"Or suiciding. Waiting for the right vehicle. Left her purse in the car. Shut her eyes and stepped out. *Bam.*"

"Which do you think?"

"I think that unless I learn more, I won't ever know which it was. Why did you have a conference with the Judge yesterday and a talk with Freddy this morning?"

"We were talking about his appeal to the electorate."

"His daddy was pleasant. Weak and pleasant and crooked. Funny thing. They say Freddy won't ever have his hand in the till because of what happened to his daddy. It did him good instead of bad. They like the way he's come up so fast."

"Too fast, Captain?"

"They changed the retirement rules when it got to be City and County of Bayside. I've got thirteen months to go. If somewhere down the road, before thirteen months are up, I get thrown off, I ride an old bicycle and eat dog food. If I last it out, I'm better off than I would have been under the old rule. If Judge Jacob Schermer and his buddies are playing poker some night and somebody at the table says they've got tired of my face, I'm through the next day."

"Scare you?"

He turned and looked at me. Those old eyes had seen everything, twice. They had looked into a lot of people. An echo of a smile touched the corners of his mouth. "Scared shitless," he murmured.

"Then I better not tell you Freddy was flying the grass from Jamaica and air-dropping it to Omaha's boat off Grand Bahama."

"No, you shouldn't tell me because it would fit too close with the arithmetic I've worked up about Freddy. He dresses fancy, drinks fancy, drives fancy. He's got the ranch and the airplane and forty pair of boots. But then you got to remember that Miss Janie has ten thousand acres of grove, and under management it must turn her sixty dollar an acre a year net, on which she can afford Fred Van Harn as a play toy, but if I were Jake I wouldn't be hoping my niece would marry up with a fellow with some kind of wrong twist in his head. Two years ago something got hushed up. They got delay after delay so by the time it was ready to go to court that girl had grown some inches taller. It's said he claims he never had any idea she was only fourteen. Anyway, she got taller and older and smarter, and settled for the money. They've been grooming him for politics, first the State Senate, then maybe Governor. They really don't give a damn what kind of a man he is. What they care about is that, he goes on local television on a public issue, you never seen such mail as comes in. Begging him to run for office. That's all they care about. In fact the other stuff kind of helps them out because it makes it easier to control him. Oh, they'll have him married to Miss Janie, and she'll be a good hostess, and she'll bear him some healthy kids, and there you are. He can turn that charm on. He can charm a five-thousand-dollar fee out of a five-hundred-dollar case and make the sucker come back for more advice. What did he tell you?"

"He told me he didn't kill anybody."

"My hunch is he probably didn't. But he sure got into the pants of just about ever' woman involved in it. You got a list?"

"Carrie Milligan. Joanna Freeler. Betty Joller. Chris Omaha. He made a try at Miz Birdsong, but she bit him."

"Good for her."

"And Susan Dobrovsky."

He stared at me, registering shock. "That girl too? Son of a *bitch!*"

"He took her out to the ranch. She was supposed to leave for home this morning. Jason was going to see her off."

"Ever since that boy was fourteen damn years old, he's been lifting every skirt he sees. There's stories about him. He goes after ever' one as if there was never going to be any more. And there's something about him, they say. The ones you'd never expect, their eyes cross and they lay back and put their heels in the air for him. There's no law against it, at least no law anybody enforces. And he doesn't seem to ever get tired of looking for it. And he finds it places you wouldn't even think of."

I had to admit to myself there were, indeed, a lot of places I would never think of. And a fair portion of every day when I did not think of it at all, at all.

"Vote for Van Harn," I said.

"They'll do that. Senator Van Harn. They need a man up there riding point on what they want around here. Deepwater port for the phosphate down in the south county. Refinery. And all the goodies that go along with it that only a few fellows get a piece of."

"The Judge offered me twenty-five big ones to go away and forget all about Freddy."

Harry Max Scorf looked mildly startled. "What do they think you know?"

"No more than I've told you. That he's a kink. He rapes people and kills people and spends too much money and flies grass in."

He stood up and carefully fitted his white hat back

over the pointy skull, tugging it to the right angle. He
gave me a sharklike smile. "What the hell do they want
for a front-runner? Some kind of nance fellow? See
you around, son."

When I went into the office, Cindy looked up with
her customer face, cool and polite. Then the great
warm smile came. "Hello," she said. It was just one
word, but it was about fifteen words long.

"And hello to you. Books balance?"

"They do now. What I did, I wrote a hundred and
sixteen dollars when it was supposed to be a hundred
and sixty-one. I saw you out there. Captain Scorf has
been around forever, and they say he's always looked
exactly the same. Was he being rough with you?"

"No. He says I've got cop sense."

"Is that a good thing to have?"

"They have finished the noisy parts of repairing the
Flush. I think I better pay my motel bill and move my
toothbrush back to the boat."

She showed quick sharp dismay and disappointment
before she caught herself. "Anything you wish, dear."

"If you want to bring a small portable fire extin-
guisher, I'll talk Meyer into cooking some of his re-
nowned chili tonight."

"That would be nice," she said, forcing it.

"Anything wrong?"

"Nothing at all, thank you."

"Are you sure?"

"Certainly I'm sure!"

There is no going past that point. All the roads are

barricaded and all the bridges are blown. The fields are mined and the artillery has every sector zeroed in.

So I went and moved my toothbrush and accessories out of the unit, went to the front, and paid a fat lady my accumulated charges. She asked me if I was feeling better, and I said I was feeling just great. She said, "It's so nice that Mrs. Birdsong has a friend nearby in her time of need. Have you known her long?"

"A very long time."

"He drank, you know."

"Yes. Cal drank."

"In a way, it's a blessing."

"There are a lot of ways of looking at everything, I guess."

"Oh, yes, that's so true."

A small fire fight, with no decision. Both sides retreated.

When I got to the boat, the glass people had arrived. There were four of them, in white coveralls, with the pieces all cut to size, tempered glass for marine use. The foreman said they would be through by four at the latest. Jason and Meyer were celebrating the completion of the vinyl job on the sun deck by having a cold beer in the shade of the canopy over the topside control panel. I inspected the job and gave my approval.

I am skeptical of all of the so-termed marvelous advances of science. And I am suspicious of anything which tries to look like something it isn't. Thus it would seem that a coal-tar derivative patterned to look like bleached teak would turn me totally off. But it is so damned practical. If you should ever have an artery which can't be repaired, it can be replaced with woven Dacron. And, wearing that in your gut, it would be unseemly to go about muttering about the plastic world full of plastic people.

So I stand on my plastic deck and mutter whatever I please. When did I make any claim about being consistent? Or even reasonable?

I went below and checked out my stereo set. I put on the new record, Ruby Braff and George Barnes. It is nice to have one that is just out and know that it is destined to become one of the great jazz classics. I knew I had lost one speaker. I suspected I had lost more. Delicate microcircuitry cannot take that kind of explosive compression. When the noise came out, sounding like someone gargling a throatful of crickets, I snapped it off in haste.

Back to the shop. No new components. Get the Marantz stuff fixed. I did not think I could placidly endure another gleaming salesman tell me that I had to have quadraphony sound, coming at me from all directions. I have never felt any urge to stand in the middle of a group of musicians. They belong over there, damn it, and I belong over here, listening to what they are doing over there. Music that enfolds you, coming from some undetectable set of sources, is gimmicky, unreal, and eminently forgettable.

Jason went back to work his turn in the office. Meyer and I made some sardine sandwiches. He was glad to learn I was back aboard for good. We sat at the booth in the galley and ate. And compared notes and reports.

"We are absolutely nowhere," Meyer said.

"A perfect summary."

"Are you sure you feel okay?"

"Don't I look okay?"

"Glassy. You stare at me in a . . . goggly way."

"Come to think of it, I feel goggly and glassy."

"Just this minute. Or . . ."

"Most of the time. The light seems too bright."

"When the windows are done—"

"The ports."

"When the windows are done, we could go."

"Home?"

"And forget this whole mess, Travis."

"Tempting. Who are we supposed to be, going around finding out who did what and why?"

"That's why they have police."

"Right!"

We beamed at each other, but we both knew we were talking nonsense. The habit of involvement is not easily broken. It is even more pervasive than the habit of noninvolvement, the habit of walking away when the action starts.

I told him we couldn't leave because we had a guest coming for dinner. I told him he was cooking chili.

14

WE three had sat with tears running down our cheeks and told each other in choked voices that the chili was truly delicious. She and Meyer had cleaned up, telling me that I was still on semi-invalid status.

By the time they were through, there was a large dark night outside, wide as a country, high as the stars, and hot with the night winds of June.

We killed the lights and went topside to a shadowed part of the sun deck, out of the reach of dock lights. The sky was pink orange over Bayside, all its outdoor advertising glowing against a mist made of hydrocarbon fartings of trucks and other vehicles. We aligned deck chairs on the newly repaired decking so as to look out at the stars over the Atlantic. We were into the rainy season now. The night of June tenth. Bulbous black lay low to the southeast, sullenly flickering an unseen artillery of lightning.

She on my left, Meyer on my right, the night air stirring across us and then fluttering back to stillness. Her hand had crept over to my thigh, stealthily, nudged a welcome, and was enclosed by my hand, unseen by

Meyer, as if we were children in church. With my thumb I rubbed the thick warm pads at the base of her fingers. I wondered if she had been told or had guessed that her husband had not died of natural causes. They would have to tell her, sooner or later, no matter how pessimistic the law felt about catching whoever had done it. Harry Max Scorf had indicated quite plainly that she was on his list of suspects. Though I knew her very well in certain limited ways, I knew her not at all in many aspects. But I could not imagine her killing in that stealthy way, jabbing a wire into the great chest while the king slept.

Harry Max Scorf, in a dogged and plodding pattern, would have long since established the identity of every person who could have gotten close to Cal Birdsong long enough to do him in.

"It always seems such a waste when it rains way out there," she said. "Sort of badly managed, to rain into the sea."

"It's moving this way," Meyer said. "But your average thunderstorm has a total life span of fifty-five minutes."

She sat up and looked across me at Meyer. "You've got to be kidding."

"Believe him," I said.

"When the conditions are right a pod will be forming in the area as the older pod is dissipating its energies. Thus we get the impression of one single storm lasting for hours. Not so."

She settled back and made a small sound of mirth and wryness. "The rest of my life," she said, "I'll see a thunderstorm and say to myself they only last fifty-five minutes."

Her hand still rested on mine, her hand warm and dry. I thought of lies and polygraphs and biofeedback. One type of biofeedback machine requires strapping a pair of electrodes to the palm of your hand. When you are tense and nervous, your palm is moist and cool and the conductivity of your skin is increased. The machine has a dial and a little electronic tone, thin and insectile. As you make yourself more calm your hand becomes more dry, the dial needle swings slowly downward, and the electronic note moves down the scale. By giving you the visible and audible results of different mental and emotional postures, in time you learn, without the machine, how to impose a great calm upon yourself, an alpha state, if you will.

Soon she would be told her husband had been murdered. The required Grand Jury hearing could not be delayed indefinitely. I rubbed my thumb back and forth across the pads on the palm of her hand, and tried to think of how to word my trick remark, and felt disgusted with myself. A rotten game to play with this woman.

Suddenly, without a word being said, I felt her palm go cold and wet. She tugged her hand away and got up and moved over to the rail and turned to lean against it, her arms folded, her shoulders hunched forward.

"What's wrong, Cindy?"

"I guess somebody walked over my grave."

She was silhouetted against the intermittent glow of distant lightning. "Did you think of something that upset you?"

"I think I'll go home now," she said.

"I'll walk you."

"I'm okay."

"No trouble."

I tried to make conversation as we walked to the motel, but she gave one-word responses. She unlocked the door and pushed it open and turned to me. I took her in my arms. Her lips were cool and firm. There was no response in lips or body, and then there was a lot. A hungry lot.

We went in and the door clicked shut. "No lights," she said. "Don't let me think about anything. Don't give me time to think about anything. Please."

The bed was by big windows. The draperies were open. The storm moved closer. The lightning flashes were vivid. Each one made a still picture of her in black and white. Black eyes and lips and hair and nipples and groin. White, white, white all the rest of her. The lightning arrested movement. It caught her in a fluid turning, mouth agape with harsh breath and effort. It froze a leg, lifting. It stopped her, astride, arms braced, halting the elliptical swing of hips, turning her into a pen and ink drawing of greatest clarity. I kept her for a long time within the prison of her own tensions, though she escaped to partial release from time to time. Each lightning stroke seemed to be brighter, each stroke bringing the thunder closer and sharper. At last the lightning made a ticking sound, filled the room with a strange hard blue light, and the great following bang of thunder made her gasp and leap. The ensuing crashing downpour of the rain was like a signal to us.

We lay damp and slack in a close and sweaty embrace, content, heavy-breathing, detumescent. The storm air moved across us, cooling our bodies. The intensity of the downpour began to slacken, but it was still a heavy tropic rain.

"Ruthie took those pills," she said.

"What?"

"You didn't know her. It was a long time ago. Bud—he was her husband—ran off a curve and hit a big tree. They gave her pills to make it easier. God, she took so many pills you couldn't talk to her, hardly. Huh? She'd say. Huh? Wha'? And sleep? She'd sleep twenty hours a day. Toby—you didn't know him either —his wife went back to see her sick mother and the airplane fell out of the sky. For Toby it was booze. After a year they had to put him away and dry him out. People use things, don't they? I'm using sex. I want it to be more and more, every time with you. It was more this time than ever. When it's so much, I can't think about anything else. The thing about me is, I'm not like this. Not really. I told you Cal hadn't touched me in ever so long. But it didn't make me feel . . . deprived. I mean it was okay. I guess I'm the way I am now, with you, because I try so hard to get my mind turned off. I try so hard, I get way way into the sex thing, like I couldn't before. I always felt a little odd about it. Ashamed, almost. I mean being so big and strong and healthy and looking . . . as if I would like it."

"You need never feel odd again."

"I won't. I won't."

"And you've got a talking jag."

"I know. And you have to listen, don't you? We don't really know each other. It's strange. I guess the way men think about these things, without me sounding like an egomaniac, what you did was luck out. You came along at the time when any presentable and sympathetic guy would be right where you are right now, doing what you were doing."

"Flattery will get you everywhere."

"Trav, please don't make flip little remarks. What our relationship is, it's backassward. It started at the end, and I want to find our beginnings. I want to know you as a person, not just want you terrible for the way you can turn my head off. It's a genuine compulsion, really."

"Okay. No flip remarks. No bedroom comedy. I saw the vulnerability and I took advantage. So that makes it seem unreal to me too. But it's more than pure physical hunger."

"What else is it?"

"Liking you. Wanting things to be right for you. Wanting the world to be a special place for you. Also, there's guilt."

"About what?"

"About knowing that Cal was murdered. Harry Max Scorf told me. I don't know if he knew I'd tell you."

She sat up, with sharp hissing exhalation. "How?" she whispered.

I told her. She made a sick sound and closed her fingers around my arm with impressive force.

"Jason," she whispered.

"Are you sure?"

"I can't prove anything. Once . . . after things had been very bad—Cal was drunk and he beat me—Jason came to me and said that there were ways Cal could be killed that nobody would ever know. I made him be still. I knew he was going to say he'd do it for me. And he would have. He's a strange boy. He can't stand any kind of cruelty. He was a battered child. He nearly died of it. And he has been . . . a little bit in love with me, I think."

"It showed, after Cal knocked you out."

She settled slowly back down again, cheek against my chest, arm heavy across me. "I thought I saw him at the hospital the evening Cal died. I was going out to eat. I thought I saw Jason riding his bike toward the hospital at the far end of the parking lot. I didn't think any more about it until now. When I came back from eating, all those people were working on Cal so frantically. What it probably was was a piece of stiff leader wire. Cal was in one of those security rooms, single rooms, but he wasn't guarded. But I don't really *know*. So I don't have to go and tell anyone, do I?"

"Are you angry at Jason?"

"I don't *know*. Cal was killing himself in any case. They'd told him his liver was going bad and he shouldn't drink at all. I can understand why Jason did it. If he did it. Trav, help me."

"Captain Scorf will ask questions of you, sooner or later. It would look better if you went to him. Ask him if your husband died of natural causes. If he levels with you, register shock and then tell your suspicions. It will have to be your choice as to whether you tell Jason you're going to see Scorf and, if Jason runs, how much lead time you give him."

"Okay. I'll do it that way. But I wish you hadn't told me anything, dear."

"Why did you get upset tonight when we were looking at the stars and the storm?"

"Upset? Oh, I just remembered a nightmare Cal had, about a week before he died. He woke up roaring. I couldn't seem to make him wake up. I looked up at the dark sky and remembered. He had a nightmare about something falling toward him out of the sky that was going to kill him, that was going to land on him and kill him, and he couldn't get out from underneath it. He was so really terrified that I guess it left a mark on me. Half nightmare and half delirium, I guess it was. His mind had gone all warped and nasty from the drinking. Then he didn't want me to tell anybody about his nightmare! As if anybody in the world would give a damn! Tonight I remembered, and it made me feel weird and crawly."

The rain stopped. Another pod formed and came grumbling toward us through the night. She talked in a slumbrous, murmurous voice, and then the voice ended and her breathing changed, slow, deep, and warm against my throat. I watched the flashes against the window and against the ceiling. The new storm moved closer, and at last the thunder became loud enough to awaken her. She started, then settled back. "I was dreaming," she said.

"Pleasant dreams?"

"Not really. I was in front of a judge's bench. It was very high, so high I couldn't see him at all. They wouldn't let me move back to where I could see him, and it made me angry. I knew he would never believe me unless I could see him and he could see me. I was accused of something about Jason, doing something wrong."

"Such as?"

"I don't *know*. I guess I was guilty of something, all right. I mean when somebody is attracted to you, you know about it. And it feels good to be admired that

way. So you . . . respond to it. Do you know what I
mean? It changes the way you look at the other person,
and the way you walk when you walk away from them,
and it changes the pitch of your voice when you laugh.
So I guess . . . those little things would add up, and
maybe that's why he did what he did. *If* he did it."

"Don't go around looking for guilt."

"I miss Cal. I miss him every single day of my life. It
had gotten to be a rotten marriage, and I miss him terribly."

"Involvement doesn't have to be good or bad. It just
is. It exists. And when it stops, it leaves emptiness."

"Something happens, and I think how I'll have to tell
Cal about that. Then I know I can't. Oh, hell."

She began to weep, without particular emphasis.
Gentle tears for a rainy night. When they subsided she
began an imitation of need, a faking of desire. But the
textures of her mouth were unconvincing. The storm
time had worn us both out. I was glad she did not per-
sist, as male pride would have made the responsive effort obligatory. The second storm was upon us, the wet
wind blowing across weary bodies. I covered us with
the sheet. The lightning once again took still pictures of
the room, of her head on the pillow beside me. After
the crashing downpour turned to a diminishing rain,
she slept. When the rain stopped I slipped out of the
bed, closed the draperies, groped my way into my
clothes, and left without awakening her, testing the
door to be sure it had locked behind me.

The storm had knocked the power out. There were
stars in half the sky. My eyes were accustomed to
darkness. I found the path without difficulty and

walked between the black shapes of shrubbery, down the slope past the office, and out onto the dock.

Meyer had locked the *Flush* and gone to bed. I found the right key by touch. In the darkness of the lounge I gave my left shin a nasty rap against the new coffee table. I limped to the head and, by darkness, took a long hot sudsy shower. The great bed swallowed me up like a toad flicking a fly into the black belly.

15

*B*Y the time I came out to fix my breakfast, Meyer was having his second cup of coffee.

"You are running for office?" he asked.

"I thought you knew I owned a white shirt and a tie."

"I guess I'd forgotten."

"I want to look safe and plausible."

"To whom?"

I poured my orange juice and selected a handful of eggs.

"Five eggs?" he asked.

"These are the super supreme extra large eggs, which means they are just a little bit bigger than robin eggs. Stop all this idle criticism and take a look at the back of my head, please. I took the dressing off."

I sat on my heels. He came from the booth and stood behind me and turned my head toward the light. "Mmm. Looks sort of like the stitching on a baseball. Nice and clean, though. No redness that I can see."

He went back to his coffee. I broke the eggs into the

small skillet, sliced some sharp cheddar and dropped it in, chopped some mild onion and dropped it in, folded that stuff in with a fork, took a couple of stirs, and in a couple of minutes it was done.

When I sat down to my breakfast Meyer said, "You were saying?"

"I'm saying something new now. We've been playing with a short deck. With a card missing, the tricks won't work. Maybe it is a variation of your invisible planet theory. I'll describe the missing card to you. The Van Harn airplane comes winging through the blue, and in the late afternoon it spots the Bertram off the north shore of Grand Bahama, as before. There are eight or nine bags of gage, plastic-wrapped to keep the water out. They are about a hundred pounds each. Van Harn makes a big circle at an altitude of a couple of hundred feet. The circle is big so that each time he comes around, Carrie has time to pull and tug and wrestle one of the bags to the passenger door and shove it out on his signal. That would be the way to do it, right? Nine passes. They hope to drop them close enough so they can be picked up quickly with a little maneuvering and a boat hook. Cal Birdsong and Jack Omaha are busily and happily hooking the bags aboard. Probably Birdsong is running the boat and Omaha is doing the stevedore job. Van Harn and Carrie are having a dandy time too. A little bit of adventure, a nice piece of money, and all the bugs have been worked out of the system. The payoff is big. Have you got the picture?"

"It seems plausible. What are you getting at?"

"Cindy told me that a week before he died Cal had a nightmare about something falling out of the sky and killing him."

I saw Meyer's face change. I saw the comprehension, the nod, the pursing of lips.

"One drop was too good," he said.

"And Jack Omaha was careless. He wasn't watching. He was maybe leaning to get the boat hook into a floating bag. There would be a hell of a lot of impact. A good guess would be that it hit him in the back of the head and snapped his neck. And all of a sudden it wasn't a party any more. It wasn't fun any more."

Nodding. Meyer spoke in an introspective monotone. "So Birdsong wired weights to the body and dropped it into the deeps, after dark. Van Harn flew back to the ranch with Carrie. When Birdsong was due in, she was waiting here at the marina with one of the little panel trucks Birdsong loaded the sacks into the truck. They got their stories straight. She drove to Fifteen Hundred where the truck was unloaded and Walter J. Demos paid her off. She drove the truck down to Superior Building Supplies. She had probably left her car there. She put the money into the safe and took her share, because she knew the game was over. And she brought her share to you to hold. Travis, how do you read Van Harn's reaction?"

"Sudden total terror. I don't think the money mattered one damn to him any more. Marrying Jane Schermer would take care of the money problem forevermore. He knew he had been taking a stupid chance, perhaps rebelling against a career of fronting for Uncle Jake and his good old boys. He would know that if it all came out, it would finish him. It wasn't a prank. He was involved in the death of a prominent local man while committing a felony. Good old Jack Omaha of

Rotary, Kiwanis, and the Junior Chamber. He wouldn't even keep his ticket to practice law. So I think that all of a sudden he was very anxious to please Uncle Jake."

"The eyewitnesses were Carrie Milligan and Cal Birdsong."

"Exactly, Meyer. A hustling lady and a drunk. I just thought of something else: Freddy's matinee with Chris Omaha. There probably isn't a better way of finding out how much the lady knows about anything. He wanted to know how much Jack had told her about the smuggling, or if he had told her anything at all. He evidently hadn't."

"And the burgled apartment?" Meyer said.

"Same reason. Find and remove any written evidence."

"What about Joanna and the bomb?"

"That won't make any sense until we know more."

"If you can ever make sense out of a bomb. The Irish tried it. Except for the people getting killed, it's turned into a farce to amuse the world. The Irish have forgotten why they set off bombs, if indeed they ever knew. It's probably because there's so damned little else to do in that dreary land."

"You won't be popular in Ireland."

"I've never had any urge to go back, thank you."

"Joanna came aboard bearing goodies. A little feast left off at the cottage for her. Meyer, we were both moving toward her as she started to open the box. If she had been a string-saver, a careful untier of knots, we'd both be dead. But she was the rip and tear type. God, I can still smell the stink of explosion in here."

"I know. It's a little less every day."

After I finished off the eggs, I answered his first question. "I am going to visit the brilliant young attorney at his place of business. And I may have to see Judge Schermer. And I may have to see the Judge's niece."

"With what objective?"

"Application of pressure."

"What do you want me to do?"

"Be right here where I can get you if and when I need you."

Cindy Birdsong was alone in the office when I walked up there from the docks. She got up from the desk and came around the end of the counter quickly, then glanced guiltily out of each of the windows before tiptoeing to be kissed. A brief kiss, but very personal and emphatic. "You sneaked away," she said.

"Like a thief in the night."

"I slept like dead. I woke up and didn't know where I was or who I was, darling."

"I'll try to keep track."

She became more brisk and businesslike as she backed away from me. "Something strange, Travis. Jason was supposed to tend the office this morning. Ollie says he isn't around. And Ritchie has got some kind of a bug."

"Where does Jason stay?"

"He and Ollie have been living aboard the *Wanderer*. Over there at the end. It's ours . . . mine, I mean. But she needs new engines and an awful lot of other things."

I could see that the *Wanderer* was an old Egg Harbor fly bridge sedan, white hull and a rather unhappy shade of green topsides, something under forty feet in length.

Ollie came into the office, round, brown, and sweat-shiny, and gave me a good morning and gave Cindy a dock slip and said, "I put that Jacksonville Hatteras in Thirty-three instead of Twenty-six. It's new and he can't handle it worth a damn. It's easier to get in and out of Thirty-three. Okay?"

"Of course."

"They'll sign in personally when they get it hosed down. They're very fat people, both of them. Not real old. Just fat."

"Oliver," I said, "do you think Jason took off for good?"

He stared at me. "Why would he do that?"

"I don't know. He's missing. That's one possibility, isn't it?"

"I didn't think of him exactly as being missing, Mr. McGee."

"Did you notice if his personal gear was gone?"

"I didn't even think to look."

"Could we take a look right now?"

He looked at Cindy and when she nodded he said, "Why not?"

We both stepped aboard the *Wanderer* at the same moment, making it rub and creak against the fenders. As we went below Oliver said, "We slept here in the main cabin, Jason in the port bunk and me over here. If anybody was entertaining anybody, the other person slept up in the bow. There's two bunks up there. You can see that he slept in his bunk at least for a while and

. . . you know something? I don't see his guitar any-place."

We checked the locker and stowage area. His per-sonal gear was gone.

"What kind of car does he have?"

"No car. A bicycle. Ten speed. Schwinn Sports Tourer. Blue. He keeps it chained to a post behind the office under the overhang. His duffel bags are the kind that hang off the back rack on a bike. Panniers, they call them. The guitar has a long strap so that he can sling it around his shoulder so it hangs down his back. He loves that bike. He does the whole bit. Toe straps. Racing saddle. Hundred miles a day. That's how come those fantastic leg muscles."

I sat on Jason's bunk and said, "I don't even know his last name."

"Breen. Jason Breen," he said, sitting facing me.

"Okay to work with?"

"Sure. Why?" He looked defiant.

"How much do you really know about him?"

"What business is it of yours?"

"The boss lady has had enough trouble, don't you think?"

He looked uncertain. "I know. But what has that—?"

"Jason could have done something very bad and very stupid, because he thought he was helping Mrs. Birdsong. I want to get a reading from you about his capacities. You strike me as being very bright and ob-servant, Ollie."

He blushed. "Well, not as bright as Jason. He reads very heavy things and he has very heavy thoughts."

"About what?"

"Free will, destiny, reincarnation. Stuff like that."

"What kind of person is he?"

Oliver pondered, his forehead wrinkling. "Well, he's a mixture. He likes to be with people. People like him. When there's a group, people end up doing what he wants to do without him having to push. When he's having a good time, everybody is having a good time, and when he isn't, nobody is. At the same time he's a loner. You never really know what he's thinking. He does nice things for people without making a big fuss about it. The ladies really like him a lot. You saw how he sort of stepped in and took care of Carrie's sister, Susan. Got her on the plane and everything. About doing anything wrong, I don't think he'd do anything he thought was wrong. But there would be no way in God's world of stopping him from doing something if he thought it was right."

"Did he have a thing about Mrs. Birdsong?"

Oliver blushed more deeply. "No more than . . . anybody. I mean she's a very decent person. And she looks . . . so great. And Cal was such a son of a bitch to her. Really dirty mean. He's no loss to anybody."

"Except to her. She misses him."

"That's her, all right. She's the kind of a person who could even forgive that rotten bastard. Look, I know what's going on with you two. If you give her a hard time, I'm going to take my best shot."

"I think you really would."

"Believe it."

"What do you think is going on, anyway?"

"Jason told me. He's never wrong about things like that. He sleeps a couple of hours at a time. He prowls around a lot. He always knows what's going on over at the cottage and on the boats and in the motel and the whole neighborhood."

"How did he act about it when he told you? Just how did he tell you? Can you remember the words?"

"Close enough. I came in the other night and he was in the bunk reading and he looked over and said, 'McGee is screwing Cindy.' It was just a statement of fact. It stung me, you know. I said you were a bastard to be laying her so soon after Cal died, and he told me that was a sentimental and stupid attitude. I couldn't tell what he thought about it."

"Current girl friend?"

"He hasn't got any particular person at the moment that I know of. He goes over and sees Betty Joller. You know, she's alone in the cottage now. Unless she can get somebody to come in with her, a couple of girls, she can't swing the rent and upkeep."

"Wasn't there another girl there?"

"Two. Nat Weiss and Flossie Speck. After the bombing, Nat went back to Miami and Floss decided to try it out in California. She was bored with her job here anyway. She was working for the phone company."

"Didn't Jason have something going with Carrie and with Joanna?"

"Probably. Sure. It wouldn't be any great big deal in either direction. It would just have to be the right time and place is all, and it would just happen."

"Would Carrie have confided in him?"

"What about?"

"Anything that might have bugged her."

"I don't see why not. People talk to Jason about the goddamnedest things. He doesn't pass it along. You know you can tell him things. Funny, come to think of

it, how he never tells things about himself to other
people. I guess he's had a hard life. He was in foster
homes. They took him away from his own folks because they nearly killed him beating him. He wasn't
even two years old. That's the only thing he did ever
tell me. He had about six broken bones. Maybe
more. I forget."

"Did the storms wake you up last night?"

"Hell, yes!"

"Was Jason in this bunk?"

"Let me think. No, he wasn't. I could see in the
flashes of lightning. I mean it wasn't anything unusual.
He's always roaming around by himself. Or visiting
people. He's a very restless person."

"But he's been here two years, ever since they
opened."

"I don't mean restless like that. We've talked about
moving on, but we never do. You get kind of hooked.
Boats and water and working outside mostly."

"But now he's packed his gear and moved on."

"I can't believe he'd just go without a word. But
maybe he would. Maybe he would. He'd have pay
coming. I don't know why he'd leave without picking
up his pay. Maybe he figures on sending for it. Or
maybe he didn't leave. Maybe he moved into the cottage."

"Want to check that out for me?"

"For myself too. Sure."

As I walked slowly back to the office, alone, I could
guess at what would convince Jason Breen it was time
to pack and leave. If he had been under the open awn-
ing windows, crouched a couple of feet from the bed,
he would have heard a conversation about Cal's

murder. A little bonus for the restless voyeur of the marina. A little lead time on the blue bike. I wondered if he had sheathed his guitar in rain-proof plastic.

I briefed Cindy and we waited for Oliver. He came back panting for breath, overheated. "Not there," he said. "Betty hasn't . . . gone to work yet. She said . . . she hasn't . . . seen Jason."

After Oliver left Cindy said, "You don't suppose Jason . . . could have listened?"

"Could be. He'd know you were going to talk to Scorf."

"But does a person . . . flee on a bicycle?"

"A person flees on what they have at hand, if they are anxious to flee."

"It makes me feel . . . sort of rotten to think anybody could have been listening."

"Ollie says Jason did a lot of prowling."

"But he seemed so nice!"

"We like the people who like us."

"I suppose. Rats. Phone call? Sure. Here's the book."

I phoned the offices of Frederick Van Harn, Attorney-at-Law, in the Kaufman Building. A soft-voiced girl answered by speaking the number I had just dialed.

"May I speak to Mr. Van Harn, please?"

"Who is calling?"

"A certain Mr. McGee, my dear."

"Is it a business call or a personal call?"

"Let's say business."

"He won't be in the office today."

"Out of town?"

"No, sir. He won't be in today."

"Where can I get in touch with him?"

"You could phone here tomorrow, Mr. McGee."

"What if I said personal instead of business?"

"You already picked one, sir."

"Is he out at the ranch? What's the number there, please?"

"Sorry, sir. That is an unlisted number. You can reach him here tomorrow morning."

I thanked her and hung up. I wondered vaguely if Freddy was stupid enough to be making another run to Jamaica and decided he wasn't. I asked Cindy if she could aim me toward the Van Harn ranch. She was blank on that, but she knew the road to take to get to Jane Schermer country, out amongst the grapefruits, and Meyer had told me they were adjacent.

I threw jacket and tie into the back seat of the bright little oven, opened all windows, and headed a little bit south and then turned west on Central Avenue. At first it was a six-lane avenue fringed with motels, the Colonel's chicken, steak houses, gift shops, dress shops, savings and loans, and small office buildings. After a few blocks of this, I was in used-car country speckled with tired old shopping centers and convenience stores. After a mile or so of that, the road became divided and I went through a long expanse of decaying residential. The pseudo-Moorish and old frame houses had once been impressive—and expensive. They were cut up into apartments and rooming houses. The yards were rank and littered, and the palms in the medial strip looked sickly. The road became two lane, and I went through an area of huge new shopping centers and small dreary-looking developments where, on the flatlands, the developers had peeled off every tree and had big bonfires before putting in the boxy little houses. As these dwindled I saw For Sale signs on raw acreage, and at about nine miles from where I had made my turn, I came to the first ranchlands, with some Brahman, some Black Angus, some Charolais. Windmills flapped near the water holes. Salt blocks were set out in little open sheds. Where there were trees, the cattle had eaten the bottoms of the boughs off in a straight line, so that at a distance it had something of the look of African landscape.

There was more contour to the land on the right of the road, and more of that was used for geometric groves, laid out with a painful precision. I saw some spray trucks working in the groves, tall booms hissing white into the trees, agitating the leaves and the young fruit.

Big trucks used the narrow road and used it fast. Their windy wake snapped at my little rental. The landscape was beginning to turn a rich and glorious green with the heavy rains. Kingfishers sat on high wires, looking optimistically down into the drainage ditches. Grease-fat bugs burst on my windshield.

The entrance was so inconspicuous I nearly missed it. The narrow driveway was marked with two gray posts. A varnished sign not much larger than a license tag was nailed to one post, saying V-H Ranch. The entrance drive was lumpy and muddy. Wire fencing was snugged close on each side of it. Ahead was a distant grove of pines. On either side was a hell of a lot of empty space, flat as a drafting table, with some faraway clots of cattle wavering in the heat shimmer. The fencing on both sides turned away from the road just before

the grove. The grove was a huge stand of ancient loblolly, home for hawk and crow and mockingbird and
some huge fox squirrels which menaced me with fang
and gesture of profane chatter. Once through the grove
I could see the house a couple of hundred yards away,
spotted in the middle of giant live oaks hung with moss.

It was squarish, two stories, with two broad verandas
which encircled it completely, one at each level. Steep
tin roof, big overhang. Porch furniture. The house
looked rough and comfortable. A pair of dogs came
around the corner of the house at a full run, arfing toward me. They were part German shepherd, but
broader across chest and brow. One put his feet up on
the side of the yellow Gremlin and grinned at me,
tongue lolling. He lifted his lips to show me more tooth
and made a sound like a big generator running in a
deep basement. My window was up before he could
draw breath.

An old man came out onto the porch, shaded his
eyes, and then put fingers in his mouth and blew a
piercing blast which silenced birds and dogs and could
possibly have stopped traffic on the distant highway.
The dogs backed away and dwindled. They walked
sideways, knees bent, tails tucked under. They swallowed, lapped their jowls, and looked apologetic.

"Git on out back!" he yelled, and they did git, in
scuttling fashion. Then he stood on the porch, feet
planted, arms crossed, and waited for me to approach,
and waited for me to say the first word. He was a tall
scrawny bald man with tufts of white over his ears. He
was all strings, except for his watermelon belly, and he
wore crisp khakis and new blue sneakers.

"It's nice to see animals pay attention," I said.

"They know I kicks their ass nine feet in the air ef'n they don't. State your business."

"I would like to see Mr. Van Harn."

"Sorry."

"He isn't here?"

"I didn't say that, did I?"

"Then he is here?"

"He could be."

"My name is Travis McGee. To whom am I speaking?"

"I'm Mr. Smith."

"Mr. Smith, your loyalty is commendable. I would like you to take a short message to Mr. Van Harn. I think he will want to talk to me."

"I don't know as I want to do that. He's in a real bad temper this morning. He had to shoot Sultan. Busted his fool leg. Fifteen-thousand-dollar horse. He don't want no help with it. He's got a backhoe down there, and a jeep with a blade, and he's burying that fool horse by himself. He sent Rowdy and the boys off to string fence. Wants to be alone with the fool dead horse. I don't want to mess into that, Mister McGee."

"The message is very important to him."

Smith studied me for long long seconds. This was a character reading. "You say you snuck by here after I told you to git?"

"I put my car back in the pines and snuck by. Where did I go to when I snuck by, Mr. Smith?"

"You followed the ruts there to the side of the house. Two hundred yards, you came to a plank bridge. Cross it and turn left past a stand of live oaks and you can see the stables and some storage sheds, and past that the hangar and the landing strip. He'll be on high ground right across from the stables. You'll see the backhoe and jeep before you can make him out."

"Mr. Smith?"

"Yes."

"What about those dogs?"

He took me around the house. The dogs crawled forward and I extended my hand. They both snuffed my hand. "Leave him alone, hear?" Smith roared. The dogs nodded. "They won't bother you none," he said.

Smith was right. I saw the vehicles first. The yellow jeep with a front-end blade was crawling slowly across the infield of a rough track, dragging the glossy red-brown body toward the slight rise and the cabbage palms at the far side, where the backhoe stood near a large mound of dirt.

Van Harn saw me walking toward him and stopped the jeep.

"What are you doing here, McGee? How'd you get past the house?"

"Smith told me to get lost. I parked in the pines and snuck around. Sorry about your horse."

He had wrapped chain around the hind legs and fastened it to the tow hook on the back of the jeep. The great head of the horse was at rest. I had seen it bobbling across the stubble. The visible eye bulged nastily from the socket. The shot had been perfectly centered, above and between the eyes, making a caked mess of the brown gloss. A swarm of bluebottle flies settled onto the horse when the jeep stopped. He was a grotesque parody of a horse at a full run, front legs reaching, back legs extended, head high.

"What do you want?"

"I tried the office first."

"What do you want?"

"Why don't you go ahead and bury the horse and then . . ."

"What do you want?"

He wanted the leverage right away, right in the blazing sun of midmorning, in the infield of his little track. He wore big oval sunglasses, aviator type, and a white canvas cap. He was stripped to the waist. He wore dirty khaki pants and old white boat shoes. I was surprised at how tanned his body was, and how slender and fit he looked. Thin tough musculature made ridges and knots under the tan hide at each slight move. He had a medallion of black hair in the middle of his chest, big as a saucer, turning into a thin line of black hair that disappeared behind his brass belt buckle.

Plausibility is the key. I said, "When we had our little talk in the limousine, there was an area we didn't get to."

"Such as?"

"Uncle Jake offered me twenty-five thousand to pack and leave. I wanted to talk to you about whether it is all the traffic will bear."

"It sounds like too much as it is. What can you do?"

"I can put things together. Carrie gave me enough to go on. It's a case of filling in the blanks."

"Blanks?"

"Such as who decided to fasten ballast to Jack Omaha and drop him in the sea after he got hit by the bag of grass when you and Carrie were air-dropping the stuff to Cal and Jack aboard the *Christina III*."

He opened his mouth and closed it, opened it again, and said, "You lost me on the first curve, McGee."

"I think you waited too long."

"Maybe I did. I've got to bury Sultan." He started the jeep up and once more the big head bounced along the ground, tongue protruding between the big square teeth. I followed along at walking speed. He went to the left of the big hole, as close as he could get to it, and cut to the right as soon as he was past it. When he stopped, the horse lay with his back at the edge of the hole. He backed to slack off on the chain, got out and unfastened it from the jeep and the horse's legs, and dropped it into the jeep. Next he bent and picked up the hind legs and pushed at them, rolling the horse onto its back. It slipped over the edge of the hole and fell four feet, turning the rest of the way over, gases bursting out of its body as it thudded against the bottom.

I backed out of the way when he got back into the jeep, after setting the blade to its low position, and began shoving dirt into the hole. It was pale dirt, a mix of sand, topsoil, and surface limestone which contained billions of small fossil shells.

A buzzard began a big lazy circle overhead. I squinted up at it against blue sky, wondering how it knew. The abrupt roaring of the jeep shocked me out of my stupid trance. The onrushing blade was a yard from my legs by the time I took a frantic sideways leap, like a man going into second base in a headlong slide. I sprawled and rolled and came up onto my feet with the jeep right behind me. I feinted one way and dived the other way, came to my feet, and ran around to the other side of the horse grave.

He idled down and stopped. Oval lenses looked at me from under the stubby bill of the white cap.

"You move good for the size of you," he said.

"Thanks. And what's one more dead person?"

"At this point in time, not very much."

"But you can't make it, not the way you've tried to make it, Freddy. You dropped the rock in the water, and you can't move around fast enough to flatten out all the ripples."

"I can give it a goddamn good try. I didn't know if you had a gun. I guess you don't."

"I should have. It was an oversight."

"Final mistake."

"What was Carrie's final mistake?"

He seemed puzzled. "Mistake? Walking in front of a truck?"

"Didn't you close her mouth for good?"

"Didn't have to. Carrie was bright. She was involved in Jack's death too, you know. And she had less leverage than I have."

It was convincing. I felt confused. I couldn't see him as the murderer of Cal Birdsong or the builder of the bomb which killed Joanna. So why was he so obviously intent on doing away with me?

"I think we ought to talk," I said.

"Make your move."

"What move? Run for it? How far would I get?"

He gunned the jeep toward the right. I lunged to the left, dipping to scoop up a handful of ancient oyster shells from the pile of dirt. They were thick, calcified and heavy, dating back to the time when the V-H Ranch had been on the bottom of a shallow sea. I wound up quickly, stuck my leg in the air, threw a shell with a followthrough that brought my knuckles to within an inch of the ground. I really whistled it, but it curved low and outside, missing his right shoulder narrowly. He backed away quickly and, out of range, stood up and pulled the windshield up and fastened the wing nuts before rolling back to position.

"That was very cute," he said.

"Freddy, I've talked to a lot of people about you."

"I'm sorry about that. But it doesn't change anything."

"Your odds are impossible already."

"You don't know how bad they really are, McGee. But they are the only odds I've got, and it's the only game there is."

I tossed the other shells away. They weren't going to help me. I could guess what he would do. He would start circling that big grave as fast as he could go. I could stay out in front but not for long, not in such heat. And as soon as I slowed, or headed for the trees or the stables, he'd have me. I didn't have much time to do any thinking.

In such a situation it is difficult to believe it is completely serious. A yellow jeep is a jolly vehicle. Pastureland is not menacing. The hour before noon is not a likely time for dying. It was some odd game of tag, and when it ended the eventual loser would congratulate the winner. Let's try it again someday, pal.

But it was real. A jeep with or without a blade is a lethal weapon. I could tell from the way it tracked that he had it in four-wheel drive. He was skilled, and the jeep was agile.

I thought of alternatives and discarded them as fast as they came up. I could head across the field and try to trap him into a circle out in the open. I could turn a smaller circle than he and maybe get near enough to the side of the jeep to jump him. No chance. He would

read it, accelerate out of the circle, and swing around
and come back at me. Or I could slow him enough,
maybe, to go up over the blade and hood and drop in
on him. But how do I slow him down that much?

Suddenly I thought of one slim chance. If I couldn't
make it work, I was going to be no worse off. I was
going to be dead. And if I didn't try it, I was going to
be dead. A mockingbird flew over, singing on the wing,
a melody so painfully sweet it pinched the heart. I do
not want to leave the world of mockingbirds, boats,
beaches, ladies, love, and peanut butter from Deaf
Smith County. Especially do I not want to leave it at
the hands of a fool, at the hands of this Van Harn who
thought he could wipe out an event by killing anybody
who knew anything about it. It has been tried. It never
works. Any lawyer should know that.

I had to get him going counterclockwise around the
horse grave. So I moved to my left and he gunned the
motor and took the bait. He came on so fast he gave
me a very bad moment. The big hole was a sloppy rectangle about ten feet by eight feet. Before I could get
my feet untangled and get around the first corner, he
nearly clipped me. He had shoved about three blade
loads in on top of the dead horse, and so that side was
filled to within about two feet of the original ground
level, the whole front half of the horse still uncovered.

He pressed me. I had to lope around pretty good,
with a constant fear I might slip and fall on the
corners. He held it in an almost continuous controlled
skid, the back wheels staying farther away from the
hole than the front wheels. His reasoning was obvious.
In such heat I could only make so many circuits. I had
to make enough circuits to lull him. The sweat was

running into my eyes. Each time I passed the decision point, I mentally rehearsed exactly how to do it. And I had to do it soon, before I was exhausted.

At last I felt ready. I rounded the corner, dropped down two feet onto the loose dirt, spun and leapt up beside the jeep, and dived for the top of the wheel. He tried to accelerate but I was able to stretch the necessary few inches. I snapped my right hand onto the top of the wheel and pulled it hard over, toward me. The jeep swerved into the horse grave, dropped, and piled into the straight side of the hole, over where it was deeper.

The left rear fender had popped me in the side of the thigh, throwing me into a deep corner of the hole, in considerable torment. I scrabbled and pulled myself up and saw Van Harn fold slowly sideways out of the jeep. The four wheels were still turning, settling it deeper, and then it stalled out.

His legs were still hung up in the jeep. One eye was half open, the other closed. He had a high white knot in the middle of his forehead, growing visibly. I hobbled to him and bent over him. He hit me in the mouth and knocked me back into the same corner of the hole. Before I could get up, he sprang out of the hole and went racing toward the backhoe. I came lumping along behind him, with no hope of closing the distance.

He went to the back of it and wrenched a spade out of some spring clips, a spade I wished I had seen earlier.

He darted to meet me and swung the spade, blade edgeways, at my middle. During my screeching halt I managed to suck my stomach back out of the way. He swung back the other way, from left to right, aiming at

my head. I couldn't back away in time. I dropped
under it, dropped to my hands and knees, felt it whip
the hair at the crown of my head. That made everything real and deadly. A tenth of a second faster and he
would have cleaved my skull.

From knuckles and knees I launched myself forward,
getting one foot under me, coming up under him like a
submarining guard, getting a shoulder tucked cozily
into his gut, clapping an arm around his heels as he
tried to bicycle backward. He smacked down hard and
lost his spade. I crawled up him, straddled him. He was
yipping, bucking, writhing. I didn't want to break my
hands on the bones of his skull or face. I came down
with a forearm across his throat, my other hand locked
on my wrist for leverage. I tucked my face into the
curve of my arm as protection from his flailings. After
a frantic spasm he fluttered a little and went still. I kept
the pressure on to be sure of him. Then I rolled off and
got onto my knees and sat back on my heels, blowing
hard. His white cap lay nearby. I picked it up and
wiped the sweat off my face and out of my eyes.

His face was puffy and suffused with blood. His
chest was moving. It seemed very quiet out there in
that pastureland. I listened to the songs of the midday
bugs and the liquid call of a distant meadowlark. Time
to wrap him up and make delivery.

16

WHEN at last I felt partially restored and was not gagging with each breath, I got up onto my feet. My right thigh was cramping with the muscle bruise the jeep had given me. I managed a deep knee bend without screaming, and the second one did not hurt quite as much.

The jeep offered the best chance of something with which I could tie him up. I trudged toward the horse grave. If he could have come the whole distance across grass, he would have had me. He had to cross some of that dirt from the hole. The brittle limestone crackled under his running feet. I jumped sideways, ducked, and spun all in a single terrified bound. I heard the spade hiss past my head. His momentum carried him toward the hole. He tried to turn, tripped, stumbled, fell and rolled down the slope, and ended up beside the jeep.

I was after him quickly and got there as he lifted the spade over his head. I reached up and got hold of the handle. As soon as I had the handle he let go of it and hit me three very fast and very good shots. He had screwed his feet into the dirt. He had very good leverage, and he was too able to attempt the roundhouse blows of the beginner. He slammed them home, very close straight shots. They darkened the sky. The spade slid out of my hand. I stepped into him and hugged him like a big sick bear. I bore him down and suddenly he was in back of me instead of in front of me. I was on my hands and knees in the soft dirt and he had a wiry arm locked around my throat.

My air was shut off. Dazed as I was, I could not get the leverage to get out of that position or to throw him off. I tried to crawl to the jeep. He somehow held me back. I scraped with both hands like a dog digging a hole as I tried to plunge forward. The world swam. My lungs heaved against the obstruction. I began to feel a lazy floating pleasure. Oxygen starvation. Rapture of the deeps. I folded down and with darkening sight stared into the hole I had dug with my hands. I saw a piece of blue pipe, very pretty blue pipe. And just under it, as in some grotesque still life, I saw an unmistakable segment of suntanned wrist, dirt caught in the sun-bleached curling hair.

The dimming brain works slowly and with difficulty. Clean blue tubing. An azure blue. The size used for a bicycle frame. And why was that fellow under it, under the dry dirt that had come from a hole too deep for all the recent rain to reach? There was a stupid rhyme in the fading brain: Jason Breen and his Azure Machine.

The realization pierced the darkness that was closing in on me. What happened in my mind was not fright, not anger. It was an overwhelming dismay. A veritable crescendo of dismay, enough to galvanize my slackening body into a few moments of a terrible, terminal strength. I will never know how I was able to come to my feet with Van Harn plastered to my back. I took a single wobbly step and then fell toward the jeep, turning as I fell, so that I smashed him against the metal. I rebounded onto hands and knees, the stricture gone from my throat. I stretched out and breathed until the shadows lightened and the sun came out again. In sudden fright I pushed myself up and spun around. Freddy lay on his side.

I had the feeling he was going to bound to his feet and we were going to have to do it all over again, as if he were some mythological creature which could not be slain.

First I got the chain from the jeep. I rolled him onto his face, and chained his wrists together, tying a clumsy knot, and used the surplus to chain his ankles.

Then I knelt by the hole and carefully pulled the dirt away until I could see a hand, and most of a forearm, and more of the tubing of the blue bicycle.

From the angle, rest of him was under the jeep, and under a foot of dirt. Somewhere under there could be found the stillness of the Jesus face, the wire glasses, the crushed guitar, the brown legs sturdy with the bicycle muscles. And somewhere in his head, lost forever in the death of the synapses, were the jellied memories of why he had come out here and what Van Harn had done to him. The idea had been splendid. Dig a big hole and bury the body under a horse. Who would ever look farther than the horse?

I dragged Van Harn up the slope toward the back of the jeep and left him in the shade of the rear overhang. I felt his throat. The pulse was strong and regular. Except for the knot on his forehead, there wasn't a mark on his face. The left side of my underlip felt like half a hot plum. When I opened my mouth to yawn width, experimentally, the hinges creaked. I had a dull headache behind my eyes. He could blow them in pretty good. His dark glasses were missing. I looked around and found them, stomped flat.

Just as I climbed out of the hole I heard the oncoming drumbeat of a galloping horse. It was one great big dark brown horse, and she looked good in her cowgirl hat, yellow shirt, and twill britches. But when she pulled it up short and slid off, she turned back into Jane Schermer, with pudding face, minimal neck, and neuter body.

"Smith said Frederick had to shoot . . ." She saw Freddy in the shade of the jeep. "What are you doing to him?"

"Nothing, at the moment. But he's kept me pretty busy."

"Get that chain off him at once!"

"First come take a look at this."

She hesitated, then dropped down into the hole. She had let the reins hang free. The big horse made munching and ripping sounds in the stubbly grass. I pointed to the hole, big around as a bushel basket and half as deep, with the arm and hand and the portion of blue bike in the bottom of it.

She stared and sprang back and turned quickly, making a shallow, gagging little coughing sound. "Who? What—"

"I'm pretty sure it's Jason Breen. He worked at Westway Harbor Marina."

"But did you . . ."

"Did I? For God's sake! Sure, I came out here and sort of borrowed that backhoe, which I don't know how to operate. Then I dug this big son of a bitch of a hole. Then I put Jason and all his gear in the bottom of said hole and covered him over good. Then I shot this horse and . . . look. Forget it."

"But Frederick couldn't have done it."

"Lady Jane, I don't think there's anything in this world that you or I could think of that Freddy wouldn't do, if he happened to feel like it."

She hustled over and knelt by Freddy. She felt his forehead with the back of her hand. She put her ear against his bare chest to hear his heart. She stood up and looked at the visible half of the horse. "Poor darling," she said softly. "Poor Sultan. Poor beast. My Graciela foaled him. He grew up on my place. I gave him to Frederick."

"That's nice."

She went to the front legs of the horse, lifted, and tested with strong hands. "Must be a hind leg," she said. "Take that stupid chain off of Frederick right away!"

"I don't think it's a hind leg either."

She stared at me. "What do you mean?"

"I think Freddy needed a dead horse."

"He has other horses here. Sultan was valuable."

"He needed a dead horse that was so valuable and he liked so much that it made sense for him to send his ranch hands off on other work while he took care of it himself."

"What makes you think a hind leg isn't broken?"

"I watched him slide it up to the edge of the hole and roll it in. By then he didn't care what I saw because he had already decided to put me in the hole next to Jason. Under the horse."

"You make him sound like a . . . Could you uncover those back legs? Please?"

I walked over and got the spade and went to work. Once I got into the rhythm of it, it didn't take long. Before I finished, her fool horse finally caught on to the fact there was a dead horse in the area. He came over and stared into the hole, then screamed and backed away, shaking his head, rolling his eyes, and clacking his teeth. Jane hustled and caught him and led him all the way to the trees and tied him to a branch and left him there, squealing and pawing at the ground.

She hunkered down and checked each back leg in turn, then stood up and dusted her hands and climbed up out of the hole. I followed her. She looked thoughtfully down at Freddy, and she didn't say anything about the chain.

"I raised Sultan," she said.

"I better go to the house and use the phone."

"Phone?"

"To report a body."

"Oh, of course. There's one in the tack room, an extension. Are you going to leave Frederick . . . like this?"

"I know. That chain looks as if I'm overreacting. But I feel a lot better with it wrapped right where it is."

She looked at me and through me. Her eyes were small and of no particular color. Dull hazel, perhaps. "The things people said about him. I knew they were all lies. They were jealous." She focused on me. "Is this all some kind of terrible trick? Did you shoot Sultan?"

"I am not terribly fond of horses, but I've never shot one."

"I have to believe somebody."

"It might as well be me. Freddy tried to kill me. He made some good tries. He tried with the jeep. He tried with the spade. He tried manual strangulation. He is a very tough animal. He is about twice as strong as he looks."

"Jane?" Freddy said weakly. "Jane, dear?"

"Yes?"

"Help me, please."

"You shot Sultan because he broke his leg?"

"No other choice, dear. Please help me. Unfasten the chain, please."

She moved closer, looking down at him. "I don't think I can help you, darling. I don't think anybody can help you. Just be patient. We're going to make a phone call. You won't have to stay there very long."

I was halfway to the stables and the tack room before I could no longer hear his voice calling her name. She cantered past me when I was almost there. I found the phone while she was shooing her horse into an empty box stall.

Captain Scorf was not available, so I asked for someone to whom I could report a dead body, a murdered body. Then I gave a very simple report and explicit directions.

Jane Schermer sat with her back against the box stall door, her knees hiked up. There was a broad overhang shading the walk which led by the stalls. I sat beside her.

After a long time she said, "They were telling the truth and he was telling the lies."

"What?"

"Nothing. I've been going over things that troubled me, that I asked him about. I've been such a fool."

"That is a very convincing fellow when he wants to sell you."

"I was too easy to sell. I wanted to get married."

"So you'll get married. But not to Freddy."

She turned and looked at me. "Men have never paid much attention to me. I know when it's the money. A person can tell. I wondered about him. I was never sure."

"Maybe it wasn't."

"You're trying so hard to be kind, aren't you? Why would he . . . spoil everything for himself?"

"In big ways, and little ways too, people do that all the time to themselves. We can't stand prosperity. We have to tinker with the machinery."

She looked out across the track at the distant scene, at the canted top half of the yellow jeep. She touched my arm suddenly. "Look!"

I looked out there and saw that Freddy had performed a feat I would have called impossible. With wrists chained behind him and ankles chained together, he had managed to worm his way out from under the back end of the jeep and get himself up out of the hole and onto his feet. He was on the far side of the hole, hopping up and down with terrible demonic energy, managing somehow to retain his balance, though without seeming to make any progress. He was springing high into the air. I thought I heard a distant shouting. Then we saw him fall, roll, and disappear back into the hole.

We both got up. Jane said, "Something's the matter with him."

"I could make you a list."

But she had started off at a flat-out run, too concerned to remember she could ride that big horse out to him. I loped along, feeling the lumpy pain in my thigh with each stride. When we got there she jumped down into the hole where he was flapping and churning around and yelled, "Fire ants! Fire ants! Help me with him."

I think he had five thousand ants on his face, arms, and torso, swarming and biting with that dedicated aggression peculiar to that innocent-looking little red-brown ant.

I jumped down and grabbed him and wrestled him up out of the hole and half carried, half dragged him about forty feet and put him down on the grass. All this while he was moaning, cawing, and whimpering, and Jane was slapping and brushing at the ants. About a hundred turned their eager attentions to me, so after I dropped him I hopped and slapped and brushed until the frequency dropped to a random nip from time to time. They are called fire ants because the bite feels like a very tiny red-hot coal on the surface of your skin.

She kept on getting rid of the ants while I quickly took the chain off ankles and wrists. He had stopped being a dangerous person. Though his gestures seemed weak and uncertain, he was of some help in removing the ants. The ones that were being brushed off were climbing back onto him, so I got him onto his feet and trundled him another fifty feet before he stumbled and fell.

When he was down I pulled his shoes and socks off, undid the brass buckle, and pulled his khaki trousers off. The ants were thick on his legs, way up to the upper thigh and the groin. I pulled his underwear shorts off and wadded them up and used them to brush away the ants. I noted that, dimensionally, he more than lived up to the billing Joanna had given him. I rolled him over and over, away from the area where the brushed-off ants could get back on him.

They are aggressive, these red ants, but they are certainly not the menace the farming fraternity and the petrochemical industry would have us believe. If you stand too near a nest, they will come out and climb up your shoes and sting your ankles. You know immediately, and you move away and knock them off. The bites make little white blisters which, if untended, are likely to fester. The easiest remedy is rubbing alcohol applied as soon as possible after being bitten. Vodka or gin will do.

Ninety-nine out of a hundred fire-ant horror stories are false. Freddy was the one in a hundred. I had never heard of anybody being so completely bitten. We had him free of the ants at last. He made sad weak sounds as he rolled his head from side to side. He was gray and sweaty. I wedged him back into his pants and clinched the big brass buckle.

I now knew why he had been so anxious to do me in. But it seemed idiotic to have killed Jason Breen.

I leaned close to him and said, "Hey! Why did Jason come out here?"

"Money," he said in a dull voice. "Called me at four in the morning on the private line. I chained the dogs. Waited in the grove. Twenty thousand."

"Why?"

"He'd snooped. Figured it all out. Saw the *Christina* come in without Jack. Told me he had killed Cal with a wire and he had to run, and unless I gave him money he'd claim I paid him to kill Cal. I said okay. He was very jumpy. Then he said he was going to beat up on me anyway, on account of what happened with the Dobrovsky girl. He hit me and I hit him. I caught him in the throat. It broke something. He grabbed his throat. Tried to breathe. Fell onto his knees. Made choking noises. Fell over dead in less than two minutes. By dawn light his face was black and his eyes bulged out. I dragged him down to the stables. Wheeled his bike down. Oh, Christ, everything is getting so . . . so far away."

He was looking worse by the moment, face bloating, tongue thickening. His lips were fat. He was close to blacking out.

"He told me once a bee sting can make him real sick," Jane said. "What's *keeping* . . . them."

A moment later we both heard the distant hooting as a cruiser blew its way through the highway traffic. When in another minute it hove into sight around the stand of trees, I stood up and waved my arms at it. It came bounding across the track and the infield, stopped near us, and two deputies piled out, very smart in pale blue shirts, dark blue pants, and trooper hats. They were big, young and ruddy, creaking with equipment.

"Hey, Miz Jane!" one of them said.

"Why, hello, Harvey!"

"Now just who is this here, Miz Jane?"

"You know him! This is Frederick Van Harn."

Harvey stared. "You've got to be kidding," he said in an awed voice. "What in hell *happened* to him?"

"He got into fire ants," I said, "and he's allergic. He's going into shock. Can you get a radio patch through to hospital emergency?"

"Yes, but—"

"You better get on it and tell them you're heading in there wide open. Tell them it's shock from insect bites. They'll know what to have ready. I think it's called anaphylactic shock."

"But—"

Jane stepped closer to him and said, "Maybe you *want* to explain to my Uncle Jake why you let Frederick die?"

That is one of the interesting things about power. Everybody who really has it seems to know exactly how to use it. The ones who pretend to have it make the wrong moves.

While he was on the radio, the other deputy and I lifted Freddy and put him in the back of the cruiser, on his back on the seat. The deputy said, "There's supposed to be a body here?"

"There is."

"Harv, I'll stay here and look into what the call was about. You come back or have them send somebody, okay?"

Jane had gotten in the back and she was kneeling on the floor, holding Freddy's hand. Harvey made a tight circle and went bucketing out of there. We heard him hooting his way down the highway toward the city.

The one left behind said, "Those far ants are mean."

I inspected the bites on the backs of my hands and between the fingers. "They're very convincing."

He took out his notebook. "Who was it phoned in?"

"Me. Travis McGee."

"My name is Simmons. Frank Simmons." He almost started to shake hands and apparently decided it wasn't professional.

"Have you been a deputy long?"

"Just over three weeks. Address, Mr. McGee?"

He wrote the ID information down, slowly and care-fully. "Now where'd this dead body be?"

"Over there in that hole."

"Is it a real old dead body? I mean dead long?"

"Only since last night."

We walked to the hole. In a higher voice he said, "That there is a dead *horse!* You funnin' me? What's that jeep doing in there?"

"Frank, there's a small hole I want you to look in, there by the front of the jeep."

He went over and looked down into the smaller hole. There were some flies on the brown arm. He swayed slightly, then whirled and took two big steps and threw up. When he was finished he straightened up slowly and said, "That didn't give me a damn bit of warning. It just come on me all at once."

"It can happen that way."

"This is my first one on duty. Jesus! Look, don't tell Harv about my barfin', okay?"

"I'd have no reason to."

"He rides me. He thinks I won't make it. I'll make it. Now, who discovered the body? You or Miz Schermer or Mr. Van Harn?"

"I discovered it."

"Who put it there?"

"Mr. Van Harn."

"The *hell* you say!" He bent and slapped at his an-kles. "Far ants all over the place. Let's get out of this here hole. You think there's a water tap around here anyplace?"

"Over there at the stables."

"Let's us walk over there. Now, you got any idea who the deceased is?"

"I think it is a fellow named Jason Breen."

"From Westway Harbor? With the beard?"

"Right."

"I'll be a son of a bitch," he said softly and stopped long enough to write the name in his notebook.

17

C APTAIN Harry Max Scorf questioned me at the scene. By the time he was through they had Jason and his bike and his smashed guitar and his duffel bags out of the ground. I followed Scorf over and took a look at the body. The eyes glared up at the sky. The beard was chalked with limestone dust, giving me a hint of what he would have looked like as an old man, had the world given him a chance to live that long.

It had taken Mr. Smith a long time to notice that something was wrong. He came trotting across the field as they were loading Jason. "What are all these damn cars coming in and out? Is that fellow dead? He looks dead. Where is Mister Fred? Who's in charge here anyways?"

Scorf settled Smith down with an admirable economy of word and gesture. Then he suggested that I drive him to the hospital in my rental car, which would give him a chance to go over my story with me once more.

We turned the vent windows so the hot air blew in. I drove slowly. I went through the play-by-play description of our battle again. He chuckled and I told him that it did not seem funny at the time, and it did not get any funnier with the passage of time. I told him that he could maybe think of a nice funny way to tell Uncle Jake that he was going to have to arrest Frederick Van Harn.

"While we're both being funny, McGee, you can tell me how you happened to know that Breen was buried under that dead horse."

"As I said, Captain, I was scrabbling in the dirt, trying to get a purchase, trying to crawl to the jeep so I could grab onto it and stand up. Which I finally did. But I uncovered part of Breen and the bike first."

"It's nothing you can prove, and I want to see just how Van Harn's story matches yours. I'll buy the story about how he killed Jason, because Jane Schermer heard that part of it too. And maybe the autopsy will verify. We know the autopsy verifies the way Birdsong died. But I would be a happier man if I could get a better way to tie Breen to that killing. He was on my list and looking better every day. But it isn't solid."

"I can make you happier. I think Cindy Birdsong will be willing to tell you without much urging that once upon a time after Cal beat her up, Breen went to her and said he could arrange to kill Birdsong very quietly for her. No one would suspect. She was horrified and told him to forget it. The same day I arrived, when Birdsong got ugly with me, he backhanded his wife in the office and knocked her cold. Jason Breen was the one who got to her and picked her off the floor."

He turned in the seat and I could feel him looking at me. "That means that I can't let you go back there alone. You could coach her. I want to come up on her cold with this."

"Captain, what difference does it make anyway? You don't have to build a case against Jason Breen. It doesn't have to stand up in court. It gets Birdsong off your books."

"I am a careful man, McGee. I like people, alive or dead, to get charged with what they did, not what somebody else did."

When we got to the hospital, we were told that Frederick Van Harn was in Intensive Care. I followed Scorf up to the fourth floor. A young doctor was sitting in the small waiting room outside the closed double doors, talking quietly to Jane Schermer. Tears were running down her prematurely middle-aged face. The doctor came and talked to us in the corridor. He said they had tried, but they just couldn't reverse the severe shock, not even with every radical treatment they could think of. He had responded slightly to massive injections of digitalis but had faded again until his heart had stopped and they had been unable to restart it. An intense allergic reaction, he said. Massive fluid imbalance. A pity, he said. Such a young man.

Harry Max Scorf looked indignant. One cannot ask questions of the dead. People were eluding him. He acted as if he thought it was unfair, a kind of trickery.

The murder and the poetic justice of the macabre death made the event a twenty-four-hour sensation. The wire services picked it up. It had the right words. Prominent attorney. Political hopeful. Possible blackmail. Involvement in drug smuggling suspected. Murdered man believed intimate of ex-model recently slain by bomb aboard houseboat.

But a news story is a fragile thing. It is like a hot air balloon. It needs a constant additive of more hot air in the form of new revelations, new actions, new suspicions. Without this the air cools, the big bag wrinkles, sighs, settles to the ground, and disappears.

Judge Jacob Schermer put the clamp on any flow of additives. He and his minions spread the word. They apparently had leverage to use on the local radio stations and the Bayside television station and the monopoly newspaper. They also had the City and County Police Department, the banks, the Chamber of Commerce, the service clubs, and every phase of local government.

No one knew a thing about anything. A blank stare was better than no comment. The reporters who had come in from Jacksonville, Miami, and Orlando went hurrying right back out of town toward the next story. People could barely remember what Van Harn looked like or what he did. The usual eruption of sick, sad, violent events continued throughout the nation and the world, like an unending, eternal string of those little Chinese firecrackers called ladyfingers.

By Saturday morning, when Harry Max Scorf came to see us aboard the *Flush,* the news story was so dead it might as well have happened in some other year.

He sat in the cool lounge, took his spotless white hat off and wiped the sweatband with a bandanna, and placed it back on his head carefully, at exactly the right angle.

"My feeling," he said to us, "is that I ought to waltz you people to and fro and bounce you up and down gentle-like until you let loose of something that makes sense out of where you fit in this picture. But it's one of those feelings I don't get to enjoy."

"Orders?" I asked.

"The official position is that there's no loose ends at all. Everything is solved and filed away. The Milligan woman was an accident. Jack Omaha lit out for places unknown. Jason kilt the Freeler girl with the bomb and kilt Birdsong with a wire. Then Freddy kilt Jason and the ants kilt him. And that's all she wrote, boys. You two fellas know, just like I know, that it adds up to a crock of shit."

"We really can't help you at all," Meyer said.

He sighed. "Anyway, one thing looks better. There's pretty fair grass coming in at a reasonable price. Somebody has knocked all them amateur wholesalers into a tight line. Some professional outfit has moved in like overnight and took over the whole county. Speaking purely as a cop, it's a relief. It's the amateurs screw everything up. With these pros, I know which way they'll jump, and what will make them jump and what won't. If they keep it tidy, we'll lay back and let it roll. When customs picks up forty-two tons at a time on the Mexican border, it's a signal that it is too big a business to hope to stop entire. If these pros start to get into any heavier action around here, then what we'll do is make their operation so expensive it'll take the cream off, and they'll back off to what they've got right now. It's the amateurs who drive you crazy. That Walter J. Demos would drive anybody crazy, the damned fool. Every time I try to talk to the son of a bitch, he starts crying. He sits down, wraps his arms around his bald head, and starts bellering. What I come by for is to say you can make everybody very happy by going back where you come from, as soon as you can untie your ropes and start your engine."

"This is a roust, Captain?" I asked.

"Not right at this minute, it isn't. It starts to be a roust when I tell somebody you won't move. Then that somebody goes to all the city and county departments that have got anything to do with boats and navigation. Then they come around here and they check you and your boat for every little paragraph in city, county, state, and federal law going back to when Lincoln got shot. Like any boat operating in county waters has got to carry two brass kerosene lanterns at least fourteen inches high as spare equipment, one with green glass and one with red glass, and if you can't show them to the inspector, it's a hundred dollars a day and costs for every day of violation, whether you're tied up or running. That's when it gets to be a roust. Want any more?"

"When you want us to move out, Captain," I said, "you just give the word and we'll move. You've convinced us."

He looked puzzled. "I thought I'd just given you the word."

Meyer cleared his throat and said, "I suppose you could change that official position you described if you could come up with something new?"

Scorf frowned. "It would have to be hard evidence. Very hard. I told you, people want this all forgot. Right now. If anything gets stirred up and it comes to nothing, I am retired with no pension."

"Sometimes you can't help thinking," I said.

"About what?"

Meyer said, "We did a lot of thinking and talking last night, Captain. We decided to check just a little bit further and then bring it to you. But you've rushed us. It's still all theory."

"Theory," he said, and seemed to be looking around for a place to spit.

I said, "Carrie Milligan's share of the ill-gotten gains was a little better than a hundred thousand dollars."

He snapped his head around and stared at me. "That sounds more like a fact than a theory, McGee."

"She gave it to me to hold for her, and to give to her sister if anything happened to her."

"We can come back to that," Scorf said. "Where does it lead you?"

"We had four people in business together. Carrie Milligan, Freddy Van Harn, Jack Omaha, and Cal Birdsong. Carrie had her own kind of twisted integrity. She'd take no more than what was hers. But she was afraid somebody might take her share away from her. With Freddy supplying the plane and Jack supplying the boat, and probably the two of them supplying the financing, would Carrie have been in for a full quarter of the pie? I'd say no. I would say a top of twenty percent. Jack was the banker. He was keeping it in the safe at the business. Carrie was the bookkeeper and courier. New buys were financed out of that money in the safe. When they eventually decided to call it quits, they would have divided it up according to the formula and gone their separate ways. If a hundred thousand equals twenty percent, then there was four hundred thousand left in the safe after she took hers."

"Four hundred thousand!" Scorf said slowly.

"Maybe more," Meyer said. "It is hard to read the

motives of a dead man you never met, but it struck us last night that Jack Omaha was setting himself up for total departure, deserting hearth and home, cashing in everything, even cleaning out the partnership. Maybe he left that money in the safe with the group funds, or maybe he hid it somewhere where he could get to it quickly."

"So maybe he did take off," Scorf said, "and took Van Harn's money and Cal Birdsong's money with him."

"Or, like I told you before, a bag of grass fell on his head and killed him, and that's why Freddy told me that Jason saw the *Christina* come in without Jack Omaha."

Scorf frowned. "So . . . Van Harn would want his money and he'd know where it was and who could give it to him."

I said, "There's a chance he would want to leave it right there for the time being. Jack and Carrie had the combination. Jack was dead and he could trust Carrie. It would be there when he needed it."

"You mean it could still be there?" Scorf asked, frowning in puzzlement.

"Suppose," Meyer said, "that Harry Hascomb walked in on Carrie when she was taking her share out of the pot that night of the day Jack Omaha died. He would know there was big money there, but no way to get to it. Harry was the outside man. Because Omaha and Carrie handled all the accounts and financial records, they would be the only ones who needed to know the combination of the safe. Insurance people like to ask that the number of people with access be kept to a minimum. Two is ideal. Because Harry saw her take the money, it would account for her being uneasy and leaving the money with Travis McGee in Lauderdale. Just in case."

Scorf displayed the quickness of the cop mind by saying, "And after he found out that Omaha was planning to clean him out, and maybe guessed from the Milligan woman's reactions that Omaha was already dead, the simplest way into the safe would be to have the Milligan woman die by accident so he could call the safe company and have them drill it open. It would be the reasonable thing for him to do."

I said, "We can assume Van Harn went there as soon as he heard of Carrie's accident. All Harry would have to do is act totally blank about there being any money in the safe. Van Harn wouldn't dare press it. Besides, Uncle Jake had already taken him out of his financial bind."

Scorf sighed. "All theory. Pretty theory."

"How about some fact?" Meyer asked him. "In the building supply and construction supply business, Hascomb either handled dynamite and caps and wire and batteries or knew how to get what he needed. He was the outside man, not the desk man, and apparently had some mechanical training or ability."

"And," I said, "Joanna Freeler told me she could retire, if she played it right."

"Are you trying to say she could have known that Hascomb killed Carrie, and she would blackm—"

"No! It really shook her when I told her I thought Carrie had been pushed in front of that truck. I think Carrie told Joanna there was a bundle of money in the office safe. They were the only two girls working in that office. And that would give her some leverage to use on Harry Hascomb. That could have been her retirement. If she played it right."

"She didn't play it right," Scorf said.

Meyer said, "We decided last night that if Harry had asked Joanna for a date she would have accepted. They'd had an intimate relationship for several years. Then, if he couldn't keep the date, he could have left off a consolation prize, a box of wine and cheese."

"Loud wine and cheese," Scorf said. He got up and roamed the lounge. He stopped and looked around. "This place was one damn mess when I checked it out. Sickened me. Dead girls get to me. A bomb is a cruel and ugly thing. Any kind of death is cruel and ugly, I guess. Except as a merciful end to pain. The worst are bombs and fire and knives. Look, I know about girls in offices. Jack Omaha and the Milligan woman were the two supposed to have the combination. Bet you a white hat Joanna Freeler knew it too, or knew where Miz Milligan had it wrote down. Know where every damn person in America writes down the combination to a safe? They write it on tape and stick it to the backside or underside of the top middle desk drawer. Half the safe jobs in the country are easy because everybody knows where to look for the combination."

"We don't want to start the voyage home just yet," I said.

"Whatever you've given me, I can handle," he said. "It's all theory. If Joanna let it be known to Hascomb that she accepted the date so they could have a little chat about how the Milligan woman died, she set herself up with wine and cheese."

"If we worked it out right," Meyer said, "it would be
. . . gratifying if we could be present when you interview Mr. Hascomb."

Scorf looked bleakly at him. "Gratifying, eh?"

"So few things in life work out neatly, Captain Scorf,
it would be reassuring to be in on one that does."

"And you think that this whole mess is neat?"

Meyer looked trouble. "Not in the usual sense of the
word."

Scorf thought it over. "It's hardly one damn thing to
go on. I don't want a committee, for God's sake.
McGee, you can come along with me and watch me
mess it up. Meyer, you better stay right here and get
this thing ready to move on out into the channel. My
orders are clear. I have to get you started on your way.
And we'll be back soon."

I had expected Scorf to sit bolt upright behind the
wheel of the dark blue unmarked Cougar and fumble it
along at a stilted thirty-five. Instead, after he had belt-
ed himself in, he tipped his white hat forward to his
eyebrows, lounged back into the corner of the driver's
seat, put his fingertips on the wheel, and slid through
heavy traffic like an oiled eel. He moved to where the
holes were, moving the oncoming traffic over, and was
able to avoid accelerations, decelerations, and the use
of the brakes. He had looked too underprivileged to be
an expert, but he was, indubitably. And I said so.

With mirthless smile he said, "I wasted a lot of time
and money ramming stocks around the dirt circuits. I
felt easy riding with you the other day. Except you're
not good on picking lanes at the lights."

"Is there a secret I don't know?"

"Always haul in behind local plates on older cars with kids driving and crowd them a little so they'll pile on out of your way. Haul in behind local delivery trucks. On three lanes run the middle one, and swing to the curb lane when you're going to miss the light. A man turning is out of your way fast."

"Where are we going?"

"Pineview Lakes Estates. Twenty-one Loblolly Lane."

It was low land, five miles out. The developers had used the fill from the dug lakes to lift the ranch-type homes out of the swamp. It was eleven in the morning when we pulled into the river-pebble driveway of number 21, a long low cypress house with a shake roof out of some kind of fireproof imitation of cedar. It was stained pale silver and had faded blue blinds by the windows, the kind that are fixed in place and never cover the windows.

Two tanned skinny boys were working on a stripped VW with wide oversized tires. They gave us a sidelong glance and no further acknowledgment of our existence, even when we stood beside the VW.

"Either of you a Hascomb?" Scorf asked.

"Me," the skinnier one said.

"Your daddy around?"

"No."

"Miz Hascomb?"

"No."

"If it wouldn't strain your brain, sonny, maybe you could break down and tell me where I could find your daddy."

The boy straightened up and stared at him in bleak

silence. "What's this shit about brain strain, gramps?"

"I am Captain Harry Max Scorf, and I am tired of the hard-guy act from young trash. I get cooperation from you, and I get manners from you, and I get respect from you, sonny, or you go downtown for obstructing a police officer in his line of duty."

The bleak stare did not change. "Oh, goodness me," the boy said in a flat voice. "I did not for one moment realize. Tsk tsk. From what I overheard I believe you will find my dear father down at his place of business, Superior Building Supplies, at Junction Park. Actually it is no longer his place of business because the silly shit has lost it because he didn't know how to run it, and his partner screwed him and ran with the cash. But Cowboy Harry is just as bigmouth as ever. He is down there because some pigeon from Port Fierce wants to buy the junk that didn't get cleared out in the clearance sale. And now if you will give me your gracious permission to get back to work here."

Scorf smiled sadly and shook his head. "Thank you kindly, sonny. I am sure we will meet professionally one day."

"You can count on it," the boy said.

As we drove out Scorf said, "What makes so many of them so damned angry at everything lately?"

"It's a new preservative they put in the fried meat sold at drive-ins."

"As good an answer as any."

There was one car behind Superior Building Supplies, a recent-model Ford wagon with local plates, dinged and dusty, with a cracked window and a soft tire. One of the big sliding doors that opened onto the loading dock was ajar about three feet. We climbed onto the dock and went into the shadowy echoing areas of the empty warehouse. The air conditioning was off.

"Hascomb?" Scorf shouted.

"Yo! Who is it?"

Harry came out of the shadows, a pair of pliers in his hand. He peered and said, "Oh, hey, Harry Max! You were against the light." He looked at me. "What was your name, friend?"

"McGee."

Hascomb was stripped to the waist, the sweat rolling off his soft torso. His cowhand pants, cinched with a wide belt, were sweat-dark around the waistline. His abundant red-brown hair was carefully coiffed and sprayed into mod position, covering his ears. His boot heels clicked on the cement floor.

"You caught me, Harry Max," Hascomb said. "What I'm doing, I'm taking off the big junction box over there. I don't rightly know if it's mine or the owner's, so in case of doubt I'm taking it. The fellow from Port Fierce offered twenty bucks, and that is twenty bucks I wouldn't otherwise have. He took a lot of the small stuff and he's sending a bigger truck back for the desks, safe, chairs, and those two generators over there. And that cleans me out."

"Sorry to hear it," Scorf said.

Hascomb sighed and shrugged. "Hard times and a thief for a partner."

"What are you going to do?"

"I think we'll head out to Wyoming. Out to the mines. I can fix any damn thing that's got moving parts. New start. The equity in the house will give us a stake. Were you boys looking for me?"

I wondered how Scorf would approach it. Suspicion without proof is a dangerous thing and a clumsy thing.

Scorf said, "Harry, I hope you won't take this wrong, I surely do. In my line of work I have to do a lot of fool things I don't believe in, but I guess every line of work is the same. Anyways, I guess your prints are on file from army duty, but it would take a time to get them out of Washington or wherever the hell they keep them, and so they said to me, Captain, you go bring Harry Hascomb in voluntary and take his prints. You won't put up a fuss, will you?"

"Me? No. Hell, no. I won't put up a fuss, but what in the world is the point of it, Harry Max?"

"Maybe I shouldn't even tell you this, but we've known each other a long time. Maybe you know or don't know, a fragment of a print isn't worth a damn. This piece they got looks like it is one half of the pad of the third finger right hand."

"A print on what?"

Scorf scuffed at the cement floor. He shook his head. "Now you've got to understand how they think, Harry. It certainly wasn't exactly a big secret around the town that you and Joanna Freeler had a lot more than a business relationship. And lovers can have quarrels. Anyway—and don't get sore—the bomb experts, they recovered a piece of battery casing about so big, and they used some kind of chemical treatment to bring out the fragment of the print enough to photograph it. Once they compare yours, then you're off the list for keeps, Harry. It's something I plain have to do, and I'm sorry. I'm really sorry."

Harry Hascomb whacked the smaller man on the shoulder. "Chrissake, Harry Max. Don't feel sorry. I know when a man has a job to do, he has to do it. Right? You want me to go in right now? Let me get my shirt."

I noticed that Harry Max Scorf drifted along behind Hascomb as the man got his shirt, and I noticed that Scorf's heavy, drab suit coat was unbuttoned, and I could guess at the presence of the belly gun clipped to the waistband of his trousers.

Hascomb shouldered into his ranch shirt and tucked it in and buttoned it as we walked out. He slid the big door shut and snapped the heavy padlock on the hasp and smiled and said, "Have to finish stealing that box later." We were parked beside the Ford wagon, just to the right of it. Hascomb started to get into the Cougar and then he said, slapping his pocket, "Just a second, Harry Max. Let me get my other pack of cigarettes."

He leaned into the wagon and thumbed the button that dropped the door of the glove compartment. He was very good. Scorf was standing outside the open door of the two-door Cougar, holding the driver's seat tilted forward so that Hascomb could climb into the back. I was opposite the hood, walking toward the door on the passenger side.

Hascomb snatched an ancient weapon out of his glove compartment. Officers have smuggled them home from the last five wars. The Colt .45 automatic. I caught a glimpse of it as he turned and fired at Scorf at point-blank range.

Scorf got his left hand up to ward off the big slow slug. He was reaching for the belly gun with his right hand. The big slug went through the palm of his left hand and hit the shelf of brow over the left eye. The resistance of the thick ridge of bone snapped his head back and broke his neck. The white hat went sailing over the hood of the car. The relentless chunk of lead plowed through the brain tissues and took off a hunk of the back of the skull as big as an apple. It was all very immediate and messy. It spattered blood and tissue over the front half of the Cougar. I saw it all in slow motion. It was in the hard and vivid light of the hour before noon. It was a day of almost stagnant air. The wind had been moving steadily from north to south, bringing to Florida's east coast all the stained and corrosive crud of Birmingham and the rest of the industrial South. The horizons were whiskey-stained, and the sky above was a pallid saffron instead of blue. The bleared sun made harsh studio lighting on the parking lot scene. And Harry Hascomb saw Captain Scorf's horrid death under the dreadful lemon sky.

Scorf lay poised halfway across the dark blue hood. Meyer had been so right about the vivid reality of death. Harry Hascomb's face was absolutely slack, his eyes blank and dulled. He had expected to see the picture of the dead grackle. Here was the genuine article, smashed, leaking, stinking, and so sickeningly vivid that it immobilized him, froze him in an incredulous horror. I was caught on tiptoe for an instant, knowing that we were in a deserted parking lot in a deserted area, knowing that I could not expect any Saturday noon curiosity-seekers.

Scorf's coat was spread, showing the gun butt. With a swift and insane delicacy, with a mind-bulging awareness of my own madness, I leaned into the field of fire of the big automatic, snatched Scorf's weapon free, and fell to the cement on the far side of the Cougar from the immobilized Hascomb. He fired as I disappeared from his view, and like an afterecho of the hefty *bam,* I heard the slug chunk into the loading dock. An instant later Scorf slid off the hood onto his side, landing with a heavy clopping and thudding.

Doubtless Harry Hascomb had some sort of a script in mind. Maybe the automatic was due to end up in my dead hand, and Harry was due to end up in Peru.

I am not one for the shootout at the O.K. or any other corral. I have no wish to stand in full view with steely nerves and draw a bead on the chap trying to blow my head in twain.

I hitched quickly into the prone position and steadied the short-barreled weapon by grasping my right wrist in my left hand and pushing outward. I aimed under the low road clearance of the Cougar, and I aimed at the front ankle creases in his Western boot and did not miss at that range. He yelled and started gimping around. I missed the other boot the first try and then got it on the second try. All of Harry Hascomb came tumbling down, making shrill sounds of total dismay. He thought to return the fire in the same manner, aiming under the car. I was after his hand or wrist, but I hit the automatic by accident. The slug spanged and went screeing off in ricochet, and the Colt killed the muffler on the Cougar before it went spinning away from him.

Without any conscious thought and without the awareness of any lapse of time, I found myself standing over Hascomb, picking a place right between his eyes.

Then I realized it would mean I would spend the best years of my life in Bayside, filling out forms and answering questions. He was not going anywhere, but to be safe I took both sets of car keys. I walked all the way to the phone booth beside the gas station, the one Carrie had patronized.

18

A wind had come up and blown all the smutch into somebody else's sky. Cindy and I sat on the deck chairs on the sun deck, side by side, and looked up at all the diamonds in the sky.

"You said they found it, Trav, but where was it?"

"In a box labeled Camp Stove. He was getting ready to go camping. And get lost in the woods. Forever."

"He said he killed Carrie?"

"Knocked her cold. Waited for the right kind of traffic and then took her by the crotch and the nape of the neck and slung her into the farm truck."

I sensed the way she shuddered.

She said, "I suppose, in a way, some of the money is mine."

"In a way. But your chances of getting it . . ."

"I know. I'll just have to make it anyway."

"Couldn't you sell out?"

"Sure. But then what?"

"What do you mean?"

"Trav, darling, I like to work. I like to run things.

270

And I like to have security. I've got a hundred thousand mortgage to pay off, and the place is worth ten times that. I am really going to have to pitch in."

"And I was going to ask you to pack a bag and come cruising."

"Well . . . someday, maybe."

"I gather that you are underwhelmed."

"Male pride talking. Can't you accept the fact that I'm tied to this place?"

"And you want to be tied to it."

"Please. I don't want to fight with you. Please, dear."

I stretched until my shoulders creaked. *"Okay,* Cindy. You are very realistic and diligent and all that. Maybe I have a grasshopper philosophy, but it strikes me there are a lot of dead people around here. Given advance warning, they could have done more living."

"We don't know each other."

"What does that mean?"

"I found out from you I'm a more physical person than I thought I was. Okay, so it makes me skeptical of myself and impatient about things. So, being a careful person, I need time. I just can't go mooning and dreaming around here and letting important things slide."

"Mooning and dreaming are very good stuff."

"Sure, sure, sure. We really don't know each other at all. And I am a drone. A worker. A builder. Maybe I can learn to play someday. But I have to have something solid, all built, before I'll dare. Please understand."

I gave up. I lifted her hand up and opened it and

kissed the palm. She shivered. I said, "Give me a call when you get all your ducks in a row. When you feel like getting acquainted."

"Could you call me?"

"I suppose so. Why?"

"It's very strange to feel so shy about somebody you've been to bed with. But I do."

"Cindy, I will call you. But when?"

She inhaled and exhaled deeply, a sign of relaxation and contentment and eventual anticipation.

"Just try me every once in a while, okay?"

And it was okay because it had to be. There wasn't any other choice. Sometimes it is a relief not to have a choice. I will have to get Meyer to explain this concept to me.